A Relative Murder

A RELATIVE MURDER

JUDE DEVERAUX

THORNDIKE PRESS
A part of Gale, a Cengage Company

LIBRARY OF CONGRESS CIP DATA ON FILE.
CATALOGUING IN PUBLICATION FOR THIS BOOK
IS AVAILABLE FROM THE LIBRARY OF CONGRESS.

ISBN-13: 978-1-4328-9525-9 (hardcover alk. paper)

Published in 2022 by arrangement with Harlequin Enterprises ULC.

Printed in Mexico
Print Number: 01   Print Year: 2022

A RELATIVE MURDER

■ ■ ■ ■

LACHLAN, FLORIDA
2019

■ ■ ■ ■

ONE

Sheriff Daryl Flynn was shaking so hard his teeth were chattering. Sweat was rolling down his face. In his hand was a piece of paper that was going to change his life. No! It was going to *destroy* his life.

He looked through the glass partition of his office and marveled at his three deputies calmly working away.

Peace, he thought. That's what he needed, what he was working toward. In the last few years there'd been several murders in tiny Lachlan, but for a while now, all had been calm. The only problems were noisy neighbors, lost dogs and a few speeding tickets given to people from Miami.

But everything was about to change. The paper he was holding said that in fourteen days, Randal Medlar would be released from prison — five years early.

For a moment, Sheriff Flynn closed his eyes. He had planned it all so carefully. He

9

was supposed to retire in four years, just before Randal was released. He would talk to his wife about leaving Lachlan and moving somewhere far away. He knew it would take about three minutes to persuade her. Evie carried her passport with her. "Just in case I'm offered an adventure," she liked to say. She was sick of living in their small town, where people thought nothing of calling at 3:00 a.m. to say their cat hadn't come home. Evie wanted to see the world. "Before I'm too old to enjoy it."

He looked at the paper again, hoping he'd misread it. In just two weeks, Randal Medlar would be free — and Daryl was sure he'd return to Lachlan.

Randal's wife, Ava, lived outside Chicago, and there was a tiny possibility that her husband would go to her. Throughout the years, Daryl had used his access to legal channels to keep track of what went on with Randal, and he knew Ava often visited him in prison. But then, Ava had always been a faithful and loving wife — so devoted that she'd caused a lot of the mess he was facing now.

The sheriff leaned back in his chair, still staring at the document as though he could change what was written. His hand was sweating so much that the corner of the paper was disintegrating.

He had two problems. The first was Randal's daughter, Kate. In the last years, Daryl had become quite fond of the young woman. But he knew Ava had hidden everything from her. Rather than admit her husband was in prison, Ava had told her daughter that Randal died when Kate was four years old. The child had grown up believing it was just her and her mother. It wasn't until she was an adult that she was told she had an aunt, Sara Medlar, who was a famous author and lived in little Lachlan, Florida.

Kate had taken the news quite well and had immediately contacted her aunt. Sara had welcomed her niece so enthusiastically that Kate got a job in Lachlan, drove south and moved into Sara's big house, where Jack Wyatt, the grandson of Sara's childhood sweetheart, was also living.

From what Daryl could see, the Medlar Three got along splendidly. Jack had a construction company that was rebuilding the poorest part of Lachlan, and Kate was doing well in her real estate job. Sara had retired from full-time writing and devoted herself to photography and whatever else she could use her active mind for. Yes, they did tend to stick their noses into any criminal activity in Lachlan — and from what he'd heard, in other places too — but when they weren't snooping, they caused no problems.

But how would Kate react when she found out that everything she believed about her life was a lie? Not only was her father alive but her beloved aunt had testified against him. It was Sara who sent Randal to prison. *"You did this. To your own brother. You'll never see Kate again. I swear it!"* Ava had screamed on the day of the verdict. Two security guards had dragged her out of the courtroom.

Daryl knew how Kate would react. She'd be furious. Kids always were. They were unforgiving of the errors of their elders. As judgmental as the Inquisition. Would Kate be so angry that she would leave town? Turn her back on everyone and disappear? That would break the hearts of a lot of people. Jack and Sara would probably never recover.

Daryl dropped the paper and put his head in his hands. None of that compared to his second problem, one that was a lot more serious than injured feelings. Long ago, there had been a "job." A big one. Involving millions. Daryl was only twenty-eight then. He was married and broke and desperately wanted to give Evie all that she deserved.

12

And there was Randal, forty-one and silver-tongued. He'd always been able to smile and sweet-talk and make you believe that everything would be fine. Until the very last, he *always* got away with whatever he did. For that job, Randal had been the mastermind, the genius of it all. Daryl, Walter and Jack's father, Roy, had followed Randal without questioning him. True, they had benefited, but there had been problems later.

Daryl looked at the paper. So now Randal was being released early — for good behavior, no less — and Daryl was *sure* he'd come straight to Lachlan. He'd want to see his daughter, who didn't know he was alive.

And he might want to confront his sister for helping put him in prison. How would Daryl, now the sheriff, deal with that?

Of course Randal would want to look up his old friends. Roy and Walter were dead. That left Daryl.

All Randal had to do was remind the sheriff of what they'd done together and . . . Then what? Blackmail? Would Randal threaten to tell the Broward Sheriff's Department if Daryl didn't do whatever illegal thing he came up with? Daryl would lose his pension and his good name. What would Randal want this time? Grand theft? Expen-

13

sive cars to disappear? How about a Ponzi scheme?

No doubt Randal had learned a lot about crime while he was in prison and he'd want to try everything. The word *dishonest* wasn't one Randal understood.

So how would Daryl be able to withstand him? Randal could talk anyone into anything. He could —

Daryl looked around his office. *Unless I'm not here,* he thought. *If Randal can't find me, he can't blackmail me into doing anything. And I'd have time to think about what I need to do. Early retirement? Evie would love that!*

He looked at his three deputies. Who could take over if he wasn't here? That he had no one who could replace him was the reason he gave Evie as to why he could never take a vacation.

Pete and Dave were cousins. They were good-looking young men who smiled a lot. They were so nice that people thanked them for handing out tickets.

If — no, *when* — trouble happened because of Randal Medlar, they wouldn't have a clue about what to do.

Bea was also a deputy but she did office work. She'd never be able to withstand Randal's honey charm.

Daryl began to sweat harder. If only he

14

could find someone to take his place.

The front door opened and in came Heather Wyatt, Jack's mother. She was passing out invitations to a school bake sale. She smiled at Daryl and held up the flyer. He nodded. Yes, she could hang it up. Anything to help the community.

When she turned away, he thought about her son, Jack. His father had been Roy Wyatt, the town's bad boy, part of Randal's gang — and one of Daryl's best friends when they were growing up. But thanks to Evie, Daryl had gone straight, while Roy had never changed. If there was a fight, Roy was in on it. Gambling, drinking, women, Roy was there. He and Randal had been great friends. Exactly the same but direct opposites. They —

Daryl nearly choked. Jack!

Jack Wyatt, reformed bad boy, now a good businessman, was also a sleuth of criminals. The protector of Sara and Kate. He was the only person Daryl knew who could possibly stand up to Randal Medlar. After all, Jack had stood up to Roy.

Daryl checked the date on the paper again. He had fourteen days to persuade Jack to become a deputy. *"Just while I'm gone,"* Daryl would say. *"You know Dave and Pete can't handle anything on their own."*

15

He'd add that Jack's juvenile records were sealed, so yes, he could be sworn in as a deputy. *"For Evie,"* he would say. *"She's always liked you so much."*

Yes, he thought. *Jack could do it. No! He would do it.*

He called Evie. "You know how you've always wanted us to go on a cruise? Well, I can, but there are some restrictions." He glanced at the paper. "We must leave on the eighth." It was two days before Randal was to be released. "If it's even one day later, I can't go. And let's stay away for at least six weeks." He listened. "Couldn't care less. Australia maybe?" That seemed far enough away. "Think you can do it?" When there was no answer, he smiled at his phone. She'd hung up and had started her search for a cruise that fit the requirements.

Okay, he thought. *Step one is done.* Now he just had to cajole, persuade and challenge Jack Wyatt into swearing in as a temporary deputy.

Daryl smiled. His plan was so heinous, so full of half-truths and secrets, that Randal would be proud of him. Too bad he'd never know.

TWELVE DAYS LATER

Lenny was on his belly, binoculars in hand, as he watched the house. It was his third day there and he had come to know the little family — as he was being paid to do.

The husband was in his forties, a lawyer in a fancy firm on Broward. He was what Lenny thought of as a "taken care of man." His pretty young wife — who was the one Lenny had been told to watch — managed the house, their two boys, the food and the little farm with its chickens and a screen house full of salad greens. If she disappeared, the man wouldn't be able to find his shoes.

Lenny figured the wife liked that people depended on her. From what he'd seen, she rarely left the property. Her only regular visitor was a young red-haired woman and they spent their time inside a building that was set back under the trees.

He'd been curious as to what they were

doing, so one night he went inside. The lock was easy to open. It was a workshop and to his amazement he saw that the two women were making birdhouses. Not those plain, one-hole things you saw for sale in craft shops, but big, elaborate reproductions of real houses.

Lenny had been so awed by the miniature buildings that he'd spent too much time inside. The photos, the tools, the perfect little houses, fascinated him. When he left, it was breaking dawn. He'd made a mistake! The woman, Charlene Adams, always got up early — and she was leaving her house as Lenny exited.

Silently, he slipped around the side of the workshop. When she went inside, he let out a sigh of relief. That had been close.

As he made his way to the back of the property to hide in the overgrowth, he shook his head. He'd come to *like* the little family. He really hoped he wouldn't be told to kill them.

Suddenly, he saw a movement. It was slight but it was there. He'd had years of practice in seeing what others didn't. Charlene was in her workshop and the husband was at work, the kids at school. So who was by the barn?

Lenny knew how to be still but he redoubled his efforts. Over the years he'd kept himself at minimum weight and maximum flexibility. While muscle was nice, he'd found that speed and agility were what was needed for his jobs.

The man came out of the shadows and Lenny watched as he crept around the barn. He was looking up at all the ins and outs — exactly what Lenny had done on the first day.

He was a young man, and the way he moved showed he was trained in some form of martial arts. Inwardly, Lenny groaned. Those guys were sneaky. They concealed knives everywhere and they could hit a target.

But maybe the kid was just a stalker. Charlene was very pretty and she was there alone most of the time. Neighbors who might hear screams were far away. It was a stalker's paradise.

When the young man went into the barn, Lenny gave a sigh of defeat. This was no stalker. Unless his many years of experience were worth nothing, he knew what the guy was planning to do.

Lenny waited a few moments, hoping he was wrong. In the loft was an open window for the loading of hay. If the man placed himself there, it would show his true intent.

There was a flicker of movement at the window. When Charlene left her workshop, the man would be ready. Lenny clenched his teeth. His worst fears were confirmed. Did he have a rifle? With a scope?

Lenny rolled to his back, took out his burner phone and called the one and only number on it. It was answered immediately. "You hire somebody else? To check up on me?" Lenny whispered.

"No." The man sounded as though he'd expected this. "I was afraid people would be after her, but she isn't the real target. Are you seeing the older man I told you about?"

"No. This guy is young. Early thirties, if that. He's had some training."

"Maybe he's a friend, a visitor."

Idiot! Lenny thought. "No. He's like me. He's after her or whoever is connected to her."

There was an audible sigh. "Can you find out what he wants? Just don't let him harm her! She's my ticket to —" He broke off. "I have to go." He hung up.

"Your ticket to getting whatever *you* want," Lenny muttered.

When he'd been hired, Lenny hadn't asked many questions, but the man was so nervous that he'd said too much. He'd even dropped a name as he tried to make Lenny believe he was actually a good man, that he'd never done anything like this before. Like Lenny cared.

"I just want you to watch her and tell me every person she sees."

Ah, Lenny thought. *A jealous lover. Or a wannabe lover.*

They'd sat in the diner for a few minutes more. With a weak, shaky hand, the man slid a fat envelope across the table. Lenny thought, *This is one of those "before I die" things.* A pair of crutches leaned against the booth and from the look of him, the man didn't have long to live. Lenny sat still as he watched the man make his way out of the diner on the crutches, then get in his car and drive away. From experience, Lenny knew it was better to not let anyone see the car he drove.

Annoyed with this new complication, Lenny put his phone away, then stood up. He waited a moment to get the blood flowing — damned old age! He began the trek across the property via a way where he wouldn't be seen.

In the barn, the two horses made no noise. On the first day, he'd befriended them with apples. He'd hidden a few, and with his gloved hands, he tossed them into the stalls. The noise of the foraging horses would cover him.

There was only one ladder up and Lenny wasn't about to use it. The half-floor loft had a safety rail but it was open. He would enter at the end, out of sight of anyone up there. He'd already figured out a way to go: step onto the old desk, foot on the reins rack, catch the loft floor, then swing up over the rail. He did it in near silence.

The young man was sitting on a bale of hay, eyes closed as though he was doing some sort of meditation. *Kids!* Lenny thought with a sneer. When the young man looked up, there was a flash of shock at seeing Lenny standing there. But then his training kicked in. Slowly, he stood, but he was leaning to the side, probably starting to reach for a weapon.

But Lenny had a gun. It was just a .22 but at this distance it would do the job.

The young man stood still in front of the open window. He was staring. "I know who you are." There was awe in his voice.

Lenny had a scar through his left eyebrow. Sometimes he covered it, but today he hadn't bothered.

"I've heard about you." There was a gleam in the kid's eye that said he wanted the prestige of taking out a legend.

"Look," Lenny said, "I just want info. I

don't want to hurt anybody."

The kid smiled in that way that only youth can. He seemed to be saying, *How could an old man like you hurt me?*

Lenny took a chance. "Does this have anything to do with Randal Medlar?" A slight widening of the kid's eyes showed the answer was yes. *Who the hell is this Medlar?* Lenny thought. He'd looked him up online but there was nothing. Only true VIPs could keep that kind of anonymity.

The young guy was inching forward while keeping their eyes locked. Lenny gave an internal grimace. *The kid probably thinks I'm too old, too senile, to know what he's doing.*

Lenny lunged, meaning to make the kid step away. The young man did, but he lost his balance. To Lenny's shock, the kid fell backward — straight out the big open hay door. When he hit the ground below, there was the crack of bone. *Good!* Lenny thought. *He'll be in a cast for weeks and out of my way.*

Leaning forward, he looked down. The young man was lying on the ground, his neck at an odd angle. Lenny had seen enough death to recognize it. The man's neck was broken. He was dead.

Lenny raced down the ladder, then outside, being careful to step only on the paving stones, and stood over the kid. *Now what?* he wondered. He couldn't leave the body here. Cops would be all over the place. He had to get rid of it. But how? Wood chipper? Naw. Too much trouble to find one. It was Florida, so how about alligators? There were bound to be some nearby. He liked that idea. Clean and tidy. And it had a hint of environmental protection about it.

He was so absorbed in his thoughts that he didn't hear the footsteps until too late. Charlene had left her workshop. Worse, she'd *seen* him!

As fast as he'd ever moved, Lenny disappeared. Like a puff of smoke, he was gone.

From his hiding place, he saw Charlene take a few more steps, but then she seemed to realize that she shouldn't confront a strange man. She had half turned away when she saw the young man on the ground.

Lenny had seen enough about her to know what she would do. She ran to help the kid. He stood in the background, fading into the trees, as he watched her try to revive the man. Mouth-to-mouth, plus her hands on his heart and pumping.

He had to give it to her — she really tried to bring him back to life.

Lenny was waiting for her to give up and

go back to get her phone. He knew she rarely carried it with her. When she did, he'd go to the loft and see what the kid had left behind. Weapons? His phone? Had the punk recorded the whole job and put it on his Facebook page?

To Lenny's horror, he saw a car drive up and he knew who it belonged to. It was the red-haired girl who built birdhouses with Charlene. He knew she'd call the sheriff and there'd be no way Lenny could sneak back into the barn.

Reluctantly, he climbed over the fence at the back of the property and drove to his motel. He had a deep feeling of failure. Maybe he *was* too old for this job.

He took out his burner phone. He had to report to the man with the money.

TWO

Kate snuggled deeper in her big bed. She had the day *off*! No houses to show, no contracts to sign, no new listings to memorize.

In the last year there had been some upheavals in her job as a Realtor. The best thing was that her boss, Tayla Kirkwood, had finally hired an office manager. Kate and the other three employees were so overwhelmed with work that they'd confronted Tayla. Her reply to their demands had been, "Sure. Find somebody."

All in all, her reaction was a letdown. An easy solution, right? Ha ha. It had taken weeks of work and two hire-and-fire situations before they found the right person. She was in place now and taking over a lot of the paperwork. As a result, Kate could have some time off.

She was going to spend the day with Charlene and work on building birdhouses.

There was an Art Deco house that Kate wanted to try. She knew nothing about tools or even the wood, but Charlene was a patient teacher, and they were both glad for the company.

It had been Sara and Jack who'd encouraged Kate to befriend someone other than them.

"You shouldn't spend so much time with just us," Sara said. "Outside of work, you don't see anyone else."

"Neither do you," Kate said.

Sara smiled. "I'm a pure introvert. Reading, creating stories, photography, Reddit confessions. They're all I need. But you . . ." She didn't finish.

"Maybe I should date." Kate gave Jack a sideways look.

"Where do you want us to go?" he shot back.

When they were in England recently, she and Jack had kissed. It would have made sense that when they got home, they'd go further. But they didn't. It was a silent agreement between them that they had time and there was no need to rush. Kate was only twenty-five. It was early to get serious.

Besides, they liked the way things were. The three of them living together in the big house, laughing, teasing, working, enjoying their lives. They didn't want to change what was so very good.

Also, there was their other "job" of solving murders. There'd been three of them so far, and they had been complicated, frustrating and sometimes scary. When Kate had seen a man hanging in the corner of a room . . . She didn't want to remember that. But in the end, solving the murders had been oh, so satisfying.

All that seemed to be over now. When Jack told Sara and Kate that Sheriff Flynn wanted him to temporarily become a deputy, they had laughed hard. What a great joke! It had taken them a while to realize he was serious.

"But Sheriff Flynn doesn't *like* you," Kate blurted.

"That hasn't changed." Jack was gloomy, his face long. He hadn't shaved in days and his whiskers were as black as the way he seemed to feel.

"Why?" Sara sounded suspicious. "What is Daryl Flynn up to now?"

Jack shrugged. "I think his wife is threatening to divorce him if he doesn't take her on a vacation."

"One of his other deputies could take over. They could —" Kate stopped. Dave and Pete couldn't handle the office on their own. If there were any real problems, they'd probably panic.

"Can't Broward send someone?" Sara asked, then put up her hand. "Sorry, dumb question." The big Broward County Sheriff's Department in Fort Lauderdale would probably enjoy sending someone to take over. With the multiple murders in Lachlan in recent years, the town was considered "dangerous." And an object of ridicule. The county would probably change everything and make the residents of Lachlan miserable. "So you're going to do it?"

"I guess," Jack said. "My father and Flynn had a hand in keeping my juvie records sealed. I guess I do owe them." Around town, Jack's father's criminal activities were legendary, and Jack had been a rebellious teen.

"You'll look cute in the uniform." Kate's eyes were twinkling.

He glowered at her. "You get to iron them."

"Like hell I will!" she said. "You can —"
He was smiling at her.

"You'll have access to all the files of past cases." Sara sounded dreamy.

Kate understood her aunt. "There are sure to be lots of cold cases. All those unsolved crimes and missing people. We can —"

29

"No!" Jack shouted as he stood up. "I'm sure *this* is the real reason Flynn wants *me* to run the place. To protect you two from yourselves. There will be no digging into files. No attempts at righting wrongs. No injustices to be fixed. No to everything." He glared at them in warning, but the women kept smiling. He sighed. "I'm going to hit the bag. Anybody want to join me?"

"Sure." The women left to change clothes and get their boxing gloves. They knew that Jack often needed a release for the anger that lived inside him.

Days later, Jack was sworn in as a deputy, and Sheriff Flynn boarded a cruise ship in big Fort Lauderdale that adjoined Lachlan. He wouldn't be back for six weeks.

For all that Jack made jokes about sleepy little Lachlan, they knew he was worried about doing a good job. One of his main goals in life was to clean up the Wyatt name.

And also, Kate knew that one of Jack's concerns was that Kate was worried about her mother. Ava Medlar seemed to have disappeared.

As a child, Kate had to deal with her mother's bouts of depression that were so deep that they consumed the woman. When Kate got home from school — elementary, high school, university — she often found her mother curled up somewhere, unable to eat or drink.

Dealing with her mother's moods had been the biggest problem of Kate's life. Sometimes it would take days to get her mother to the stage where she could speak — and then it was always about her deceased husband. "I just miss him so much. He was my life. He was my reason for being," she'd say.

Kate never let herself be hurt by the comments that left her out of her mother's life. Kate saw it as a different kind of love than what was between a mother and daughter.

It wasn't until Kate was a college graduate and had a good job as a Realtor that her mother shocked her with the revelation that Kate had an aunt — and Ava had nothing good to say about her. "A selfish, senile old woman who cast us out of her rich life," was only part of what Ava said about her sister-in-law.

Feeling like a traitor, Kate had looked up Sara Medlar online. She found that her aunt was a very successful author. But that hadn't mattered. Kate just wanted what she'd always dreamed of: a loving family. She very much wanted to meet her unknown aunt. In secret, she'd contacted a

Realtor, Tayla Kirkwood, in Lachlan, explained who she was and asked if she had an opening in her firm. Tayla had replied with an enthusiastic, "Yes!"

The only thing left to do was tell her mother — and Kate had dreaded it. She prepared herself for her mother's biggest, most serious fit. But to Kate's shock, her mother encouraged her to leave Chicago and Ava's religious fanatic brothers, to go to sunny Florida, where Aunt Sara lived. Kate almost chickened out when Ava talked of Sara's violent temper.

But moving had been the best thing Kate could have done. She'd now had a few years of extreme happiness and contentment — and therein lay the problem. Something was up with her mother and Kate knew she was going to have to deal with it.

Usually, Kate and her mother had frequent contact: phone calls, texts, videos. Kate often had to endure her mother's bashing of Sara. Out of self-protection, she'd silently withstood all Ava dished out. Standing up for her aunt would have sent Ava into one of her depressions, then Kate would have to fly back to Chicago to console her.

So far, Kate had resisted that urge. But something had changed. Last month, Ava had begun hounding Kate to return to Chicago "for a visit." Kate wasn't fooled. Her mother wanted Kate to move back "home." For them to live together. She didn't dare say, "This is my home now." That would have put Ava in the hospital.

Instead, Kate used work as her excuse not to be able to return. But Ava had been adamant. She came up with a hundred reasons why Kate should return. She could go to grad school, see her old friends. And in winter she could wear her pretty sweaters. Anything Ava could come up with, she used.

During one video chat, Kate had suggested that Ava move to Lachlan. "I'll find you a pretty apartment and —"

"You want me to live *alone* while you live with *her*?" Ava went purple with anger.

After every call, Jack handed Kate a frosty margarita.

Both Jack and Sara had volunteered to call Ava to try to soothe her. "No!" Kate had blurted. She knew that outside influences would make things worse.

But everything had ended abruptly. Ten days ago, her mother had sent a text.

I have to go away. Good things happening. See you soon.

Kate had not heard from her mother since. Ten whole days and not a word. There had been no replies to any form of communication Kate used.

Of course, she'd told Sara and Jack everything.

Sara had called one of her publishing friends who lived in Chicago and asked her to check on Ava's house. The friend's son had entered the house. Sara wisely didn't ask how he got in. He said the house was clean and neat and empty. He sent photos of the closets and Kate saw that half of her mother's clothes were gone, but her winter coats were there.

"At least she went somewhere warm," Sara said.

Jack said, "I'll fly up there and ask questions."

"No," Kate said. "I'll wait a while longer."

Jack didn't say so, but she knew that part of the reason he'd taken the deputy job was because of Ava. Jack could now call for help from the Chicago Police Department.

Sighing, Kate got out of bed. It was late, although in their household, *late* was a relative term. Jack was usually at his construction business by seven and now he was at the Lachlan sheriff's office by then. As for

34

Sara, it wasn't unusual to see a light under her door at 4:00 a.m.

Kate got dressed, went into the kitchen and ate a bowl of cereal. She was peeling an orange when Sara opened the double doors to her bedroom. She was a small woman, with short blond hair and a remarkably unlined face, considering her age. They didn't speak of any numbers, but Sara had protested the Vietnam War.

"Jack's gone?"

"Oh yeah," Kate answered. "He's probably there, reading all those delicious files."

"More likely, he's fighting off girls. He does look good in that uniform." Sara was an honorary grandmother to Jack and in her eyes he could do no wrong. "You heading to Charlene's?"

"Yes."

"Getting any info out of her?"

Kate laughed. She couldn't fool her aunt. Many years ago, Charlene had known Kate's late father, Randal. All her life, Kate had been obsessed with her father, but she'd never been able to get anything from her mother. At least not anything *real*. To Ava, Randal Medlar had been a saint, too good for the earth. "God took him," she'd say with tears.

One of the reasons Kate had wanted to

meet her aunt was to find out about her father. What was he really like? Kate wanted to know everything from his favorite foods to his politics.

But Sara had been evasive. She'd let out snippets about her brother but nothing much. The only solid thing Kate had learned was that her father wasn't exactly the most honorable of men. Maybe he was even a bit of a scoundrel — and that was being kind.

Kate had been told he'd died of a heart attack but sometimes she wondered if that was the real cause of his death. If she ever did get access to the files in the Lachlan sheriff's office, she was going to look up Randal Medlar and find out some truths.

"You look serious," Sara said. "What's going on? Charlene tell you something bad?"

"She talks about my father less than you do."

Instead of accepting the guilt, Sara smiled. "Clever girl. So you'll be there all day?"

"Guess so. I enjoy it. I don't know what it is, but Charlene and I fit together. Sometimes she hands me things before I need them. And I'll be thinking about something and she'll start talking about it."

"Probably a past life bond."

Kate smiled. Sara's book plots had often dealt with reincarnation. "Hope it was the eighteenth century. I love those clothes."

"And how are the boys?"

They both knew Sara meant Leland as well as the children. "He adores Charlene. He's always watching her to see if she's okay."

Sara nodded at that. They knew what was behind Leland's solicitation.

"The kids are wild." Kate was smiling. "Charlene keeps a firm hand on them or they'd be swinging from the barn rafters. They love the horses and —" She looked at Sara. "Why are you smiling so hard?"

"Glad to see you're happy. Why don't you invite them over and Jack can grill fish?"

"That sounds great. How about next Saturday?"

"Perfect."

Kate looked at her watch. "I have to go. I told Charlene I'd be there by nine."

"Have a good time," Sara said. "A peaceful and safe time."

Smiling, Kate kissed her aunt's cheek and went to the garage to her car. She was tempted to ask if she could take Sara's powerful little MINI Cooper JCW but she didn't. She'd make do with the big, comfortable sedan she used to drive clients around town.

It wasn't far to Southwest Ranches, the

community that used to be small family farms. They'd been bought by rich people who built multimillion dollar homes that completely covered the plots. It had become an exclusive area.

But Charlene had kept the original one-story house. Years ago, Jack had remodeled it and built the chicken coop, a barn, a screen house where Charlene grew lettuces for local restaurants, and the beautiful workshop.

Kate drove down the long driveway and punched in the code to open the gate. She watched in her rearview mirror to make sure it closed.

She drove up to the side of Charlene's house, parked, got out and opened the trunk. Jack had given her a box of wood scraps for Charlene's birdhouses. She was headed toward the workshop when she heard her name being called.

"Kate! Help!"

She dropped the box and ran toward the barn, then halted. It took a moment to realize what she was seeing. Charlene was trying to revive a man who was on the ground. She was alternating between mouth-to-mouth and hard chest pumps.

Due to her recent experiences with murder investigations, Kate could see that the man was dead.

Kate's phone was always with her. She called Jack and he answered before the first ring finished. "I can't talk now," he said. "Idiot Dave has —"

"There's a dead man at Charlene's."

"On my way. Call Sara," Jack said.

Kate didn't call; she sent a text. Sara tended to ignore ringing phones but she couldn't resist any form of the written word.

Charlene's NOW. Camera.

Kate turned her attention to Charlene. "You need to stop," she said softly.

"But I think I can —"

"No," Kate said. "You can't. Who is he?"

"I don't know." Charlene leaned back until she was sitting on her heels, her eyes never leaving the man.

Kate looked up at the barn. It appeared as though the man had fallen out of the open window of the loft. Usually, there was a safety gate across the open space, but today it wasn't there. A few strands of hay were straggling down. "Jack and Sara will be here soon. I'm going to check out the loft."

Charlene barely nodded that she'd heard.

Inside the barn, Kate said hello to the two horses, then climbed up the ladder. She used her phone to take a few photos, then walked around the edge so as not to disturb anything.

Even as she did it, she chided herself. She was treating it like a murder scene. She was becoming too suspicious. Maybe the man came over the high wooden fence that surrounded the property to see the horses. Maybe he happened to fall out the window. There were reasons for this other than murder.

She looked out the window to the ground below. From this angle she could see the man clearly. He had on dark, formfitting gym clothes and running shoes. It looked like he was prepared to move easily and quickly. He was in excellent physical shape. It would have taken years of training to get his body that defined.

When she saw Jack's sheriff's car pull into the driveway, with Sara's fast little JCW right behind it, she let out a sigh of relief. Multiple people here were safer than just her and Charlene alone.

When Kate turned away from the window, she saw a shiny piece of wood sticking out from beneath the straw. Using the tip of her foot, she moved a few strands away. It was the end of a rifle stock. "I wish I hadn't been right," she muttered, then retraced her steps and went back down the ladder.

Jack was questioning Charlene. Did she know him? Ever seen him anywhere? Was she sure?

Charlene just shook her head and murmured, "No," to all his questions.

Sara was photographing every inch of the body and the place.

"I'll have to call this in," Jack said, but Kate put her hand over his phone. He understood that there was something she didn't want to say in front of Charlene. "Go in the house and call Leland to come home," he said kindly.

Charlene nodded, then walked away. Her pace wasn't steady.

Jack turned to Kate. "Show me."

Sara was already in the barn and taking photos. "I think you should see something."

"The rifle?" Kate asked.

Sara and Jack turned to her with wide eyes.

"I, uh . . ."

"Don't tell me what you did," Jack said, then looked at Sara. "What do you have?"

They followed her to the back of the barn to the alcove with the old desk. Sara pointed. On the edge, very faint, was a footprint.

"That print is from a very flexible shoe,"

41

Sara said. "It's not from one of those big Nike clodhoppers like the dead guy is wearing. If this were twenty-some years ago, I'd say it was from a hightop Reebok."

Jack was looking at her. "Not something a young whippersnapper would wear?"

"Exactly." She nodded toward the rack of leather reins. One of them wasn't hanging straight. "Onto the desk, foot up there, then up to the loft."

Kate was imagining the movement. "I'm five-seven and that would be too far of a stretch for me."

"And a lift like that takes strength," Sara said. "He or she would have to do a full body lift."

"That means a lightweight butt," Kate said.

Jack gave a one-sided grin. "Old timey shoes, skinny and tall. Do I have it right?"

The women nodded.

Jack looked at Kate. "Since you've already been snooping and have contaminated the crime scene, you can lead the way up."

She didn't move. "So now I'm a contaminator? In the past you would have congratulated me for thinking ahead. But now that you're a big shot deputy, you —"

"Now that I'm on the other side, things are different. I had to take an oath to uphold the law. To —" He broke off because Sara was halfway up the ladder.

Kate hurried up behind her. With a groan, Jack followed them.

"I went around the edge," Kate said to her aunt.

"Like a killer wouldn't do that," Jack muttered.

Kate turned on him. "Since no one knew he was here, he seems to have been smack in the middle of the barn."

"That's what the victim did," Jack said. "That means someone else went around the side. If the guy was pushed, it could have been a killer, and he —"

"It's here," Sara said loudly. She was at the edge of the open window near the tip of the rifle that was peeping out from under the straw.

"Maybe he was after Charlene," Kate whispered, and they looked at each other. They didn't have to say that there were *reasons* for someone to be after Charlene.

They went down the ladder and back outside. They stood by the body lying on the ground, looking at it in silence — but they knew their thoughts were the same.

When Charlene was sixteen years old, she did something she shouldn't have. Her aunt Tayla got her out of it and had managed to keep it a secret for many years, so Charlene was never caught. But they knew there were still case files — which meant there was possible DNA. With modern technology, a match could be made.

"Did she touch him?" Sara asked.

"When I drove up, she was giving him mouth-to-mouth."

"Lord!" Jack whispered. "I need to report this. So how are we going to play it?"

"So now you're part of *us*?" Kate asked. "Not hiding behind a badge?"

Before he could answer, they heard a car. It was Leland.

"We must protect Charlene," Jack said as he took out his phone and called the Broward County office. Soon they would be inundated with high-ranking officers who would delight in ridiculing them. Yet another mysterious death in little Lachlan.

With triple sighs, they waited for Leland to come to them.

Leland Adams was a very handsome man. Not like Jack, a man who made women's hearts beat a little faster, but old-fashioned handsome. Like a 1950s movie star.

He was about ten years older than Charlene. He'd made them remember how a fifteen-year-old Charlene had developed a major crush on Sara's younger brother,

Randal, who was in his thirties at the time. "Tastes never change," Sara had muttered.

Leland's face was a deep frown as he stared at the body lying on the ground. He turned to Jack. "Who is he and why is he here?" He was using his lawyer tone.

"We don't know," Jack said. "Charlene tried to revive him but he was already dead."

For a moment, Jack and Leland locked eyes in understanding of what the ramifications of this act could be.

"I'll take her away," Leland said. "She —"

"No!" Kate and Sara said in unison.

"Right," Jack added. "That would be too suspicious. We don't want anyone digging into this. Why don't you and the kids go away? Charlene can stay here. I'll make sure she's protected."

With a nod, Leland turned and went to the house.

As soon as they were alone, Kate asked, "Now what?"

"The county guys will be here soon. They'll —"

"Make a mess of everything," Sara said. "Who do *we* think this is? And why was he here?"

For a moment they were silent but they were thinking of Charlene.

"It's a cold case," Jack said. "*Very* cold.

45

After Dakon died, no one cared."

He was referring to the Atlanta police officer who'd been obsessed with the White Lily Kidnapping.

"Yes, it was a long time ago," Kate said. "Surely no one today wants to know about it."

"Does Everett still want to write a book about it?" Sara asked, since Kate frequently visited the man.

"I think you scared him away from the project," Kate said. "Uh-oh." Pulling into the drive through the gate Leland had left open were two Broward County sheriff's cars. Getting out of one of them was Detective Cotilla, a good-looking man of Cuban descent, midforties.

Jack groaned. The officer had given them a lot of trouble in the past.

"Well, well, well," Cotilla said as he looked Jack up and down in his brown uniform. "Looks good on you, doesn't it? That why you agreed to do it? To get Badge Bunnies?"

Jack clenched his jaw shut.

Chuckling, Detective Cotilla looked at the body on the ground. "So what do we have here?" He glanced up at the barn opening. "Looks like an accident. Fell out the window and landed on his head. They should put a rail across that window."

46

"There usually is one." Kate stepped forward. "I think you should look inside the loft."

Cotilla glared at her in a way that made Kate step back.

"Sorry," she murmured. "Just trying to help."

"I thought maybe Flynn swore the lot of you in as deputies." He was being sarcastic. "But there seems to be only one. Too bad, as Lachlan sure does seem to need a homicide squad." He looked at Jack. "Let me guess. You think this was a murder and you Nosy Three plan to solve it."

"I'm leaving that for you to decide." Jack was obviously trying to hold in his temper.

"You have a motive for this guy? Do you even know who he is?"

"No," Jack said.

"Just what I thought. Jumping to conclusions with no evidence." Cotilla went into the barn while the others stayed outside. Minutes later, he was standing in the open window, rifle in hand. At least he had a cloth between his hand and the weapon. He was looking out above their heads, not down at the body. Sara took photos of him.

When he returned, he handed the rifle to his deputy. "Bag it." He turned back to Jack. "You can see halfway to Sawgrass from up

there. He was probably some tourist looking for gators or an anaconda to shoot."

"In a suburban area?" Sara asked.

"I never underestimate tourists. Who
knows what he wanted? So who found the
body?"

"Charlene Adams," Jack said. "He was just
lying there when she —"

"I'll ask her myself. When does Flynn get
back?"

"Six weeks," Jack replied.

"Must be nice to get time off. You two go
home. You, Wyatt, just wait out here and I'll
tell you what to do next. But I assure you
that we'll take care of this." Detective Cotilla waited until he saw the three of them
walk to their cars before he went into the
house to talk to Charlene.

Sara and Kate stopped at Jack's car.

"This is good," he said. "Maybe it was an
accident. Tourists do some crazy things, so
maybe —" His phone buzzed. "It's Tayla."
He didn't answer but looked back at Sara
and Kate. "I think we should be cautious.
I'm going to have this place wrapped in
security. Cameras, alarms, the works."

Jack's phone buzzed again.

"Tayla will be hysterical about Charlene,"
Kate said.

"She'll want her niece to stay with her,"

Sara added.

"Only if she has a guard with her," Jack snapped. "At least Tayla doesn't live in that big house alone anymore." He turned to Kate. "Ask Gil if he'll stay here and take care of Charlene's menagerie."

"Quinn will love being here," Kate said. Gil was Jack's best friend and his foreman, and Quinn was Gil's young son.

"You don't think this has anything to do with Quinn's mother, do you?" Sara asked.

"She knows the money stops if she shows up, but I'll check on it anyway. Anything else you two can come up with?"

"I hope it was an accident," Kate said. "I mean, I'm sorry for the man, but . . ." She took a breath. "I'm going to call Tayla and tell her what happened. Think you can find a bodyguard for her?"

"Yes," Jack said. "I'll see you two later." He paused. "I'm going to find out whatever I can. I wish —"

Sara put her hand on his arm. "Wish Daryl were here?"

"Right now I do, yes." He looked at Sara. "What are you planning to do?"

"Nothing dangerous."

He kept looking at her, waiting for the truth.

"Okay, I think I'll prepare a little package

49

for the skeptical detective. I thought I'd write a detailed report of everything we saw and did. And I'll put the photos on a thumb drive to give to the county officers."

She sounded so innocent, so sincere, that Jack and Kate stared at her.

Kate blinked. "Did you get a good picture of the footprint on the desk and the re-arranged bridles?"

Sara grimaced. "I didn't. There wasn't enough light. I need to work on my low light skills." She smiled up at Jack.

"I didn't hear a word of that."

"Maybe this afternoon I could check your files," Kate said to Jack. "I'd like to see if Charlene's DNA is in there."

"It isn't," Jack said quickly.

"I take it you already looked?" Sara asked.

Jack shrugged in answer. "Okay, now go before Cotilla comes out and rips me apart."

The women were backing away. "You'll tell us whatever you hear from Charlene?" Sara asked.

"Maybe. If it's legal."

Kate was at her car. "I'll go to Tayla and fix it for Charlene to stay with her. And I'll talk to Gil and help him and Quinn pack."

"Don't flirt with him." Jack had a pained look on his face. "Gil's had enough women problems to last him a lifetime."

"Why, Jack," Kate said, fluttering her lashes, "I would never be a problem to any man. I would —" She cut off her words because the door to the house opened. Cotilla was coming out. In an instant, Kate and Sara were in their cars and leaving so fast that gravel spewed.

THREE

Sara thought the most beautiful thing in the world was a blank sheet of paper. After she left Charlene's house, she made a quick stop at Time Paused, the local gift/stationery/bookstore to buy a new journal. Mr. Wilkens, the owner, had had to carry more than books to be able to stay in business. Sara was one of his best customers so he kept a lovely selection of journals. He knew she preferred the ones from Italy.

Her quick stop turned into over an hour as she picked up a biography of an Edwardian countess, a thick photo book of Steve McCurry in India, and a journal with a cover of embossed red leather. She liked having a different notebook for each of her many projects.

At the register, Mr. Wilkens talked her into buying two new pens. This simply involved putting them where she could see them.

"Anything new coming out?" he asked.

"My wife wants another book from you."

"Maybe," Sara said. "Right now I have some ideas I want to write down."

"Oh good. Got a pub date yet?"

Sara managed to keep smiling. TV and movies showed authors turning in a thin manuscript held together with clips, then the "book" coming out two weeks later. People couldn't believe it took a year to write a hundred thousand words, then another year before it was published. Unless you were extremely lucky, a week after it came out, it was all over. "Not yet," she said, "but I'll let you know."

"What's going on at Charlene's house?"

Sara gasped. Lachlan already knew about the body?

He understood her surprise. "My wife's cousin knows . . ." He trailed off at Sara's look. "I'm sure no one else has heard."

Sara didn't reply, just put her credit card away, took the bag and left.

She put the bag in her car, removed the notebook and pens, then walked to the bakery. The feeling of "new" as in pens and blank paper was cheering her up. Paper could be filled with anything she wanted: garden plans, camera settings, a plot for another novel or character sketches. She loved to sit somewhere quiet, hidden away, and watch people and imagine their lives. A love life or not? Occupation? Brave or a coward? In the last years, she'd added "Capable of murder or not?" to her sketches.

She went to Mitford Tea Room. That it was named after the fascinating Mitford sisters had always pleased her.

However, in the first years after she'd returned to Lachlan, the owner, Bessie Owens, had been less than friendly. She said a low-class Medlar had no right to pretend to be part of Lachlan society. Blah, blah, blah. Since then, some things had happened that made Bessie see that she'd been wrong. In apology, she'd invited Sara to her tearoom, but Sara had turned her down. "I don't blame you for being angry," Bessie said contritely.

"It's not that," Sara said. "I live on a keto diet. Few carbs and no sugar. Those divine little tea cakes of yours would destroy my blood sugar. I'd be ravenous for days."

Two weeks later, Bessie sent her an invitation with a note. She said she'd researched and experimented until she'd made scones from almond flour, chocolate chips, heavy cream and sweetener from the stevia plant. Pure keto. She asked Sara to please come and sample them. Sara was there the next afternoon. With the keto-allowed butter and clotted cream, the scones were divine.

Bessie had put the leftovers in a corner of her display case with a little handwritten sign saying No Sugar, Almost No Carbs, But Lots Of Fat. She figured no one would buy them and she'd have to throw them away. But they sold out in minutes. She now had keto cookies, cupcakes and three kinds of scones.

Sara was a frequent visitor. Locals knew to nod hello, then leave Sara alone, but tourists weren't kind. They thought nothing of plopping down at Sara's table and telling her all about their lives. They pretty much always ended with, "There's something I've always wanted to ask a writer. Where do you get your ideas?"

After several such encounters, Sara stopped going to the tearoom. But Bessie's sales had increased due to Sara's presence and the introduction of the low carb cakes. To lure her back, Bessie set up a tiny table far from the door and in the shadows. She even put up a pretty screen beside the table in case Sara felt she needed to hide from anyone.

When Sara entered the shop, she smiled at Bessie, said, "Same," then went to her table in the back. She let out a sigh of satisfaction. New pen, blank notebook, a pot of Assam tea and two chocolate chip scones with dollops of thick cream. Life couldn't get any better.

As Sara ate, she began to write down everything she could think of that might be related to the case. First was why Charlene could be the reason someone was hiding in the loft with a rifle. But she didn't write that. If her notebook was found by someone she didn't want that information in there.

It wasn't necessarily planned to be a murder, she wrote. *Could be something to do with Leland. Maybe it was an angry client of his. Big question: Did someone push the man out of the barn or did he fall? Could he have —*

She looked up when someone noisily put a chair at her table and sat down. It was Everett Gage and Sara's surprise turned to a glare of *Go away.*

"And hello to you too," he said.

He was a pudgy, pale-skinned man and he *always* wanted something.

"What do you want?" Sara's eyes narrowed.

"Do you mind?" He picked up a scone and bit into it before she could answer.

"I have work to do and I need peace."

His mouth was full. Good table manners were not his forte. "Our book is finished."

56

Like she hadn't been told that a dozen times already. Everett considered himself a journalist-with-a-mission, meaning that he wrote what he saw as "the truth." Actually, his many past books had merely sensationalized some old crime cases. He got his small publishing house to declare there was new information inside, but there never was. Big surprise, his books didn't sell.

It was through Sara, Jack and Kate that Everett had met Arthur Niederman. Arthur was in a wheelchair, had money from a settlement and he wanted to write murder mysteries. The two men decided to collaborate.

Everett moved into Arthur's beautiful house, and together they wrote the first book of a series of mysteries. Sara had been bullied into helping them with the plot, getting an agent and a publishing house. After that, she told them they were on their own.

But Everett always wanted *more.* She repeated, "What do you want?"

"I was talking to my agent and —"

"The agent I got for you."

"Yes you did, which is why I feel that I can ask for one more small thing from you. It's about the publication."

"You want a cover quote."

"Yes, but also something bigger."

"You already have two names on the cover. Mine wouldn't fit."

He frowned. "Author names come with royalty splits. We aren't going to share the money."

Sara's hair stood up in rage, her teeth clamped. "I have *never* asked you for *money.*" She picked up her notebook and pen to leave.

"Sorry." He clamped down on her forearm.

She looked at his hand and he released his grip.

Bessie came to the table and glared at Everett. "Maybe you'd do better at your own table."

Everett sighed. "I'll behave." He gave his sad, helpless look to Sara. "Please listen to me? For Arthur?"

With a grimace, Sara gave a nod, then turned to Bessie. "It's okay. Could I have more scones, please? He ate mine."

With a sniff, Bessie turned on her heel and left.

"She didn't even ask what kind I want," Everett whined.

"Beggars, et cetera," Sara muttered. "So state your case. I have work to do."

"Writing about the dead body found at Charlene Adams's house?"

Sara wasn't surprised by this second mention of it. "It was an accident. A man fell out of the barn window. His neck broke on impact."

"Charlene had an opening of a second-story window with no bars across it? With those hellion kids of hers? Who was the man?"

"A tourist."

"Doesn't Charlene have a fence around the whole place?"

Sara leaned back in her chair and crossed her arms tightly. She wasn't going to give him any more information.

"All right, I'll come clean. My agent and I thought it might be nice if you did a little publicity for our book. After all, it's kind of your plot. Detective in a wheelchair, lawyer nephew, pretty girl gardener. And of course the retired romance writer who pulls it all together."

She narrowed her eyes at him. "You used *my* plot and now I owe *you*?"

"It is kind of your baby so I thought you might want to, uh, nurture it."

"I —" Sara began but Bessie dropped a plate of four scones on the table and gave Everett a dirty look before she left.

"Judgmental, isn't she?"

"You have no idea. I need to go." With

pen and journal in hand, she stood up. When the front door opened, she glanced toward the light.

There are moments when events are so traumatic that they make time stand still. This was one of them. Standing in the doorway, blinking from having left the brilliant Florida sunshine, was Ava, her sister-in-law. Kate's mother.

It was a full second before Sara could think, and when she did, she acted. She did a boxing duck, dropping into a squat as though to avoid being hit. In the next second, she did a three-step crabwalk to get behind the screen and hid from sight.

"What the hell?" Everett turned toward the door. Instantly, his plump face became a study in shock and disbelief.

With a lightning-speed grab, he picked up the plate of scones, bent over as far as his belly allowed and scurried behind the screen with Sara.

"Get out!" she hissed.

"And face Ava? No thank you."

Yet again, Sara was shocked. Her eyes were nearly the size of the scones.

"Don't look at me like that." Everett was trying to stuff two whole scones into his mouth at once. He succeeded.

Sara, squatting so she was barely two feet

60

off the ground, peered around the screen.

Ava was at the counter, looking into the big glass case and pointing to one pastry after another as Bessie bagged them. One thing Sara truly *hated* about her sister-in-law was that she could eat as much as she wanted, of anything she wanted, and stay as thin as a worm.

Everett pressed close to Sara and looked around her. "She eats brownies and ice cream for breakfast." His tone was of disgust and envy.

"How do you know that?"

"I interviewed her about Randal."

Sara twisted around to glare at him.

In spite of a full mouth, Everett managed to look smug. "Didn't know I knew about him, did you?"

They watched in silence as Ava paid cash for her big bag of little sandwiches, cupcakes and lots of the beautifully colored macarons. They didn't fully exhale until she left the shop.

Everett was the first to speak. "I don't think I can get up."

Sara stood up easily. Forty-plus years of lifting weights had kept her strong. "Too bad. Bessie has strawberry scones using the recipe from the Father Brown mysteries."

Everett stood. He was still holding the

plate, which was now empty.

Bessie came over with two pots of fresh, hot tea. More Assam for Sara and jasmine for Everett. She wasn't smiling but neither was she glaring. She left quickly.

"Looks like I passed some test," Everett said. "This tea smells divine."

"She probably thought you were protecting me." Sara filled her cup, added full cream, then looked at him. "Out with it."

"I don't mean to be an I-told-you-so, but you've always dismissed me as a writer who is not of equal worth to you. Just because I haven't sold millions as you have, you think —"

Sara looked ready to hit him. "The first time I met you, you were shouting that I was that despicable thing called a 'romance writer.' Lowest of the low. Stupid, incompetent and worthless."

Everett waved his hand in dismissal. "Well, I had been told some things about you before that."

Sara looked at him as she tried to put together the pieces of all that she'd seen and heard. "Ava. She bad-mouthed me to you."

Everett smiled. "There! See? That's proof that you're smart and clever as well as being very successful. I bet you can —"

62

"Stop sucking up to me and tell me how you know her."

"I wrote a book about your brother."

Sara stared, barely able to speak. "When?" she whispered.

"Years ago. About 2001, I think. And before you ask, I never used his name. I wanted to, but . . ." He shrugged. "Lawyers, you know."

"How? Why?" Sara's voice was low.

Everett took his time answering. "First of all, I want some credit for keeping this secret. I was shocked when Kate spoke of her 'late' father. Poor girl. She still thinks he died when she was what? Six? Seven?"

"Four." Sara was almost choking.

He finished his cup of tea and poured another. "That book was my first attempt at fiction and I will admit that it was a failure. I wanted to write about a *real* cat burglar. You know, true crime, what I'm good at. I'm not like you, who can make up stories out of nothing. I need a foundation in truth."

"You elaborate on old crimes. You don't 'make up' anything."

"It depends on how you look at it. Anyway, I prefer the unsolved ones. I like to think that my work helps bring justice."

63

"Tell me what you did." She wasn't smiling.

"I guess you've heard of the big jewelry theft in Las Olas in 1995? At the Oliver Mansion?"

Sara didn't answer. "Go on."

"It was a case that was never solved. Old, rich Mrs. Oliver owned a veritable hoard of jewels. There were priceless items, some of historic value. Think of Wallis Simpson's great pile. While she was dying in a hospital, all of them went missing. Her stepson reported the robbery to the police and the insurance company. But he was adamant his stepmother knew more about the robbery than she was telling. He said everyone — her relatives, lawyers, et cetera — questioned her night and day but she died without telling anything. He was a *very* angry man."

Sara was sitting in silence but her eyes showed she was listening to every word.

"I spent months trying to find cases of other burglaries like that one, hoping for a clue. But I came up empty. One day, I thought that if I had relatives as nasty and greedy as hers, I'd be glad someone else got the jewels. That's when I thought that I'd try to find someone she *liked.*"

Sara was listening, but saying nothing.

"I had to go way back in her life to find someone who fit the bill. I looked on microfiche. Remember those rolls? My neck still aches from that machine. But I found something. Back in the late sixties, there was a grainy newspaper photo of the rich Mrs. Oliver attending a gala on the arm of a tall, handsome young man. It took a lot of digging to find out who he was. He was a teenager by the name of Randal Medlar. I was intrigued."

Everett picked up the last scone. "It wasn't easy to find out about him. By then Randal was in prison and, oddly, I could find out very little about what put him there."

"Not jewelry theft," Sara said.

"No. He got the maximum sentence for something that could have been a misunderstanding." He was looking hard at Sara.

"I didn't turn him in or set him up if that's what you're implying."

"Of course not." His voice hinted that she was lying.

Sara clenched her fists so hard her nails embedded in her palms.

"I wanted to write a nonfiction account," he said, "so I wrote Randal a letter, asking if I could interview him. I will say that it was a very flattering letter. If he'd pulled off that job, I was truly impressed."

65

"You thought he'd confess to you?" Sara was looking at him in disbelief.

"I've done several true crime books and yes, many perpetrators love to brag."

"But not my brother."

"No, not him. He never answered me directly but I did receive a letter from a lawyer named Melvin Hopkins who was in the same prison. It said I was to cease and desist all my inquiries. If I didn't, he would sue me. He added that he was bored and would love doing it. Lawyer humor, I guess."

"You changed the book to fiction."

"I did. I took what I had imagined, but could find no proof of, and wrote it. It's titled *Rooftops of Gold* and was touted as being about one of the greatest cat burglars of all time." Everett's eyes twinkled. "I called my cat Rowan Bletley because . . ." He looked at Sara.

"Because the fruit of the Medlar tree has to be bletted before it's edible."

Everett smiled as though they were colleagues and sharing a happy memory.

"What did Ava tell you?"

Everett's skin seemed to pale about three shades. "She is, uh, a passionate woman. Great emotion."

"Blamed me for everything?"

"Yes. Vehemently." Everett gave Sara a

look of sympathy. "Every time she went off about, well, about *you,* I tried to direct her back to the subject. Didn't work. She called her brothers on me."

At that, Sara did give a look of sympathy. Ava's three older brothers, religious zealots, didn't have any concept of courtesy or understanding — or abiding by any laws. "Did they put you in the hospital?"

"Almost. They didn't hit me, just shoved me a lot, grabbed my arms, that sort of thing, while they threatened me. I had some serious bruises."

"A lawsuit and the brothers," Sara said. "I can understand why you backed off. The question is 'What now?' "

"If you're asking if I'm going to tell Kate the truth about her father, the answer is no."

All Sara could do was nod. They were speaking of her biggest fear in life. Her beautiful, caring, smart niece had become her reason for living. And Sara knew that when — not if — Kate found out the truth, she'd be furious. Sara could almost hear her. *"Why did you lie to me? Why didn't you tell me the truth?"* Lies and truth. Nothing was more essential than those two.

At the thought of what would happen when Kate found out, Sara began to blink back tears of fear.

Everett lost his pleased-with-himself expression. "I'm sorry," he said softly. "In these last years Kate has been a great friend to Arthur and me. We look forward to her visits. She reads our pages and praises them and tells us what to change. We had the Jack character so macho he wasn't real. Kate made us tone him down." He took a breath. "We wouldn't ever hurt her. I can't imagine your pain when Ava denied you access to Kate." He nodded toward the door. "If Ava is here in Lachlan in secret, I'm sure it's for a no-good purpose."

"She wants Kate to move back to Chicago with her."

Everett gave an involuntary shudder. "And live at the mercy of those uncles and Angry Ava?"

"Yes," Sara said softly.

Reaching out, Everett took Sara's hand and squeezed it. "Sometimes it may not seem so, but you and I are on the same team. If you can think of a way for me to help with this, I'll be there. And Arthur loves a good fight. We are at your service."

Sara swallowed against the lump in her throat. "Thank you."

Everett gave a smile, then looked at his watch. "I have to go. I'm meeting Arthur for lunch. Thanks for the appetizers."

At other times, Sara would have made a snide remark about an uncountable number of pastries being an "appetizer." But not today. "Tell him hello for me."

"Tell him yourself when you send over a really great book endorsement." His eyes twinkled at having changed it from a one-sentence quote to a full blurb for the back of the book. "And maybe you have some notes about a plot for the second book." He hurried away before Sara could reply.

Bessie came to the table. "I see he left you with the check."

"It's okay." Sara handed Bessie her credit card and added an equal amount as a tip.

As she left, Sara asked Bessie, "That woman who came in here? I haven't seen her before. Did she just move here?"

Bessie smiled. "Trying to get business for Kate? A house to buy?"

Sara smiled back. "Exactly. You know me so well."

"She's been here a couple of weeks, I guess. I've tried to welcome her to Lachlan but she won't say much. I couldn't even get her to tell me her name."

Sara knew the relentless inquiries of Lachlan residents. It was much worse when she was a child and people didn't move around so much, but it was still bad.

"You want me to work harder at finding out about her?"

"No!" Sara said, then calmed. "I mean I like my privacy so I guess she does too."

"If she plans to move here, I'm sure she can find Tayla's office. Let's hope she goes to Kate and not that Melissa," Bessie said. "My daughter told me Melissa was at the Brigade two nights ago and dancing with all the firefighters. It was shameful."

Sara gave a weak smile and left the tea-room. When she got to her car, she fell back against the seat. What the hell was going on? A man fell out of Charlene's barn loft and died. A few hours later she saw Ava. In Lachlan. And it seemed that she'd been here ever since she'd sent Kate a cryptic note saying something good was about to happen.

What did that mean? Ava *was* going to move to Lachlan? Sara couldn't imagine her leaving the "protection" of her brothers. After the trial, even Randal hadn't been able to persuade her to leave the Chicago area. "Sara will take care of you two," he'd said just before he was led away to prison. He well knew his wife's refusal to get a job.

Randal hadn't envisioned that Ava would manage to get Sara to support them but that she'd also deny his sister access to little Kate.

Sara looked out the windshield. It appeared that everything was soon going to end. Ava would use her weapon of Randal being alive against Sara. When Ava had first told Kate she had an aunt, Ava had said that Sara left them. Dropped them flat, abandoned them. Sara could almost hear what Ava would scream now. "It was your aunt Sara who put your father in prison. It's *her* fault he's in there."

Ava was always and forever the victim.

Sara started the car and pulled out. It would make sense to go home but she couldn't do it. For years now it had been a place of happiness. But that was based on the trio of Jack, Kate and her. That was about to end.

She turned left and went to the opposite side of town, to the almost-slum where she'd grown up. Jack had purchased several of the run-down houses and had restored them beautifully. He'd bought the two that had been owned by Sara's family and Jack's grandfather. But he hadn't started work on them. He said he wanted Sara's input but she hadn't been able to put her mind to the job.

Jack and Kate seemed to understand that

restoring the two little houses, no matter how tastefully they did it, would destroy the memories in the place.

"We'd chase away the ghosts," Kate said one night.

"It's time they went," Sara had replied, but she wasn't sure she meant it. She'd dealt with it all by procrastinating every aspect. She didn't visit the place and didn't answer Jack's questions about what she wanted to do.

Right now, all Sara wanted was to talk to Cal, Jack's grandfather. If he were still on the earth, he'd know how to handle everything.

She drove down the street where she'd grown up, admiring the houses Jack had remodeled. They looked great!

Past them were the two almost-derelict houses where the Wyatts and the Medlars had lived. Jack had repaired them enough that the roofs didn't leak and he'd had exterminators come in, but not much else had been done.

"Tell me when you're ready," he'd told Sara.

She parked her car so it couldn't be viewed from the road, then she went to the back, where she and Cal used to meet.

FOUR

By the time Jack got away from Charlene's house, it was after one o'clock. He wanted to get a sandwich, then visit his three construction jobs. He'd like to strap on a tool belt and climb a ladder, preferably with two fifty-pound bags of cement on his shoulders.

Instead, he needed to go back to the Lachlan Sheriff's Office and fill out paperwork.

"Just write whatever you can remember," Cotilla had said in a way that insinuated Jack might not be able to read or write.

Jack was acutely aware that in real life he could punch the detective in the face. He'd be handcuffed, then have to go before a judge, but it might be worth it. Now that he was in a uniform and had taken an oath, he could do nothing.

"And give me those photos," Cotilla ordered.

Jack wanted to point out that Sara was a private citizen and wasn't obligated to turn them over, but he said nothing.

Now he was in the patrol car and headed toward the office. Like a good boy.

On impulse, he turned left and went to a burger joint. Maybe he'd find Gil, they'd have lunch together, and Jack could spend an hour venting his frustration. He ordered two of everything, all the most greasy, high-calorie things he could get. Since living with two women, "healthy" had become a daily way of life. Sometimes a man needed more.

He took the bag — already grease soaked — from the pretty girl at the window, then called Gil. It went straight to voice mail.

So now what should he do? Find Kate? Sara? And answer their thousands of questions? Was he to keep his oath and reveal nothing and therefore make them feel betrayed? Or did he squeal?

As he drove, he realized he was going away from the office. Maybe he'd park somewhere and eat. But he'd already learned that his patrol car drew lots of attention. People tapped on his window. "Could you help me find my dog?"

"Has anyone turned in a brown jacket to your office?"

"I can't find my phone anywhere!"

Several minutes passed before Jack realized where he was heading. This morning Bea had said someone reported seeing a light on inside Sheriff Flynn's empty house. "Maybe he set the lights on a timer," Jack had replied.

Bea gave him a look. She was in her fifties and knew all about the town — and certainly everything about Daryl Flynn.

"So maybe Evie did it," Jack said.

Bea didn't say anything, just kept looking at him.

He surrendered. "I will check on it." During the chaos at Charlene's house, Bea had sent two texts reminding him to look in on the sheriff's house.

Jack was close so he went there. He'd never been inside the house. It was a nice one story with palm trees and a rock garden in front.

When Jack saw that the driveway curved around to the back, he smiled. He could hide the car with the writing that seemed to say, *I'll do anything you want. Ask me.*

He got the food bag, the cardboard tray of drinks, and thought he'd sit outside. There was no pool, and no cover over the patio area, not even chairs. With Florida weather, it was best to put them away if you were out of town.

When it started to rain, Jack muttered, "Oh the hell with it." There were no signs warning of an alarm system so he wouldn't set it off. He had a few tools on his key chain so he jimmied the lock on the back door.

As soon as he saw the kitchen, he knew that someone had been in the house. It wasn't a mess, but it was headed that way with all of the pizza boxes, Chinese food cartons, a recycling bin full of beer cans.

What was more, he could hear the faint, muffled sounds of a TV.

Silently, he put the food on the kitchen counter, drew out his gun and went through the house.

At the back was a den. Three sides were covered in dark oak bookcases that held every award the sheriff had ever received. Jack could almost hear Kate and Sara laughing. "It's a man cave," they'd say.

In front of the TV, someone was reclining in a big leather chair. Jack couldn't see the face but the ottoman had been raised and the left foot was in a plaster cast.

Jack would recognize those stubby legs anywhere. Without a sound, he reholstered his gun, then went back to the kitchen, got the food and took it to the den.

He dropped a foil-wrapped burger in

76

Sheriff Flynn's lap, then sat down in the matching leather chair.

" 'Fraid the rain would melt you?" the sheriff asked.

Jack handed him a drink the size of a washtub and a half shoebox of fries. "You aren't supposed to be here, but don't worry. I won't blab." He nodded toward the cast, eyebrows raised.

"Mishap."

Jack didn't reply as he bit into his giant, grease-dripping burger.

"You allowed to eat that?" Flynn asked. "There are none of those little green cabbages anywhere."

"Brussels sprouts. And no broccoli either." The men smiled at each other.

"So how'd you find me?"

"Bea said somebody saw a light on in your house and she strongly suggested that I should go check."

Flynn groaned. "That means she knows I'm here."

"Knows you lied about going on a cruise?"

"I meant to go! I was just hours away from leaving, then this happened." He nodded toward his cast.

"Gunfight? Ninja attack? You can tell me. I won't judge."

Flynn grimaced at his joke. "I dropped a

very heavy suitcase on my foot."

"Poor Evie. She must have been upset about missing her cruise. She around here?"

Flynn took his time answering. "She, uh . . . She was kind of angry, even hinted that I did it on purpose. She picked up that damned suitcase and carried it to the Uber. Then she went to Port Everglades and boarded the ship."

Jack was envisioning it all. "I guess you took yourself to the hospital."

"Yeah, in Boca."

"So you wouldn't see anyone you know?"

"Right."

Jack was trying not to laugh. "She having a good time on her cruise?"

"Time of her life is what she says. Texts me every hour to tell me who she's met, some cocktail she's had, what she's seen. Her photos are great."

Jack couldn't contain his laughter any longer.

Flynn acted hurt but one side of his mouth twitched.

"You got room for a fried pie?" Jack asked.

"Only if it's guaranteed not to be healthy."

"It'll clog your arteries after one bite."

"Give me two of 'em."

Jack gave him a pie and took the other. "So what are you watching?" The TV was

78

on so low they'd paid no attention to it. It was a game show.

Sheriff Flynn was licking thick cherry syrup that was running down his wrist. He touched the remote button and turned off the TV. "So why are you here?"

"Just came to check if your house was safe. I had a gun drawn on you."

"I saw your reflection in the TV. You sure can be quiet when you want to be. My guess is that you came here to escape. You and feisty little Kate get into a fight? She tell you she wanted a man who wasn't half criminal? Someone who was *respected* in town?"

Before Kate came into his life, those words would have sent Jack into an infamous "Wyatt rage." But not now. "I hate this job," he said.

"Let me guess. Today at a suspicious death, you were treated to a Broward Bashing. Dismissed as a small town nobody even though you've solved previous murders."

Jack was startled. "How'd you find out about that?"

Flynn shoved his empty papers into the big bag. "I have a few tricks. What did you and the girls see that you didn't tell anybody about?"

Jack shook his head. "Smart old hound

dog, aren't you?"

Sheriff Flynn waited until Jack told him about the footprint and the out of order reins.

"Maybe the dead guy did it," the sheriff said.

"Could be." Jack was silent for a moment. He and the sheriff had never been friends. When Kate first came to Lachlan, Jack and the sheriff were closer to being enemies. Flynn often said that Jack was just like his lying, thieving father.

Maybe he had been for a while. But when Jack was eighteen, enormous responsibility had been dumped on him. He'd been put in a position where he had to take care of his mother and his young sister, so he'd started Wyatt Construction.

Gradually, Jack started gaining some respectability for the Wyatt name — but not to Flynn's generation. They remembered Roy too well.

"I know some things from the past," Jack said softly.

"About Charlene?"

Again, Jack looked startled.

"Don't tell me the details," Flynn said. "Wait until I'm retired and no longer wear a badge. I figured out some of it back when Tayla was in jail, but I thought it was better to keep quiet. So you think the man in her barn was there for a reason?"

"Yes. We saw —"

Flynn put up his hand. "Before we start with confessions, you and I need to make a deal. If it's known that I'm here, I'll have to get involved. That means whatever we talk about is official police business."

"So I'm to keep my mouth shut about you being here?"

"If I'm not here, then you're talking to a ghost. And ghosts can't reveal things we've discussed."

"Then I guess I can tell you anything and all of it." His head came up. "You're not saying I'm not to tell Sara and Kate that you're here, are you?"

"I leave that to your discretion. A need-to-know basis."

Jack was beginning to understand. "Do you have something important to tell me?"

"Yeah, I do. It's why I planned to leave town, why I'm hiding and why I bullied you into putting on the badge." He swallowed. "Sometimes it may seem that I don't trust you, but you're the only person I know who can handle this."

"I'm not sure I want to hear what it is. Will it harm Sara or Kate?"

Flynn took his time answering. "It will affect them greatly, but maybe you can keep them from actual harm. It will help if you're forewarned."

"Then tell me," Jack said. "I want to hear every word."

Flynn took a deep breath. "Sara's brother? Kate's father?"

"Yeah? Randal. Died when Kate was four."

"No, he didn't. He's been in prison all these years. He's been released early and I believe he's headed this way. Wherever Randal goes, trouble follows."

Jack leaned back in the chair, eyes straight ahead, and prepared to listen to every word the sheriff had to tell him. "I want to know everything."

FIVE

It took Kate hours to get it all organized. She went to her boss, Tayla — who was nearly hysterical — and answered all of her zillion questions about her niece and what had happened. The answers were mostly, "We don't know."

Kate tried to stick to the facts: dead body found outside the barn. "We don't know who he was or why he was there."

Finally, Kate suggested Tayla needed to think about getting her house ready for Charlene to stay. Tayla's former house had been huge, but this one was smaller, simpler and would be easier to protect. There were three bedrooms, but one was quite small. The only things in it were Tayla's suitcases.

"Jack suggested hiring a security person. Maybe he can stay in here?"

Tayla readily agreed.

"Why don't you go buy a frame and mattress and some sheets?" *That will keep her busy,* Kate thought.

"Yes, that would be good," Tayla said. Minutes later, she was out the door.

One down, one to go. Kate's next step was to visit Gil at work. The construction site was a divine cacophony of saws, hammering, drills going, men yelling.

"Looking for me?" Gil asked. "At least I hope so." He was shorter than Jack and thicker. A concrete block of a man. Best was that Gil Underhill had an air about him that made people feel safe, cared about.

She laughed and was glad to do so. "We need your help."

His handsome face became solemn. They never spoke of it, but he owed the Three his life. He nodded toward his truck. It would give them a private place to talk.

As they closed the doors, Kate thought about lying through omission. She couldn't tell Gil about the past, only the present. She described finding the dead body and concluded with what was becoming a mantra: "We don't know who he is or why he was there."

Gil didn't hesitate. "Whatever the reason, the creep was trespassing. You want to get Charlene the hell out of there, don't you?"

Kate breathed a sigh of relief. "Yes. Could you and Quinn look after the place?"

84

"Love to. Quinn will be ecstatic. I'll take care of the plants and animals. All of it."

"Thanks. Jack is having security cameras and alarms put in. I don't know exactly what's being done, just that it'll be safer."

"I've got some cousins. I'm the smallest one. Maybe they'd like to stay there with us until you guys solve this."

"That sounds great! But just so you know, while Jack is a deputy sheriff, Aunt Sara and I are staying out of it."

Gil laughed. "Good one, Kate."

She tried to look serious but couldn't. "Maybe Aunt Sara and I will ask a few questions here and there, but that's all." She was grinning.

"Gonna make Jack think he's the boss?"

"We always try to do that. Haven't made any progress so far." She opened the truck door. "Thank you so much for this. Leland's taking the boys out of state, and Charlene should be out of their house by this evening. The house and all the critters are yours tonight."

"I'll call my cousins now."

Smiling, she got out and went to her car. It was nearly one. Maybe she'd take herself out to lunch, go home and swim for a while, then snuggle up with a book. She could still salvage half of her day off.

85

When she got into her car, she looked at her phone. She'd turned it off while she was with Gil, but she had three messages from the office, each marked Urgent. She thought about not replying. This was to have been her day off! So far, it had been anything but.

With a sigh, she called. Raye, the new office manager, answered instantly.

"We have a problem."

When isn't there a problem? Kate thought but said, "What is it?"

"Melissa was supposed to show a house at one thirty but she's stuck in Aventura and can't get back in time."

Bet she's in the mall, Kate thought. "Can you call the client and ask to postpone?"

"Can't. It's one man. He's here just for today and get this — he doesn't have a cell phone. But that's okay. Maybe you could stop by and say, 'Sorry, I'm too busy having fun to show you a house. Call somebody who cares.'"

"Gee, Raye, you should do stand-up comedy."

"I'm here working on a glorious Saturday while you and yours are probably at the beach. Does Jack wear a Speedo?"

"Couldn't find any large enough," Kate shot back. "I'll do it. What's his name?"

She shuffled papers. "James Bletley. I'll text you the address. It's a half-million house."

"Oh," Kate said, "a South Florida slum." That was Realtor humor.

Raye gave a snort of laughter and clicked off.

When Kate saw the client standing on the sidewalk in front of the house, she was glad she kept a garment bag of clothes in her trunk. She'd been able to change out of her building-a-birdhouse outfit into a blue silk blouse and navy linen trousers.

The man waiting for her had that European look of casual elegance that few Americans could achieve. His black trousers were perfectly cut and didn't have a crease in them. Not easy to achieve in Florida's balmy weather.

His white shirt was of a whispery soft fabric that was the kind sold in stores that had a guard at the door. His tasteful belt could only be Hermès. He was almost as tall as Jack and seemed to be physically fit. Courtesy of some internationally famous personal trainer?

She parked on the street, two houses down. *Bet he's got enough cash in his wallet to buy the house,* she thought as she grabbed her briefcase. It was Prada. "Thank you, Aunt Sara." She was glad she wasn't showing up with an old shopping bag like Melissa sometimes carried.

As she approached him, the man watched her walk; he seemed to be appraising her. He was midfifties and a *very* handsome man. He looked perfectly groomed and exquisitely well-mannered.

"Hello," he said.

Of course he has a beautiful voice, Kate thought.

"I'm Jim Bletley."

She shook his hand. It was big, warm, strong. "Kate Medlar. I'm glad you like this house. It's —"

She didn't say more because a motorcycle roared, seemingly out of nowhere. Thinking it was Jack, Kate turned toward it.

The rider was clad in black leather with a black and red helmet and slowed to drive close to Kate. Suddenly, a hand shot out, reaching for her bag.

One of the best things about boxing was that it taught muscles so thoroughly that they remembered. No thinking required.

A hand darting toward her made Kate duck into an almost squat, then she instantly rebounded upward on the other side. As she came up, she delivered a right uppercut to the rider's rib cage.

Just as it landed, Mr. Bletley did a high kick punch that hit the rider hard in the shoulder. Another inch and his neck would have been hit.

For an instant, the startled rider struggled to regain balance, then sped off.

Kate looked at Mr. Bletley. "I'm sorry. I . . ." Her heart was pounding.

"Why don't we go inside? I believe the house is still furnished. We can sit down."

She looked at the house but couldn't remember anything about it.

"Come on," he said softly, then bent his arm for her to take and she did.

The door had a Realtor lockbox on it. He punched in the numbers and the door opened.

"How did you know?"

"Same codes everywhere."

Kate nodded. All of Melissa's listings used 1234 as the code. She tried to get her mind back on her job. "The square footage is . . ." She was too flustered to think clearly.

"Would you like to call the sheriff?" He sounded concerned.

Jack has enough to worry about today, she thought. "Sorry. I should — Oh! You're bleeding." There was a cut on his hand. "Sit down and I'll see if I can find some bandages."

He sat down on the sofa and looked around the big living room with its perfect gray and white decor.

Her senses were beginning to return. "As you can see, it was professionally decorated."

"A bit colorless for my taste," he said.

She smiled in agreement. "My aunt Sara says that's why places like this are photographed at night. The lights give the rooms some personality."

"I think your aunt and I are of the same mind."

"You couldn't do better," Kate said over her shoulder as she went to the kitchen. She opened drawers until she found a first aid kit. She hurried back to him with a dampened tea towel and the bandages.

"You really don't have to do this," he said, but he obediently held up his hand while she cleaned the blood away, then bandaged it. It wasn't very deep. She wondered how it had happened.

Stepping back, she looked down at him. "Shall we look at the rest of the house?"

He nodded toward the chair across from him. "I think we need a little time to recover."

With a grateful sigh, Kate sat down. "Thanks," she said. "That was a great kick you did."

"Just reflex. As was yours. Boxing?"

"Yes."

"Oh!" he said. "I left my shopping bag outside. Excuse me for a moment."

Kate didn't feel like moving. The trauma of what had happened was hitting her. She really should call Jack. And Aunt Sara. When she told them later, they'd be furious that she'd waited so long. She could almost hear Jack yelling. He'd say —

Mr. Bletley was standing in front of her and holding a white bag from an Apple store. "I can see that this place suits me. Is it possible that I could rent the house as is until the owners move their furniture out?"

Kate tried to remember the particulars about the listing. The owners were in Denver, looking for a house to buy. So far, they'd had no luck. "I think that could be arranged — if you do plan to buy the house."

"Then consider it done. When was the last time you ate?"

"A bowl of cereal many hours ago."

He held out his hand to her. "We're going out to lunch."

"I'm supposed to be the one offering a

meal to you." She took his hand and stood up.

"Shall we take your car? I drive?"

She didn't know this man! *Jack won't like this,* she thought, but at the same time, she felt she could trust this stranger. There was something about him that made her feel good. She nodded.

He opened the door for her. "You make me feel like I'm an eighteenth-century lady."

"Good!" he said. "Someone should."

As she could have predicted, his driving was excellent, and they went to a restaurant she'd never seen before. It was tiny, with a pretty little shaded courtyard with flowers all around.

"This is beautiful," she said.

"Reminds me of home."

"And where is that?" Of course he held her chair out for her.

He took the seat opposite her. There was no menu. "We are at the mercy of Henri. Whatever he feels like cooking today is what we'll eat. It could be sweetbreads or Kobe beef."

"That sounds good to me. I'm not a picky eater." A waiter, dressed all in black with a white apron, poured white wine.

"Looks like it's fish today," he said.

They were the only people in the courtyard. The other five tables were empty.

"We're late," he said. "For Americans."

"But not where you come from?"

He took a few moments before he answered. "I've had an odd life."

"Couldn't be stranger than mine."

"Oh?" he encouraged.

"You first."

The waiter placed a narrow plate in front of them containing eight pretty appetizers. They reached for the same one at the same time, then he withdrew his hand. "Please."

She took it and ate. Delicious. "I have inherited my aunt's love of stories so I'd like to hear yours. Besides, I've had a tough day. I need some relief."

"Really?" He was frowning — and interested in hearing more.

She smiled. "I mean it. You tell your story first."

He smiled back, showing his perfect teeth. "All right." He took a breath. "Years ago, I had a great tragedy in my life. I lost the person I loved most in the world."

"I'm sorry," she whispered.

"Thank you. Afterward, I went into a deep depression. I wanted to retire from all life." When he saw her frowning, he smiled. "This story has a happy ending, so it's all right. I heard of a place of . . . isolation, I guess

93

you'd say. It was an island where people went to heal."

"You mean a hospital?"

"Oh no. An actual island. It's not on a cruise route, meaning it's not rich enough to supply food and fuel, so few people have heard of it. It's been turned into a refuge for people like me who want to disappear. The inhabitants are out of touch with the outside world. They're good and bad, from all cultures. I believe that now the word is *diverse.*"

"You were happy there?"

"As well as I could be, I guess. I never really got over what sent me there, but I managed."

The waiter brought sizzling platters of fish cooked in brown butter. Four kinds of vegetables were on the side.

Kate said, "But you left your island."

"Yes, I did. One morning a voice seemed to say to me, *'It's time to go home.'* It took weeks to arrange everything, but I did leave. I have some relatives up north, but they aren't people I'm in a hurry to see again. Besides, it's too cold up there. I'm not used to wearing a topcoat. I decided to go south and see what was here."

"And you chose Lachlan?"

"When I stopped for lunch in Orlando, I

94

saw a brochure. I liked what I read about the renovations to this town so I decided to have a look. This town suits me."

"It was all done by my boss, Tayla Kirkwood," Kate said proudly. "I was told that you have only one day here."

"For now, yes. One of the men from the island came with me. We're to meet tomorrow to say goodbye. He's going to California. I called your office and a young woman, Melissa, said she'd love to show me houses today, but you showed up. However grateful I am for the error, I hope I haven't caused you any inconvenience."

"Absolutely not. In fact, you've cheered me up greatly."

He didn't smile. "And what happened that made your spirits need reviving?"

Kate started to answer, but the waiter came to check on them and she thought better of it. "The office manager said you didn't have a cell phone. Is that what's in the Apple bag?"

His expression changed to exasperation. "I've been told these things are a modern miracle and everyone looks at them rather than at each other, but . . ." He raised his hands in helplessness.

"You sound like Jack."

"Is he your brother?"

95

"Oh no. I'm an only child, but Jack lives with me."

He raised his eyebrows in question.

"It's not like that. It's my aunt's house and Jack is the grandson of a man she . . ." Kate felt like she was telling too much. In the realty business, it was to be all about the client.

"I just told you more than I've ever told anyone," he said. "There's something about you that makes me feel it's all right to confide."

"Thank you. I feel a bit of that too." He was looking at her in silence. "I guess it doesn't matter since it's all local gossip. Bessie at Mitfords could tell you. Or Dora. She cleans for everyone."

He was still waiting.

"Jack is the grandson of the man my aunt Sara was madly in love with."

"Ah. That's generous of her. A child born out of wedlock?"

"No! It's not like that. Sara loved him but she didn't marry him. She left Lachlan and became a famous writer. When she retired, she moved back here."

"Why didn't she marry the grandfather?"

"I have no idea and she won't tell anyone."

The waiter put a plate of hand-dipped chocolates on the table. As before, they

96

reached for the same one at the same time.

"Your turn," Kate said.

"I'd lose my gentleman's badge if I went before a lady."

She laughed.

"So tell me about this man, Jack. What does he do?"

"Right now he's a deputy sheriff, but with the actual sheriff out of town, Jack is running the office. Well, sort of. Broward County took over this morning."

His eyes grew intense. "Why?"

"I didn't mean to say that."

"If the county men are involved, whatever happened will probably be in the news tomorrow. I'd like to hear the truth before they distort it."

"That's a good point." She saw that he was waiting for her to continue. There was something about him that made her want to tell him everything. "Have you ever done interrogations? For INTERPOL, maybe?"

She expected him to laugh but he didn't. "In a manner of speaking, yes. I've had extensive dealings with higher branches of law enforcement, both here and in other countries."

"Oh." Her eyes widened. *What did that mean? FBI? Maybe he* was *with INTERPOL.* She took another chocolate. "This morning, Charlene, a friend of mine, found a dead man. He'd fallen out of the window of her barn." Kate wasn't sure, but the color in his face seemed to fade a bit. "Maybe I shouldn't tell you this."

"No, please do. I want to hear everything."

She told him what she thought would be reported online, but nothing personal. She didn't tell of the footprint or their belief that someone else had been there. She certainly didn't say that maybe there was a *reason* Charlene was a target.

Gradually, he seemed to recover his composure and by the end he was relaxed.

He leaned back in his chair. "What an extraordinary day you've had. Dead man this morning, motorcyclist attack in the afternoon."

"Sheriff Flynn would say it's normal for us. We've solved three murders." Her eyes widened. "Sorry, I shouldn't have said that." She looked at her watch. It was nearly four. "I need to go. I've taken up too much of your time." She handed him her card. "Call me so I can have your number."

"I don't know how to do that."

"Right. New phone."

Bending, he pulled the box out of the bag. "They set it up for me at the store. I believe I now have an account, but I'm not sure about that."

"May I?" At his nod, she opened the box and took out the phone. It took only seconds for her to enter her contact information. She set him up for texting and emails, then handed the phone to him and gave him some instructions. He caught on quickly.

She started to get up but he didn't move.

"What is a selfish?"

She laughed. "A selfie is a self-photo." She showed him the buttons. But he touched the wrong one and ended up photographing Kate.

She got up and went around to his side, then leaned forward, her face close to his, to show him. But he touched the button before she got out of the photo. What came up was a rather nice portrait of the two of them.

She offered to pay for lunch but he refused. Oddly, he didn't pay either. He and the waiter exchanged nods and that appeared to be the end of it.

They walked out to Kate's car but he didn't get in. "Can I give you a ride somewhere?" she asked.

"No, but thank you for the offer." He paused. "I feel that I made a friend today."

"Me too," she said.

"May I?"

She knew he meant exchanging cheek kisses. "Yes."

They exchanged formal, European-style cheek kisses, then Kate got into her car and drove away.

When she looked in her rearview mirror, he was talking on his new phone.

"He sure picked that up in a hurry!" she said aloud.

She smiled all the way home.

Six

Before Kate's car was out of sight of the restaurant — *why* didn't Sara buy her a BMW or a Mercedes! — Randal had tapped in the number he'd memorized.

Mel answered on the first ring. "I *knew* you'd call. Knew it! It's not my fault. Lenny had nothing to do with that dead guy. He doesn't know who the man was. Didn't touch him. But the guy had a rifle. Think he was after your girlfriend?"

Randal was listening, not interrupting, and trying to put it all together. For a smart lawyer, Mel was a bit of a scatter-brain. But then twenty-some years in prison hadn't helped.

"Who is Lenny?" Randal asked.

"Don't get upset but he's a hit man."

"You hired a hit man?" Randal's voice was low.

"No!" Mel shouted. "I just wanted him to watch out for *you,* that's all. Please, Randal,

101

you know what I want, and you're the only one who can do it. I want to die knowing that —"

Randal cut him off. He'd already heard every word of what Mel was about to say. "What about the motorcycle?"

"I told you! Lenny doesn't know who he is. He — Wait! What motorcycle?"

"I was with Kate and —"

"Ohhhh," Mel said in a groan of pure envy. His own children, now adults, wanted nothing to do with him — although they did cash his checks. "Is she as beautiful as her pictures? Was she glad to see you? Tell me every word she said."

Randal wasn't one for revealing what he considered his private business. "Someone on a motorcycle reached for me and almost got my daughter. He had a push dagger in his fingers. I evaded, but he cut my hand. I don't think Kate saw it. The license plate was covered so I didn't get a number."

"What did Kate say? Was she hurt?"

"No, she wasn't, and she thought he was after her handbag." Pausing, Randal smiled. "She ducked and came up punching. It was glorious! I knocked him away so I don't think Kate saw what he was holding or even realized who he was after."

"Did you do one of those high kick things

that Neil taught you?"

"Yes, I did."

"I bet she was impressed." Mel sounded lonely and sad.

"What do you know about him?"

"Nothing. I swear it. If that guy was after *you,* maybe the man in the barn was too. Ava always said you were in love with Charlene. That's how I knew where to send Lenny. Looks like Ava was right."

Randal closed his eyes for a moment. "Ava was not right. There's nothing between Charlene and me."

"But Ava said —"

"It's not true!" Randal snapped. "There's nothing between us!"

"Okay." Mel backed down. "Sorry."

"Where is this guy Lenny now?"

"Sitting in a motel and waiting for my orders. Want him to protect Kate?"

"Charlene seems to be the one in danger."

"And you."

"I can take care of myself. Where did you get this guy Lenny?"

"Buster told me about him."

"Then he's good. By the way, Buster's birthday is next week. Send him some flowers from both of us. Sunflowers. He'll like those."

"Sure. What about Lenny?"

"Tell him to find Charlene and watch out for her. Think he can do that?"

"Of course. He's old but Buster says he's still the best. Have you seen Ava yet?"

"No. She's in Chicago, and that's fine with me."

"Yeah. Take the time to get to know your kid." Mel let out a sigh. "Is Kate still solving murders?"

"Yes." Randal paused to take a cup of coffee handed to him by the waiter and took a sip. "Thanks."

The waiter nodded and went back inside.

"Who was that?" Mel asked.

"Remember Hank Crestler?"

"Hid two hundred fifty grand from his ex and her lawyer boyfriend sued?"

"Yes, he's here. Now he says he's French and calls himself Henri. He has a nice restaurant. Kate and I had lunch here."

"After what you did for Hank, I bet he didn't charge you. He owes you. Speaking of which, you owe me a favor or two. You know what I want."

Randal grimaced. "You wrote some letters for me but you want me to infiltrate —" He stopped talking as he knew it was a waste of breath. "I have some people I need to see. Find out what you can about a kid on a motorcycle. Pretty sure it was male but these days you can't be sure — or even say. Who uses a push dagger?"

"I'll ask."

"Include the question with Buster's flowers. Who sent him and why?"

"Good idea. I'll do it now. Randal, best of luck with your daughter when you *do* tell her who you are." He clicked off.

Randal couldn't help a smile. It looked like Mel had guessed that Randal hadn't told Kate the truth about who he was. But then, it was Mel's cleverness that had him put in prison in the first place. Clever, curious and honest. That was Mel.

As Sheriff Flynn got up to get another beer, he was thinking that he should buy one of those little fridges and put it in his den. But he knew Evie would veto it. She went to gym classes three times a week and kept in shape. Between sitting and all the paperwork Daryl had to do, he had "let himself go" as she said. So, okay, maybe he did have a belly but it didn't keep him from doing his job. He —

As he stepped into what was supposed to be *his* room, he tried not to let the shock he was feeling show. And to conceal that his heart was pounding.

Sitting in the big leather chair that was

probably still warm from Jack Wyatt's backside, was Randal Medlar.

To say that he'd aged well was an understatement. As a kid, Randal had looked like an adult — and he'd acted like one. Now that he was older, he looked like he'd grown into his body. Evie would say that Randal was a "fine-looking man."

Daryl couldn't help glancing at Randal's flat belly. Unless his fancy shirt was hiding it, there wasn't an ounce of fat on him. He held out the can of beer to Randal. Daryl imagined running out the back door and never being seen again.

"Thanks, but no," Randal said.

Daryl sat down in his chair and opened the beer. "Does Kate know you're not dead?"

"Not yet."

Daryl's look was intense. "Whatever scam you have planned, I'm not going to do it."

Randal gave a little smile. "How's your foot?"

"Sore."

Randal nodded. "Who made the cast for you? Jaye?"

"Her son. You've been away a long time. You've lost touch with everyone."

"Not quite." Randal was looking at the TV, which was on Mute. "You haven't changed. I knew you wouldn't leave Roy's kid in charge of a law office and not stay around to watch over him."

"He's not like his father." Daryl paused. "Not entirely anyway."

"What's between Roy's son and my daughter?"

Daryl shook his head in wonder. "Jack's so in love with her that it's painful to watch. But she tells him no. I think she wants him to prove himself."

Randal smiled. "I like that. But is he like Roy, bed 'em and leave 'em?"

"Jack used to be that way but Sara and Kate have him on a short leash. So why are you here?"

"In Lachlan or in your house?"

"Both." Daryl was studying him. "You don't look like you're broke. What'd that shirt cost you?"

"Nothing. Bernie's nephew has a store."

"And you're collecting favors."

Randal shrugged. "Why not? Perks of being locked up with white-collar criminals. There were lots of lawyers, a yoga master, accountants, a man who owned a dozen gyms. We shared information and talents."

"What did you teach? Lock picking?"

"That's not kind, Daryl, and you know that I don't share what I know."

"Ain't that the truth." He stared hard at Randal. "So why are you really here? And don't tell me it's to meet your daughter."

"I want to know who betrayed me. Who put me in prison? Who gave me the job that set me up? Who reported me to the police?"

"The investigation was done by the old captain. He didn't share info with me."

Randal narrowed his eyes. "I'm sure you've read the reports from that time."

"The caller was always kept anonymous. I'm not sure the captain knew who it was. He wanted to get you and he did."

"I didn't steal some car full of drugs!" Randal said.

"I'm sure he knew you didn't. But he also knew there were other things that you did do."

"My deal with that car was perfectly legitimate. But when I was charged, there was *no* evidence to back up what I was saying. It had all disappeared. You know I'm not careless. I showed that at Mrs. Oliver's. You remember that, right?"

"Every day I try to forget that whole thing."

Randal looked at him in disbelief. "That job got you this house. And it scared you so much you joined law enforcement. You've used your badge as a shield."

Daryl's lips tightened. "I needed some-thing to protect myself from Roy and Wal-ter. They wanted me to get you to plan another job."

"They're gone now so it's just you and me. Nothing happened to any of us after that job. No one found out anything in spite of Roy's big mouth and Walter's self-pity and your fear. But when I tried to go straight and took on a *real* job . . ."

"I know." Daryl's voice was low. "You were sent to prison for an extraordinarily long time for a small crime."

"So who did it? Who betrayed me?"

That word again, Daryl thought. *Betrayed.* "You did make a few enemies along the way. Charlene's family was pretty angry."

Randal took his time answering. "I heard about the body they found at her place. Any news about it?"

"None. But they'd call Jack, not me."

"Ah yes. You're not here. So who knows the truth about that?"

Daryl picked up his cell off the side table, brought up the photos of the dead guy that Jack had sent him and handed it to Randal.

"Never saw him before." He swiped the screen to see other photos of Charlene's place. "My sister take these?"

"Yeah. You're handy with that phone. Usually, guys just out have trouble adjusting."

"I had a good teacher." Randal's smile was dreamlike.

"So what do you have to do with a dead man at Charlene's house? Is he why you're here and not with your wife in Chicago?"

"I came here to see Kate. But . . ." Randal closed his eyes for a moment. "Ava visited me all those years. She got to know the guards and some of the men. I had to be careful what I said to her."

"About Kate?" Daryl hadn't spent much time around Ava, but it was enough to know what she was like.

"Yes. If I asked too many questions about my daughter or wanted too many photos . . ." Randal took a breath. "One day Ava got mad at me and threw a fit in the visitor's room. She yelled that I was still in love with *her*, with Charlene. Everyone heard." He looked at Daryl for sympathy.

Daryl stared hard at Randal. "What do you know that you're not telling me?"

When Randal's easygoing expression returned, Daryl knew his question wasn't going to be answered. "Kate is beautiful, isn't she? She's smart and insightful. She's everything I hoped she'd be." He stood up. "I need to go. I have some things to do."

Daryl was watching him. "You should

know that if you hurt Kate in any way, Sara will kill you. I mean really murder you, and Jack will help."

"My sister has always been a terror." Randal held up his bandaged hand. "I will protect my daughter with my life."

"Good to hear. And next time, use a door."

Silently, Randal left the room.

For a few minutes, Daryl leaned back in his chair. Curse words weren't enough to express how he felt. He'd tried so hard to deal with Randal's return. Sending Evie off with a big lie, lying to Jack, lying to the whole town.

And now, the very *worst*. He was feeling sympathy for Randal. It was true that Randal had committed several nonviolent crimes, but as he'd pointed out, he'd never suffered repercussions for them.

But someone had framed him. Yes, Sara had been a character witness, but it wasn't as Ava had shouted. It wasn't Sara who'd put her brother in prison. She wasn't the one who'd set Daryl up, who'd lied to Captain Edison.

Daryl waited a few more minutes, listening hard to make sure Randal was gone. He levered himself out of his seat and went to the wall-length cabinet he'd had built many years before.

He pulled the bottom drawer out on its metal runners, then lifted it out. On the floor was a folder. It had all the former sheriff's notes and letters and documents about Randal Medlar. The file had been started when Randal was eight years old. The report said Randal had somehow broken into the locker of the school bully. Randal had taken out all the stolen money and returned it to the owners.

To his fellow students — and to his mother — Randal had been a hero. But the bully's parents had demanded that "the Medlar trash boy" be suspended for at least a week. As the kid's father got out his checkbook to buy new sports equipment for the school, the principal had agreed.

Greatly embarrassed, Sara had been called out of class to walk her little brother home.

Daryl didn't have to be told what happened next. Ruth Medlar had coddled and caressed her precious son while she screamed at Sara that all the bad was her fault. When Sara had gone to their father asking for support, the cowardly man had withdrawn. As she always did, Sara had retreated to her hideaway in the scrub between their house and the Wyatts'. With pen and paper in hand, she wrote stories of another world, a place where there was justice and truth. Later, Cal Wyatt would show up. Sara would read her stories to him, then Cal would tell of whatever low-down, rotten, mean thing his father had done to him.

For a moment, Daryl thought about how childhoods set people up for their lives. Randal was rewarded for thievery. In writing, Sara found a way to escape her unhappy world. And through Sara, Cal saw a world other than the violence of his father, so he didn't grow up and repeat the pattern of abuse.

As Daryl put the file back in place, he was once again reassured that his part in Randal's incarceration wasn't in there. Only one person knew the whole story and he was dead. Daryl paused, struck by a terrible thought. Was it possible Walter had told someone else the whole story?

SEVEN

Kate was home at last. She'd stopped at her favorite Publix grocery and bought bags of food. As she put them away, she kept smiling.

She knew it was silly, of course. Most women her age were happy when they met a young man, preferably someone who looked like Jack. But Kate was pleased to have met Mr. Bletley.

She'd been teased about visiting Everett and Arthur so often. Melissa had been the worst. "I hear Arthur has money. Marry him, then you can inherit."

Kate knew she was supposed to laugh but she couldn't.

Even Tayla asked about her "old men." But Tayla had been perceptive. "Or maybe they're father figures." Kate had turned away so the redness of her face couldn't be seen.

So maybe she was curious about older

men — normal ones, that is. Growing up, the only older men she'd had dealings with were her three uncles. Nothing but criticism came out of their mouths. When she was seven, the uncles demanded that Ava dye Kate's hair black. "It's too *red*," they shouted. "The color of evil."

Ava said she was going to do it, but then she went away for two weeks on one of her trips to buy fabric to make Kate's clothes. She returned, saying, "No!" Not a quiet refusal, but a fierce one. The uncles had backed away.

So now maybe Kate had a new man to add to her life. Maybe he'd be like Arthur and Everett. They always had time to listen. Office politics, personalities, annoyances. They were interested in them all. And Kate was involved with the book they'd just finished. They were thanking her in the acknowledgments.

She wanted to tell Jack and Sara about the man she'd met today, but she thought it would be better not to. They were both very protective. She didn't want Jack showing up with a gun on his hip and questioning Mr. Bletley. And of course Sara would want to meet him. Inspect him. Judge him.

All in all, it would be better if Kate said nothing, at least for a while.

When she got the groceries put away, she went in search of Jack. She found him in the little courtyard that had doors opening to their rooms. It had a pretty fountain of a girl dancing in the rain. He was on the chaise, his eyes closed, and he had on jeans and a T-shirt.

"No thirty pounds of weaponry?" she asked as she took the chaise next to him.

"No." He opened one eye. "Why are you so dressed up?"

"Melissa was stuck in Aventura so I took her client."

"Ask her what she bought at the mall."

"I will, but it's her loss. It's Tayla's listing so I'll get the commission." She was looking at him. "What's wrong?"

"Other than hating the job? Finding a dead man? Worried about Charlene?"

"Yes. Other than those things."

He didn't answer for a few moments. "Can you and I have lunch tomorrow?"

"Sure. Is this about the dead guy?"

"Maybe."

"Aunt Sara will be there?"

"No."

"Jack, you're scaring me. This sounds serious." When he didn't answer, she drew in her breath. "Aunt Sara is ill."

"Not at all. Not that she'd tell us, but she

116

looks good."

"Where is she?"

"Locked up in her fortress. I haven't seen her since this morning. You hungry?"

Kate started to tell him about her big lunch but didn't. There was time for that. "I got steaks. Think you can handle some beef?"

"Gladly." As he got up, he picked up his phone. "I have to carry this with me everywhere I go." He sounded disgusted.

"Just like the rest of the world."

Dinner was dreadful. Since Kate had been living in Florida with Jack and Sara, they'd told each other everything. But not tonight.

Usually, their dinners were fun. They exchanged information about their days and they were appreciative of each other. Kate loved telling stories about her picky clients. "They said they wanted only the best," she'd say.

Jack would say, "So they bought a slum."

"Exactly." Then they'd laugh.

Sara had lots of friends, both from her writing career and the years she'd been traveling. They emailed and texted each other. She'd say, "I got an email from Sandy today. She and Tibor had a big dinner with their kids. She sent photos of her garden.

And Lynn and Bob invited us to Las Vegas." Kate and Jack had come to know all of them and loved the stories and pictures.

Jack was always full of plans for houses he wanted to remodel. When a new one came on the market, Kate would show him the specs and they would discuss whether or not he should take on the job. In the last year he'd hired four more men.

But none of that was happening tonight. Both Sara and Jack had their heads down, eating in silence. Earlier, Jack had been quiet but now he was nearly catatonic. Kate thought about blurting, "I met a man today." Of course they'd assume it was a man her own age and that she was interested in him as a boyfriend. That would send Jack into jealousy overdrive and Sara would be consumed with curiosity. Was he good enough for their Kate?

But tonight Kate was more interested in what was *wrong* with the two of them. "So what did you guys do today?" she asked. "I mean after the, you know, dead guy?"

Sara shrugged in silence.

"Called Gil," Jack mumbled. "Got no answer."

"He was with me," Kate said.

There was no response from either of them.

Kate grimaced. "Gil and I were slam banging, doing the dirty, in the back of his pickup."

Sara didn't lift her head.

Neither did Jack. "Toolbox. No room," he said flatly.

"What. Is. Wrong. With. You. Two?" Her jaw was clenched.

"I, uh . . ." Jack began but didn't finish.

Sara put her fork down but didn't look up. "Ava is in Lachlan."

That got their attention.

"My mother?" Kate whispered. "She's here? What did she say? She wants me to leave?"

"I didn't speak to her." Sara looked at Kate. "I should have. I'm sorry, but I didn't." Her voice was almost trembling.

Kate put her hand on her aunt's forearm. "It's okay. Tell us what happened."

Sara took a breath. "I was at Bessie's tea shop. I wanted to write down all we'd seen this morning, then Ava walked in."

"Maybe she'd just arrived in town," Kate said.

"Bessie said she's been coming in every morning for days."

"So maybe she wants to settle in before she sees us."

"You think she's staying at a hotel?" Sara

119

asked. "Wouldn't she want to stay here for free?"

They looked at Jack, as he hadn't said a word.

"Did you know she was here?" Sara sounded accusatory.

"No, I did not. I don't know anything about Ava," Jack said.

"But *something* is bothering you," Sara said. "I can tell."

He stood up. "Stop trying to put the attention onto *me.* You and Kate need to talk. If Ava's here, she'll show up at the front door soon. You two need to plan what to do with her. I have some files to read. Good night."

The two women watched him walk away, then heard his bedroom door shut loudly. They turned back to each other.

Sara spoke first. "I'm sorry. I should have sent you a text right away. I should have —"

"What was she doing?"

"Buying a big bag full of pastries."

Kate and Sara looked at each other with grimaces. They were alike in that they gained weight easily, while Ava ate much more than they did but weighed less.

"She didn't see you?" Kate asked.

"The table Bessie gives me is in a back

corner and there's a screen beside it. It's quite pretty. I sort of hid behind it."

Kate tried to look serious but couldn't. "I bet Bessie thought that was funny."

"And I bet that by now she's told everyone in town."

"Oh yes!" Kate let out a loud sigh. "So what do we do now?"

"I don't know. If Ava's been here awhile, what is she doing? Are you sure she hasn't been at your office? Maybe in the parking lot. Or . . . ?" She didn't finish.

"I haven't seen her." Kate looked at her plate of half-eaten food. She'd lost her appetite. "Mom said something good was happening. I guess she meant that she was coming here."

"So why hasn't she shown up at this house?"

Kate shook her head "My guess is that she's preparing a place for the two of us to live."

"Like buying a house or condo?"

"Yes." Kate put her head back, eyes closed. "This will be a battle. She'll say I have no excuse not to live with her."

"Marry Jack and I'll buy you a house in Italy."

"With a guesthouse for you?"

"Exactly," Sara said.

For a moment they smiled at each other, their minds full of thoughts of Italian sunshine. Kate recovered first. "This is horrible of me! She's my mother and I love her. It's just that she's not an easy person to live with."

"You've been away for years. It would be difficult for you to return to that."

"If she's willing to leave her brothers," Kate said, "maybe she's better now."

"Maybe . . ." Sara said but didn't finish.

"What are you thinking?"

"The man this morning. He was found at Charlene's."

Kate nodded. They knew that long ago, Charlene had had an affair with Kate's father. It was believed to have been brief, but it did happen — and Ava was notoriously jealous.

"Did you tell Ava you've been going to Charlene's to build birdhouses?"

"Absolutely not!" Kate said loudly. She pushed away from the table. "I don't know why she's here but I'm sure she has a reason — and I will be told." She started clearing the table.

"Go to bed," Sara said. "Watch TV. Read. Do something to distract yourself. I'll clean this up."

"Thanks. I think that tomorrow I'll go into

the office early. I have a client who wants to rent a house before he buys it. I'll see if I can get that going."

"Sure," Sara said, then she hugged her niece. "We'll work this out, and I'll help you in any way that's needed. I'm serious when I say that if necessary, we'll move."

"That's kind of you," Kate said and headed toward her bedroom.

"Kate?"

"Yes?"

"Where would your mother get the money to buy a house?"

"I have no idea, but she always seemed to come up with cash whenever she needed it. Maybe she sold our house in Chicago." Kate could see that her aunt had more questions but she didn't want to think about her mother's finances right now. Her mind was full of the storm that was coming.

She went to her bedroom and closed the door.

Kate thought of how hard her mother had tried to get her to move back in with her. More than once her mother had said that the only reason Kate was staying with her aunt was because of Sara's fancy house. She had no doubt that her mother would create a spiderweb to lure her daughter to her.

Kate envisioned one of those horrible houses in Miami where every wooden surface was shinier than a mirror. The furniture had steel legs and hard seats. Gray on top of gray. The curtains in those houses started at forty grand.

Oh Mother, she thought, *please don't buy one of those dreadful places. Please don't get us deeply in debt. I'll have to work seven days a week to pay it off. I'll have to . . .* She made herself quit that train of thought.

When Kate got into the shower, she had to hold back tears. Sara and Jack were so strong. They were good at telling people no. Jack had stood up to his father. Aunt Sara had stood up to the whole publishing world.

So of course they expected Kate to "just say no" to her mother. But Kate could hear her. "You chose *her* over *me?*"

"But I'm your *mother.* I nearly died giving birth to you."

"You are my whole *life.*"

Kate knew she wouldn't be able to withstand all that guilt.

As she washed her hair, she remembered Aunt Sara saying she should marry Jack. In the fantasy that they would move to Italy, there was no need for her and Jack to marry.

I wonder why she threw that in? Kate thought. *A Freudian slip?*

She was concerned that when she went to bed her worries would keep her awake, but they didn't.

The next morning, she woke early and quickly dressed in nice clothes — no yoga pants and T-shirt as was her usual Sunday gear — and left the house by the side entrance. As she went through the courtyard she and Jack shared, she held her breath, hoping he wouldn't be there. Right now she just wanted to work. She didn't want to think about why her mother was skulking around town. "Probably planning some devious thing to do to me," she muttered.

Kate was on the way to her office, but when she saw the Mitford Tea Room, she parked. She told herself she really *needed* some high-calorie, nonnutritional, sugar-loaded pastry. Yeah, right.

The shop wasn't open yet, but Bessie was loading her glass case. Sunday was her busiest day. When she saw Kate at the door, she unlocked it.

"I just pulled cinnamon cookies out of the oven. They're keto. Think your aunt will like them?"

"I'm sure she will. Let me have a dozen, please."

"Gladly."

As Bessie put them in a bag, Kate tried to sound casual. "My aunt was in here yesterday, wasn't she?"

Bessie laughed. "She sure was, and it was a riot! The whole place was staring. My cooks came out from the back and took photos. They want to do means on the internet."

"Memes?"

"That's it. It was great entertainment! Those two were hiding like spies."

"You mean Aunt Sara and the woman who was in here?"

"No. Sara and Everett. You know, that chubby writer. I shouldn't say that, should I? He put away at least six scones. I couldn't keep track. They were crouching down, with him looking over Sara's head. They looked downright terrified. In a tea shop! It was hilarious."

Kate's eyes were widening with every word. "I don't understand. Why would both of them be hiding?"

"I have no idea." She took the cash Kate held out. "I think they saw someone they didn't want to see — or to see them. Whatever, they were certainly in it together! I don't know who it was. There were four people at the counter and all the tables were full. Although . . . Sara did ask after one

126

woman. She said she was drumming up business for you."

"That's right," Kate said. "Aunt Sara mentioned her. A thin woman?"

"That's her. Most days, she comes in the morning, but yesterday she was in later." Bessie looked at her watch. "She's usually here by this time. Wait and you can meet her."

"Yeah, sure," Kate stammered, then said quickly, "I have to go. Client. Work." She grabbed the bag and raced to her car. She didn't dare look sideways for fear she'd see her mother.

"I am a bad person," she said. "What daughter doesn't want to see her own mother?" She didn't answer herself but almost ran over an orange construction cone as she drove away.

There was no one in the office when Kate got there and she was glad for the solitude. She went to work right away, doing her best to lose herself in it.

She'd contacted the owners of the house Mr. Bletley wanted and they'd replied that they were concerned about someone using their furniture. They had some antiques. "Does he have a dog?"

"An SO with kids?" They had a dozen

questions.

Kate sent Mr. Bletley a text but didn't think she'd get an answer so early. He replied right away, asking what an SO was. Significant other she replied and she could almost feel him laughing. He answered all the questions the owners could come up with. Mr. Bletley would be the only person living there.

When they asked for references, he replied, Of course.

An hour later he sent a PDF containing three letters. They were from a lawyer, a pastor and the CEO of a gym franchise, all on elegant letterheads.

"Not the president of the US?" Kate mumbled, and forwarded them. "He did a PDF. I'm impressed."

With the owners finally satisfied, Kate pulled up the appropriate contracts from the system and asked Mr. Bletley for identification. He sent her a photo of his passport. James Leighton Bletley, born in Lisbon, Portugal, 1960. "Fifty-nine years old," she said.

Kate typed everything in, sent it to the owners through DocuSign, and they immediately sent it back, completed.

She texted Mr. Bletley that all it needed was his signature and he could do it on his computer. She pressed Send and breathed a sigh of relief.

While she waited, she checked her emails and texts. No, she didn't want a side-opening bathtub. Didn't want new windows. No, she didn't want to send a poor lonely widow twenty-five dollars so five million could be deposited into her bank as soon as she gave them her account number.

Then there was a text from Jack.

Sarah's old house in 30? I'll pick up sandwiches.

She had forgotten she was to meet him for lunch — where she knew he had something important to tell her. From the way he acted yesterday, she knew it was bad. Considering that last night Jack had left the table rather than talk about Sara's announcement that she'd seen Ava, Kate had no doubt it was about her mother.

Kate corrected herself. Sara *and Everett* had seen Ava. Everyone knew Everett was the biggest blabbermouth in town. Since he'd had his gossipy books published, maybe he was the worst in the US. If his books sold via foreign rights, maybe — She stopped.

All she knew for sure was that Jack had

something to tell her that was so bad he wanted to meet her where he was sure no one would interrupt them. So Kate wouldn't be seen crying? Or yelling in anger?

When she heard the front door of the office open, Kate jumped, then went into pure terror. Her mother had found her! The battle would now begin. The rages, the guilt — and Kate's inevitable capitulation.

"Hi." It was Melissa.

Kate was so relieved she almost burst into tears.

"Oh. Bessie's shop. May I?" Melissa was opening the bag Kate had set on the counter.

"Sure. Help yourself." Kate was smiling broadly.

"Sorry about yesterday. Something personal came up."

Usually, Kate let Melissa know what she thought of her frequent irresponsibility, but she smiled broadly. "That's okay. You get something nice at the mall?"

Melissa, mouth full, blinked in wonder. "I did. I was sent a thousand-dollar gift certificate at Nordstrom's, but it expired at 3:00 p.m. It was use it or lose it. You seem like you're in a good mood. Expecting Jack to arrive?" Everyone in town knew Melissa had a crush on him.

"No. Actually, I'm glad to see *you.*"

Melissa lowered the half-eaten cookie. "What did I do wrong now? Did you tell Tayla? Please don't rat me out."

"You didn't do anything wrong. I just —" She broke off as her phone pinged for a text. It was from Mr. Bletley.

I don't have a computer. Could I sign them on paper? Is that still done? I am heading to the house to have lunch with champagne in celebration. Would you join me?

Kate started to type that she had a previous engagement but he could sign the papers on her computer so she'd stop by.

"You sure you aren't angry?" Melissa asked. "Raye said I stuck you with some old man. Sorry about that."

Kate looked at her for a moment. "I've got to do a signing." She turned back to her phone and sent a text to Jack.

Sorry. I have to work. Meet you at 4?

He must have been waiting because his answer came right away. Sure. See you then.

To Mr. Bletley she texted, I would love lunch, but only if the champagne is very cold.

Is there any other way?

131

Be there in minutes.

Kate looked back at Melissa. "I've got to go." She sent all the documents to her laptop and closed it.

Melissa was staring at her. "You're acting very strange. You aren't trying to solve another murder, are you?" Her eyes widened. "Now that Jack is the sheriff, he can use his gun."

"No, Melissa." Kate was smiling. "I'm not going to see Jack or try to solve a murder. I'm going to have *fun*. See you tomorrow." She picked up the bag of cookies and left the office.

EIGHT

There was no car in front of the house Mr. Bletley was to rent, but the door was ajar, which meant the Realtor box had been opened.

I must tell Melissa that she needs to change her code, Kate thought. The house smelled wonderful. In the pretty kitchen, Mr. Bletley had his back to her. He had on another beautiful shirt, this one light blue with darker pinstripes. A navy apron was tied at his waist. He didn't turn around.

"Lemon?" she asked.

"It's an old family recipe from Gilbert." He pronounced it as Jill-bear. "Big guy, former boxer and a truly magnificent chef. Do you like pasta?"

"If I remember correctly, I do."

He turned to her in question. As always, he seemed very glad to see her.

"With my aunt's keto diet, we don't do a lot of carbs." She paused. "Yes, I love pasta."

He used a wide strainer to drain it. It was angel hair, her favorite. It was almost as though he knew.

"I hope you don't mind that I've set up a picnic outside."

She looked out the window to see a lovely sight. Under a big tree, a snowy white cloth was on the ground, with dishes full of food, two bottles of champagne peeping out of a silver bucket and crystal flutes to the side.

"Too much?" he asked.

She smiled at him. "Not today. Today I need luxury. And nonserious talk. And . . . Sorry. I'm venting. It's all lovely but I do feel guilty. I should have brought you a gift for purchasing. At the closing I'll make it up to you."

He removed his apron and picked up two shallow bowls full of lemony pasta. "Shall we?"

"Oh yes." They went outside.

The food was all things she loved: olives, spicy peppers, cheeses, tiny garlic rolls.

Mr. Bletley poured them flutes of champagne, then leaned back against the tree. He ate little and drank even less, while Kate ate and drank heartily.

"I'm sorry," she said. "I'm not usually such a pig but I didn't have much dinner and I missed breakfast. I've hardly eaten since I had lunch with you yesterday."

He refilled her glass. "You apologize often." It wasn't a criticism, but an observation.

"I'm practicing for what's coming." She drained her glass and held it out for him to refill. "Sorry. I mean . . ." She gave a bit of a giggle. "I don't usually drink during the day. Or at night either, for that matter. Just when I'm with Jack. He can put away a six-pack and not even feel tipsy." She giggled again. "He'd hate that I used that word about him. *Tipsy.* Wonder what the origin of it is."

He skipped the unimportant parts. "What are you practicing for?"

Kate had had too much champagne. "My mother is here in Lachlan."

There was a brief widening of his eyes, then his face relaxed — and he said nothing.

Silence is a funny thing. Most people worked to fill it. Even with her fuzzy brain, Kate knew she shouldn't confess her worries. But sometimes, talking to a stranger was more satisfying than pouring your heart out to someone you knew, especially to someone who loved you.

He was sitting there, so very calm, and watching her. Waiting.

"I love my mother," she said. "I do. For so many years it was just us."

"No other friends? Relatives?"

"Well, the uncles." She gave a little laugh. "My mother has three older brothers, but they don't count." He was looking at her as though waiting for her to explain. "They're very religious. They said the red in my hair is a sign of evil. When my mother wouldn't dye it, they wanted to perform an exorcism." She was trying to make it sound funny, but it didn't come out that way. "When you grow up with something on a daily basis, you don't realize it's strange. Or even that it's different."

"And abnormal."

"Yes! In college, I tried to be like other people, but . . ." She didn't tell what she was remembering.

"Even there, you weren't released from the peculiarities of your life."

She nodded in agreement. "I didn't actually know how odd my life was until I came here." She looked away for a moment. "I've learned that being a victim hurts, but it's how you deal with it afterward that matters." She took a deep drink of her champagne.

"Tell me about your mother," he said softly.

"I shouldn't."

He made no reply, just waited. Ready to listen.

She took a breath. "My mother never got over the death of my father."

Kate wasn't sure how long she talked but she told him all of it. She'd never done that before. She'd told bits and pieces to Sara and Jack, but she'd tried to do it in an upbeat way. Jack tended to brood over his father and Sara liked to keep secrets.

But the truth was that she hadn't wanted to tell. She liked to think of her life as a sci-fi movie. When she came to Florida, she'd stepped through some dense blue liquid and everything had changed. Her past was "on the other side."

"You're happy now?" Mr. Bletley asked. "You want nothing else in life?"

"Maybe later I will, but not now." She looked at him. "I'm afraid my mother will change things back to the way they were."

"You could —"

"Do *not* say I could just tell her no. It's not possible. You don't know what she's like. She'll cry and tell me how alone she is." Kate put her hands over her face. "I don't know *why* she's here. Did the uncles send her after me?" She put her hands down. "I didn't mean to make this about me. Today

137

is a celebration of your new house."

"This is better than superficial chitchat. It's a bit like what I've had for the last years of my life."

"I would imagine that you were the resident therapist."

"In a way, I was. But we all had our roles."

Out of habit, Kate began to clear the cloth of dishes.

"I'll do that," he said.

Kate looked at her watch. "It's nearly four! I'm supposed to meet Jack and he'll be upset if I don't show up."

He lifted an eyebrow. "I've heard gossip about the Wyatt temper. He wouldn't turn it on you, would he?"

She laughed. "Far from it. It's worse. If I don't show up, Jack will *worry*. He'll call people. Send them out to look for me." When she stood up, she swayed on her feet.

"You can't drive. I'll take you to him. Where is he?"

"In what used to be the bad part of town. Jack remodeled several of the houses but he left two of them alone."

"Might I guess that one is where your aunt grew up?"

"You're very perceptive."

"Not as much as I'd like to be. I'll drive you in your car, then I'll take a . . . . What are they called?"

"An Uber."

"Right. So many new words."

As he stood beside her, she put her hand on his arm. "Thank you. I feel better."

"That's all that matters. And Kate." He locked eyes with her. "Everything *will* be all right. I promise. On my life, I swear it."

He smiled so sweetly that Kate believed him.

Mr. Bletley drove straight to the old Medlar house, no directions needed. Jack's truck was outside. "Come in and meet him," she said.

With a curt shake of his head, he fairly leaped out of the car. He said something that sounded like "gradual socialization," then he seemed to disappear, as though the wild tropical plants swallowed him.

Kate had had too much champagne to try to figure out what was going on. She went to the house.

Jack was waiting for her inside — and he was frowning.

The house was in better shape than when she'd first seen it, but not much. It had been built at the end of WWII when soldiers were returning and ready to start families. The small houses were divided into little rooms.

Kitchens were closed off. There was one bathroom and it was so tiny it was hard to turn around.

But what was good was that the air of hopelessness that used to be in the house was gone. Since Jack had bought the place, he and Sara and Kate had spent hours inside it. Their laughter, their plans for the future, had pushed the bad spirits out.

Sara said, "Happiness beats all the sage burning in the world." It seemed she was right.

Kate smiled at Jack. "Is that look for me? I'm not late, am I?"

"No."

His expression didn't change — and Kate dreaded whatever it was that he planned to tell her. She'd had a good time with Mr. Bletley and she didn't want that taken from her. She wanted to lighten Jack's mood. "When I was on the way to work I stopped at Bessie's and bought some keto cookies. Aunt Sara will love them. You'll never believe what Bessie told me."

Jack didn't reply.

"She said that when Aunt Sara was there, Everett was with her. They *both* hid from my mother. Why do you think he did that? Out of solidarity? Bessie said it was all very funny. Everyone was laughing. They took

140

photos and plan to make memes."

Jack's expression didn't change. A lawn chair was leaning against the wall. He opened it and motioned for her to sit down.

She remained standing. "Jack," she said, "I've had three glasses of champagne but even so, you're scaring me. *What* is the problem?"

"Your father."

"I know. My mother will use his memory to bully me into moving in with her. I'm prepared for that. He died a long time ago but she still —"

"No, he didn't." Jack's voice was barely a whisper. "He didn't die then or ever."

Kate wasn't understanding. When she took a step back, Jack put his hands on her shoulders and she sat down in the chair.

He began to pace the small room. "I didn't know. I was just told yesterday. Randal Medlar . . ." Halting, he looked at her. "When you were four years old, your father was sent to prison. He's been there ever since."

Kate was having trouble concentrating. "He's alive now?"

"Yes. And he's been released early. He might be on his way to Lachlan."

Kate closed her eyes — and her mind filled with images of Mr. Bletley. She looked

141

back at Jack. "Tell me everything. Why? How? Where?"

"He's been in prison in upstate New York. He —"

"New York?" Kate said. "Mother went there at least twice a year. Sometimes more. Did she visit him?"

"Yes."

"Her depressions came after her trips to see him." Kate's voice was quiet, subdued.

"Kate, I —"

"Mother is here for him, not me."

"Maybe. I don't know the details. I'm still in shock about it all." He knelt in front of her and took her hands in his. "Are you okay? Maybe I shouldn't have told you."

"Aunt Sara. What does she know?"

Jack stood up. "She . . ."

"Tell me!" Kate said.

"At your father's trial, Sara was a character witness, and she told the truth about your father. He has a tendency to . . ."

"Steal things," Kate said. "I know that." She was sobering up.

"Your mother blamed Sara for sending Randal to prison."

Kate was trying to process this information. "That explains my mother's hatred for Aunt Sara."

"I guess it does."

"And Mom took me away to punish her." Kate's head came up. "You said you were told yesterday. Who knew this to tell you?"

Jack hesitated. "Sheriff Flynn."

"He called you from a ship?"

"He's here, holed up in his house." Jack's expression turned to anger. "The bastard knew Randal was coming so he conned me into taking over." He looked at Kate. "Sorry. This is worse for you than it is for me. You haven't been, uh, approached, have you?"

"What do you mean?"

"Older man appearing out of nowhere?"

The images in Kate's mind were flooding it. Two lunches. Pouring her heart out to the man she'd just met — and all about her *mother*. His wife. "I wonder what he looks like now?"

Jack sat down on an overturned paint bucket. "No idea. But I remember that my grandmother said Randal was the most elegant man she'd ever seen. Dad said he had belts that cost as much as his truck."

Hermès can do that, Kate thought. "Aunt Sara knows that he's been released?"

"I don't think so. Of course she knows her brother isn't dead, but he wasn't supposed to get out for years."

"So she believed she was safe. For a while, anyway." Kate shook her head. "Lies on top of lies. A skyscraper built of lies."

Jack leaned forward, elbows on his knees, hands over his face. "This changes everything, doesn't it? I don't blame you if you're angry. You should be. All this was kept from you." He looked at Kate, his eyes asking what she was going to do.

But she couldn't decide anything now. "The money?" she asked. "Mother said we lived on a life insurance policy from my father's death. That was a lie, so who supported us all these years?"

"I wondered about that so I did a little forensic accounting. Sara sends a check every month."

Kate took a deep breath, then let it out slowly. "This is a lot for me to take in." She stood up. "Thank you for telling me all this, but right now I need time to figure things out. Digest them. Could we keep this between us for now? Aunt Sara hasn't adjusted to Mom being here. If she's told her brother might be here too, it could push her over the edge. She'll run away."

"I'll do whatever you need." He stood up. "Do you want to go home?"

"Not now. Not yet. I need to think." She looked at him. "I want you to drive me to Arthur's house."

Kate started to tell him that she had a

suspicion that Everett knew what was going on, but she didn't. The sheer size of the lies she'd been told, the volume, was beginning to sink in. Father alive, mother's depression, trips to visit him, her aunt blamed and cast out. The lies were deep enough to choke her. "I need time," she managed to say.

Silently, they walked to her car and Jack got in the driver's seat.

"Why has your seat been moved back?"

She gave him a look that told him it was none of his business.

He nodded in understanding, then drove to Arthur's pretty house. He turned off the engine and looked at her. "Kate —"

She put her hand up. "Let me adjust to all this before I say anything. Take my car. I'll get Everett to drive me home." *Or I'll spend the night here,* she thought.

"Whatever you need. Anything."

"Just go home and act like nothing has happened. I can't deal with other people's worries right now." She opened the car door, then looked back at him. "If my mother shows up, please text me a warning."

"I'd like to put your mother in a jail cell."

"I wouldn't object." It was the closest Kate had come to humor since Jack made

145

his announcement.

By the time she reached the house, Jack was gone. She put her finger out to ring the doorbell, but didn't. There was a little iron chair in the shade, more decorative than functional, and she sat down on it.

There were so many thoughts in her mind that it was difficult to focus on any of them.

Her mother's deep, debilitating bouts of depression had given her a lifetime of guilt. Her mother said that her trips to New York City were to buy fabric to make clothes for Kate. Everything had been for Kate. She had grown up believing her mother's fits were her fault.

When she was very young, when her mother was away, Kate had to stay with the uncles. They were tall, bearded and never smiled. Their wives and children were just like them and they'd viewed Kate as a zoo exhibit. They pointed and laughed and ridiculed her for the red in her hair, her modern clothes, her school, for everything about her. If it hadn't been for Noah . . .

When her mother returned from her trips, Kate was so glad to get away from the relatives that the inevitable fits were almost a welcome relief.

But now . . . She'd been told it was all a

lie. Her father didn't die; he had been in prison. And her mother's depression was *not* her daughter's fault.

Kate was trying to put together what Jack had told her. There had been a trial. *For what crime?* she wondered. Aunt Sara had testified to knowing that her brother had a lifetime of thievery. She and Jack had made jokes about Randal Medlar's love of diamonds. Is that what he was caught with?

After the trial, Aunt Sara had been banished from their lives. But she had financially supported them. The guilt Aunt Sara must have felt in believing that her testimony had sent her brother to prison!

Kate remembered accidently hearing Aunt Sara on the phone with her mother. At the time, Kate had just suffered a trauma and Sara threatened to force Ava to get a job if she wasn't kind to Kate.

The hate between the two women! Kate shuddered. She could see it all. Ava saying that Sara had destroyed their family. Ava using her power as the mother to separate her daughter from her aunt. Then demanding that Sara pay. Kate could almost hear her mother. "You *owe* us!" she'd shout. "You took our lives so you have to repay us."

Kate remembered that yesterday Aunt

Sara had asked where Ava got the money to buy a house in Lachlan. Kate had nonchalantly replied that her mother "always seemed to come up with cash when she needed it." Would Ava badger Aunt Sara into giving her the purchase price for a house now? Would she threaten to coerce Kate into returning to Chicago if Sara didn't give the money?

Was Aunt Sara still sending Ava money to live on? *Surely not,* Kate thought, but part of her knew it was possible. How else could her mother live if money wasn't being sent to her? Ava had never had a job in her life. She hated living with her brothers. "Too many rules!" she'd always said.

Kate glanced at the door. She should ring the bell and go in. She felt sure that Everett knew more than she did, certainly more than Jack was told by Sheriff Flynn.

Another lie, Kate thought. The sheriff had dropped the whole mess onto Jack rather than facing Randal Medlar. Why? Was the sheriff afraid his old buddy would talk him into committing a crime? Or be forced to turn a blind eye when Randal stole something?

Her thoughts were taking her back to the place she didn't really want to go: to her father.

Was the man she'd met . . . ? She didn't want to face what she was pretty sure was true. James Leighton Bletley was maybe, possibly her father. Probably was.

She put her head back and closed her eyes as she went over her two visits with Mr. Bletley. Seeing the house the first day, then lunch together. Another meal the second day.

From the first moment, she'd felt comfortable with him. They were at ease together. Talked like old friends. They seemed to like the same things.

Again, she remembered that she'd told him about *her mother.* He'd seemed very interested in that! He'd asked several questions — and she'd answered them all. Nothing had been too private to not tell him.

Abruptly, Kate sat up straight. The guy on the motorcycle! She'd nearly forgotten that. She'd assumed he was after her bag, but was he?

She put her hands to her temples and squeezed her eyes hard closed as she envisioned every second of that encounter.

The androgynous person on the bike had reached out, but to what? Mr. Bletley was holding nothing, but Kate had a Prada bag. It made sense that the rider wanted what Kate had.

No, she thought. He wasn't reaching for anything. He or she was striking. It wasn't an open-handed grab, but a closed-hand punch.

And Mr. Bletley had come away with a cut on his hand. It seemed that the rider had been hiding some sort of knife. Kate's hit in the ribs and Mr. Bletley's kick had kept the blade from reaching its target and the rider had sped away.

She opened her eyes. Her convicted-criminal father had come to town and look at all that had happened. The sheriff had suckered Jack into being deputized, then Flynn ran away and hid. Coward! A man fell out of Charlene's barn and died. There was evidence of someone else in the barn. Kate's mother had been in town for a week but had told no one she was there. And just yesterday a person on a motorcycle had tried to attack the former prisoner with a knife.

"It's all connected," she said aloud. "I *know* it is! It's all one big problem."

"And what would that be?"

She looked at the door. It was open and Arthur, in his wheelchair, was there. She wondered how long he'd been watching her.

"Everett isn't here and won't be back until tomorrow. Why don't you come in and we'll

150

share a pot of tea?"

She hesitated. "I wanted to talk to him."

"This have anything to do with him and Sara hiding from your mother? Or about your father being alive and probably here in Lachlan?"

Kate's eyes were wide. "Does *everyone* know?"

"More people by the minute. Have you met your father?"

"I think maybe I have."

"Charming, isn't he?"

"Very."

He looked serious. "Did you check your wallet afterward?"

She didn't smile. "Worse. I arranged for him to live in a beautiful, furnished house." She sighed. "And I just remembered that I forgot to get the papers signed and I didn't get a check from him."

Arthur looked like he was trying not to smile but had no success. "I tell you, you Medlars are the most exciting people I've ever met. Come in and we'll tell each other everything we know." He paused. "And I'll give you a copy of the book Everett wrote about your father."

"He did what?"

"At last I've found something you don't know." He lowered his voice. "I have Everett's box of research for that book. It contains photos of you and your father."

Kate gasped. "I've seen one picture of him. A studio portrait. My mother said the other pictures were lost in a fire. Or a flood. She couldn't remember which one."

"I so much want to meet your mother. Everett is terrified of her."

"Everyone except Aunt Sara is. Well, except maybe she is."

He wheeled his chair back. "Do come in, and let's share everything."

"I'd like that." She followed him inside.

NINE

When Arthur was a young man, he'd been in an accident that was his company's fault. He won the ensuing lawsuit but lost his battle to walk. For years his life had been one of great loneliness, but after Sara, Jack and Kate entered it, things changed. Now Everett was his roommate — or as Arthur put it "my free lodger."

Whatever the terms the two men had decided on, they now had a home and a career. And most important, they knew they owed everything to the Three.

Arthur's kitchen had been built to accommodate a man in a wheelchair. Sara, at five feet tall, said it was her dream kitchen. Jack, at six-two, replied, "No," to rebuilding the one in the house they shared.

Kate sat down at the little table at the end of the kitchen while Arthur prepared a pot of tea. She knew better than to try to help him. He didn't like being treated as an invalid.

"Any plans yet?" he asked.

"Not even close."

"So what are you dreading the most?"

"My mother and Aunt Sara getting together. They'll rip each other apart."

"What about your father?"

"From what I've seen, he runs away whenever there's even a possibility of trouble."

Arthur chuckled. "Already found that out, have you?"

"You know him?"

"Not really. He ran in circles that were above me. All the girls, young and old, liked him very much."

Kate grimaced. "I bet they confided all their secrets to him. He's just so damned *adorable.*"

Arthur couldn't help laughing. He let Kate carry the tray into the living room while he got a package of chocolate-covered cookies.

They sat down and Kate poured. She picked up a cookie. "From Bessie's?" There was bitterness in her voice. "So how does Everett know my mother?"

"From research for his book." Arthur wheeled back a couple of feet, opened a

154

cabinet door and withdrew a well-worn paperback. *Rooftops of Gold* by Everett Gage. The cover was dark, showing a man lit by the moon as he tiptoed across a rooftop.

"It didn't sell," Arthur said. "Everett was pretty angry about that."

"He makes that clear when he complains about Aunt Sara's sales."

"Everett does love to make his opinions known to everyone. Why don't you settle down on the couch and read it? It's not very long and it tells a lot about the four men."

"Which ones?"

"Randal, of course, then Roy Wyatt, Walter Kirkwood and . . ." Arthur paused. "And Daryl Flynn."

Kate's eyes widened. "The sheriff was a *criminal*?"

"Uncaught, but maybe yes. It's all explained in there. Under made-up names, of course, but they're easily recognizable."

There was nothing Kate wanted to do more than lose herself in a book. She needed the all-encompassing pleasure of reading.

After they finished their tea, she slipped off her shoes, turned to put her feet up on the couch and leaned back. Arthur, always a considerate host, spread a hand-crocheted throw over her lap.

The book started with an introduction from Everett. He said that while the main story was about a great cat burglar, it was also about four men — all of whom were given false names. Two were born into unspeakable poverty and one was as rich and as blue-blooded as you can get in the US. The fourth was willing to follow wherever the others led.

Everett went on to say that his story was as true as he could make it, and he was risking his life to tell it. He had been threatened with multiple lawsuits, but readers deserved to know the truth. *There is no drama queen like Everett,* Kate thought.

When she turned to chapter one, she was shocked to see that the name of the ringleader was Rowan Bletley.

"Bastard," she murmured. He must have laughed at his use of Everett's made-up last name. And that Kate didn't recognize it told him that she'd not read the book.

She glanced at Arthur, who was also reading. "He got a lot of information out of me," she said.

"The combination to a safe?"

"If I had one I'm sure I would have told him. But then, maybe he didn't need it. He opened the house lockbox with no help from me."

"Oh yes, that's Randal."

Kate kept reading. The whole first chapter was a character study of the four men. What they were like and how they needed each other.

Everett said Rowan was born at the wrong time and into the wrong family. "He should have been royalty, or at the very least rich. His manners were of another time, and he had a way with women. He listened to them. Rich women with abusive, neglectful husbands adored him. They'd do anything for him."

Roy Wyatt, billed as Joe Harlan, was young, poor, rough, crude, and would hit people rather than speak to them. Walter Kirkwood was the rich Wilbur Keen, a man who thought the world should obey him. Daryl Flynn was Dan Fields, young and married, but he couldn't figure out what he wanted to do in life — and he desperately needed money.

By the second chapter, Kate was ready to get on with the story. *What* had Randal done to get himself put in prison? She was tempted to flip to the end, but she didn't.

It looked like Everett had interviewed many people, all of whom were willing to tell glowingly honorable stories about their time with Randal Medlar.

What followed was a modern Robin Hood story. Yes, Rowan Bletley stole, but it had always been for a good reason. There was a chapter about an older woman who was dumped by her rich husband. He pleaded poverty so she'd get nothing. Mr. Bletley went to the Cayman Islands and somehow found the documents proving the man's massive wealth. The wife paid him a healthy percentage of her settlement.

The next chapter was about a husband who was giving his family's jewelry to his mistress while promising to marry her. Two women were being wronged.

When Mr. Bletley introduced the wife and the mistress to each other — they looked alike, twenty years apart — Kate almost laughed. The two women joined forces to get what they deserved. Of course they paid Mr. Bletley a nice fee.

There were paintings that were believed to have been stolen by Mr. Bletley. He returned them to their rightful owners.

A true hero, was Kate's sarcastic thought. She was getting impatient. How was he caught?

The next chapter was about the biggest job of all. The four men had worked together and millions of dollars' worth of jewels were taken from an elderly lady. The detectives were sure it was an inside job, but the owner, who was dying in the hospital, would tell them nothing.

Everett wrote about what happened after the crime. The character of Jack's father suddenly began making a lot of bad investments. He gambled, drank and bought a big Harley. He was soon broke. The rich man went to California and bought stores, then he dumped the actual work of running the businesses onto his long-suffering wife. The last young man was so scared by the job that he went into law enforcement.

Everett wrote that none of this could be proven. He informed the Fort Lauderdale Police of his theories but they dismissed him. They said it was all conjecture by a "hack writer." Everett's bitterness could be felt on the page.

What interested Kate was that in all the stories and whatever the job, it was clear that Randal Medlar was *always* the boss. He saw the opportunity, made the plans and ruled every detail.

Kate put down the book and looked around. It was dark outside. She heard Arthur rolling into the room.

"Had enough?"

"I haven't come to how he ended up in

jail. Where are the photos?"

"On the bed in the guest room, along with a sandwich and chips, and two cans of fizzy water. I thought maybe you'd like to spend the night."

"I think I will. If I go home, Aunt Sara will take one look at me and know that something is wrong. Maybe by morning a solution will come to me." Kate didn't sound hopeful.

Arthur led the way down the wide hall to the guest bedroom. It had a bed, a night table and a lamp. There wasn't a chair or a rug. It had a small en suite bathroom. Everything was plain and basic.

"I'm going to introduce you to Jack's sister, Ivy," Kate said. "She's an interior designer."

Arthur chuckled. "Can't imagine why you think I need her."

On the bed, beside the plate of food, was an old file box. A huge white T-shirt was laid out at the foot. "It's perfect," she said.

"I'll leave you to it then."

She kissed him good-night and closed the door behind him.

The first thing she did was text Jack that she was spending the night at Arthur's.

How's Aunt Sara?

Worried.

Any visitors?

Glad to say no. You okay?

She started to tap out that Everett had written a book about her father, but she didn't.

Just being calm. I'll see you tomorrow after work.

It was a few seconds before he responded so she knew he was considering whether to ask questions or not.

Sleep well.

You too.

She shut off her phone. She wanted a night's peace before her world broke apart tomorrow. She was going to have to tell Jack and Aunt Sara that her father was in town and she'd met him. And of course Ava would show up. Kate didn't want to think about the chaos that would follow. People yelling and accusing and dumping blame everywhere.

For all the bareness of the room, the

bathroom had a dozen little hotel-size bottles of shampoo, conditioners, some lovely moisturizers and toiletries. She took a long hot shower, washed her hair, then put on the big T-shirt.

She sat cross-legged on the bed and lifted the top off the box. Inside was an acid-free envelope marked Pictures for Gold. Kate held her breath as she opened it. There were only four personal photos. They were of her, as a toddler with long braids and . . . Kate took a breath. Her father.

He was a handsome devil! she thought.

What struck her most was that father and daughter were looking at each other with absolute love. As though they were each other's world. Be all, end all.

The photos weren't clear, probably taken with one of those cardboard-encased cameras, but the man in the picture was indeed the Mr. Bletley Kate had come to know.

She spread the pictures on the bed, then looked through the box. There was one more grainy photo of some men in a prison yard. They were in a group and seemed to be in an exercise class. It was clear enough to see that the trainer was her father.

The rest of the box was filled with papers — handwritten, typed, photocopied. At the bottom were transcriptions of oral interviews.

Kate put the papers back in the box and set it on the floor. She got under the covers, opened her drink and picked up the sandwich. She ate while she read the rest of Everett's book.

When she learned that her father had been sentenced to twenty-five years for hijacking a car, she was shocked. That seemed a lot for a petty crime.

She went on to read Everett's details. Randal's lawyer put him on the stand, hoping his personal charisma would appeal to the jury. Randal declared his innocence, saying that he'd been hired to drive the car, a Bentley, to the owner's home in Nashville. He was told that the key would be left on top of the left rear tire and that's where he found it.

Everything had gone as planned until Randal drove across the state line. He wasn't ten miles over when the state police stopped him. He went to show the papers for the job, but he couldn't find them. Everything had vanished.

Since the owner of the car said he saw Randal take the vehicle, that made it a hijacking rather than just a theft. And also, the car was very valuable. When they found cocaine in the trunk, it was all over. The jury found him guilty, but with a recommendation for leniency. They suggested a suspended sentence as Randal had a clean record, not even a parking ticket. But the judge, a friend of the former sheriff's, gave Randal the maximum sentence allowed. Everyone knew it was for past crimes that no one had been able to prove.

It was late when Kate finished the book. She knew she needed time to process everything she'd just read, so she turned off the light and immediately went to sleep.

Kate woke early and there was a moment before she realized where she was and what was going on in her life. When she did, she didn't want to get out of bed.

But she dragged herself out, dressed in yesterday's clothes and made her way into Arthur's kitchen. He was already there.

"I thought you might get up early. Going to work today?"

"I guess," she mumbled as she sat down at the table.

Arthur put a plate of bacon, eggs and toast in front of her, but she had no appetite.

He rolled to the other side of the table. "There was a time when I was so scared of what other people thought of me that I did

164

nothing."

She knew what he meant. Years ago, if Arthur had spoken up, some deaths might have been prevented. It was a heavy burden for anyone to carry.

Kate kept her head down and nodded in understanding, but she didn't think her situation was as bad as his. She pushed her plate away. "Sorry. I don't think I can eat."

He took her plate away. "Don't go to work today. Everyone will ask you questions about the dead man and what was going on with Sara and Everett at the bakery and everything else. You need to let all this settle in your mind."

She looked at him. "I dread what's coming. All the arguing and accusations. My mother and Aunt Sara. Jack angry at everyone. And what am I to do with my father? Do I yell at both my parents for lying to me? I don't know how to handle any of this."

Arthur looked at her in silence for a moment, then asked, "How is Charlene?"

Kate had to think to even remember who that was. "Fine, I guess. She's with Tayla. Jack got a security guy to stay with them."

"Good to hear." Arthur rolled away. "Why don't you go shopping? I hear Sawgrass has some big sales going on. Randal's a fancy dresser. You don't want to embarrass him."

"Maybe I should get an orange jumpsuit."

Arthur's mouth twitched in a smile. "Has to be the right shade of orange, though."

Kate didn't smile at his joke. Her sense of humor was gone. She stood up. "I think I will take today off. Melissa can take my appointments. Heaven knows I've covered for her a thousand times."

"Kate the good girl," Arthur said. "Takes care of everyone. Kate the peacemaker."

She looked at him hard, trying to figure out if he was being serious or facetious. "I think I'll go. Thank you so much for everything. I'll leave the research here."

"Good idea. They'd probably make everyone angry, then you'd have to calm them down."

Kate was still watching him, trying to understand what he was actually saying, but she couldn't figure it out. His words were good, but there was something odd underneath them.

He picked up a set of car keys from the counter that she recognized as hers. "Jack brought your car back and put these on the hall table. He opened my locked door, but he didn't speak to me or you. There sure is a lot of fear going on in the Medlar household right now."

"And it's all my fault," she said softly, then

took the keys, kissed Arthur and left. When she was in her car, she sent a text to the office. She said she wasn't feeling well and wouldn't be in today.

The office manager, Raye, texted back.

Too many scones at Bessie's?

Kate felt a surge of anger. Damned gossip! She didn't reply to Raye's snarky text. Instead, she decided to take Arthur's advice to go shopping. Maybe she'd go to a movie. Anything rather than deal with what was going on in her life. Postpone it all as long as she could. Did she confront Tayla or go searching for Charlene? It took her only seconds to decide.

Sawgrass was an enormous discount shopping center with hundreds of stores. There were high-end shops in the Colonnade and she liked those the best.

It was early, before the stores opened, so the Colonnade was barricaded. She parked under a tree, turned off the engine and waited. She wanted to block the events of the last days from her mind. But she kept envisioning what was going to happen. Everyone was going to be angry and/or hurt. There'd be screaming and accusations.

"You lied to me!" would be a constant refrain.

She tried to read a book on her phone but couldn't concentrate. She listened to four Reddit posts. Mothers-in-law seemed to be truly horrible. *Jack's mother is wonderful,* she thought, then chided herself for jumping to that idea.

When the stores were about to open, she was the first in line to go through. She parked in front of the Burberry store. Maybe she'd splurge and buy herself a new raincoat.

She got out and wandered through half a dozen stores but didn't see anything she wanted. By lunchtime, she was exhausted. She left the Colonnade to go to the Food Court and bought a plate of Chinese food, with fried rice and spring rolls.

She sat down at a table but just looked at the food. She and Aunt Sara joked about how it wasn't fair that some women under stress couldn't eat. "But the more stress I have," Sara said, "the more I eat." Kate said she had the same problem.

Kate pushed her plate away. *This kind of stress is a whole different level,* she thought. "I'm so sick of being scared," she said aloud, thinking about her entire childhood. "Just plain fed up with it."

She looked around to see if anyone had heard her. No. People were busy with their own lives.

What if I stopped? she thought. *What if I stopped being afraid of* all *of them?*

As the idea began to take shape in her mind, she pulled her plate back and ate everything on it. When she finished, she went back to the Colonnade.

What Arthur had said was ringing in her mind: "How is Charlene?" Kate looked down the row of pretty stores. "Forgotten," she said aloud. *Charlene has been forgotten.* There had been a rifle hidden and a man falling out of her barn and dying. Later, there was a slash made by a person on a motorcycle. All, just plain *forgotten*.

As she walked in the deliciously warm Florida air, she began to develop a plan. A Plan. There was a seating area nearby and she sat down on a concrete bench to think. She could envision everything she needed to do. No! That she *had* to do. Twenty minutes later, she took out her phone, and texted Jack.

I'm holding a meeting for five people at Aunt Sara's house today at four. I need drinks, food, etc. can you do it?

He texted back right away. Yes.

And please make SURE Aunt Sara is there.

Will do. You okay?

Best I've been in years.

He sent a smiley face emoji and a thumbs-up.

She called Sheriff Flynn's private mobile number. Sara and Jack had often butted heads with the sheriff, but he and Kate had become friends.

"Kate," he said happily. "What a delightful surprise. How are you doing?"

"Very well. How's your cruise?"

"Great. I've always loved the sea air."

"We're having a meeting today at Aunt Sara's house at 4:00 p.m. I believe you know where it is. I'll see you there."

"Kate, dear," he said in that patronizing voice oldies used on the young, "you just said I was out of town."

"If you don't show up, I'll call Detective Cotilla and tell him where you are and why you conned Jack into taking over *your* job." She waited but Sheriff Flynn said nothing. "By the way, Randal will be there. You know,

170

my dead father."

There was still no reply.

"What? No comment?"

"I'll be there at four," he said softly.

"And don't be late. Aunt Sara hates tardiness." She clicked off the phone.

As she brought up the number of "Mr. Bletley," she clenched her teeth. She touched the number. He picked up instantly.

"Kate, what a pleasant surprise. Can we meet for our daily lunch?"

She glowered at the phone. What presumption! "You are to be at Aunt Sara's house at 4:00 p.m."

"How kind of you to invite me but I have a previous engagement." He sounded amused, as though she was cute but not very bright.

What a smooth, practiced liar he is, she thought. She wasn't sure how her father felt about her mother, but Kate had had a lifetime of experience so she could guess. She replied in exactly the same tone as his. "If you don't show up, I'll call Mother and tell her you've been here for weeks but you haven't contacted her. And I will also tell Aunt Sara that you've been secretly wining and dining me for days. How do you think Jack will take that information? Don't forget that he's Roy's son. I can assure you that Jack has inherited the Wyatt temper."

There was a silence before Randal spoke and his voice was almost meek. "I'll be there at four. Should I bring anything?"

"Whatever you think will make Aunt Sara forgive you." She heard his gasp. Her request was impossible. Kate clicked off.

For a moment she sat still, staring ahead but seeing nothing — and she didn't think she'd ever felt better in her life.

War clothes, she thought. She was going to dress herself from the skin out. Stiletto heels were in her mind. And she'd have her hair and nails done.

"Damn them all!" She spoke too loudly.

A woman with a baby in a stroller was walking past. "I agree with you, girl," she said, and kept going.

Smiling, feeling taller and all round better, Kate headed toward the stores. She had to prepare for battle.

TEN

Kate arrived at Sara's house at ten to four. Jack was waiting inside.

"Wow! You look great." His eyes were wide. "Your shoes . . ."

She stalked past him. It looked like her new Escada suit and the red-soled Louboutins were a success. One end of the big dining table had been loaded with food and drink. She put her new red leather Kate Spade portfolio on the table. She'd made notes.

"The bar is stocked with booze," he said. "In case you want anything. Ready to tell me what this is about?"

She turned to him. "Where is Aunt Sara?"

"Locked in her room, quaking in her boots. She's dreading facing your mother."

"So you didn't tell her that her brother has been released early?"

"Nope."

"He's here and I've met him. I had lunch

with him twice."

It took Jack a moment to breathe. "What's he like?"

"Lovely. Charming. I'm going to kill him." The doorbell rang. "They're here. Go get Aunt Sara and do *not* let her run away."

"Yes, ma'am." Jack was smiling.

Kate opened the door. Her father was there, beautifully dressed as always, and smiling like he was pleased to see her again. Old friends. Behind him was Sheriff Flynn in head to foot denim, as though it was modern male armor. He looked like he was heading toward the gallows. She opened the door wide.

As Randal entered, as though it was natural, he bent to kiss Kate.

"Touch me and you die," she hissed.

With a chuckle, he went into the house.

As Daryl passed, he said, "I see you've come to know your father well."

"And *you* dumped him onto Jack."

The sheriff shrugged as though to say, *What else could I do?*

When the two men reached the living room, Randal said, "My sister's done a wonderful job remodeling this old house. But then she always was the most competent person there ever was." He made it sound like a sin.

174

The double doors opened to Sara's bedroom and she came out. Her fierce expression showed she was expecting to be hit with her sister-in-law's venom. Instead, she looked at the smiling, handsome face of her brother — who was supposed to be in prison.

Sara's face changed from warrior mode to sheer horror. "No," she whispered, and turned back to her bedroom.

But Jack was behind her. He put his hands on her shoulders and guided her toward the big dining table. As she passed her brother, she didn't look at him.

"You're to sit here," Kate said to her aunt as she held out the middle chair on the long side of the table.

Pointing to the chair on Sara's right, she looked at her father. "Sit here." Her voice was not soft. "And you are here," she said to the sheriff. The two men sat down to flank Sara, who was staring straight ahead.

Kate looked at Jack. "You're on the other side, by me."

His face lit up. "I've never been the teacher's pet before."

Daryl muttered, "Except when you were a senior in high school."

Jack took his seat. "She was a substitute, not a real teacher."

Sara said, "Kate, I never meant to keep any secret from you, especially not about your father. But I was afraid that your mother would —"

Kate, still standing, waved her hand. "I understand. But I also know that once I was away from her, you had ample opportunity to tell me the truth."

"I . . . I . . ." Sara, the wordsmith, had no words.

Kate said, "Are you still paying my mother her blackmail money?"

"Yes." Sara's voice was barely a whisper.

"Then stop." Kate opened a can of seltzer and poured herself a glass.

Sara nodded in silence.

Randal spoke softly to his sister. "She's wonderful, isn't she?"

Sara was almost in tears. "I think she hates me."

"No, she doesn't," Randal said. "I've already seen that she'll be like you and do the sensible thing, whatever that is. But the part of her that's like me will do it with grace and elegance."

Sara sneered at him. "You haven't changed at all!"

Randal smiled. "I think that's the kindest thing you've ever said to me."

Kate set her glass down and glared at the

two of them. They stopped talking. She opened her portfolio.

Jack was grinning. "For once, I'm not the bad guy."

Kate turned on him. "You didn't tell us that the sheriff was still in town. What did you two do? Hide out and drink beer? Talk about your misery?"

Both Jack and Sheriff Flynn lowered their heads and said nothing.

"All right," Kate said. "For right now, we must put aside our anger and animosity, as well as past feelings of hurt. Most of all, we have to stop the *lies.*" She was looking at her father. "The first matter of business is the house you rented through me."

Sara spoke up. "If he gave you a check, it'll bounce."

"Is that true?" Kate asked him.

Her father gave one of those shrugs that meant, *That's just me. I should be forgiven.*

Kate didn't smile. "It's my reputation that you've put in jeopardy."

Sara said, "I'll pay it. He can —"

"No you will not!" Kate said. "I'll deal with this. I'll tell the owner some tragic story and work it out."

Randal said to Sara, "I told you she was like me. Truth is a creative concept."

Kate said, "I am like *me* and no one else.

Got that?" She took a breath. "What we're all forgetting is that our number one job is to protect Charlene."

"Problems that *you* caused," Sara said to her brother.

Randal looked affronted. "To be fair, she did make the first move."

Sara snarled, teeth bared. "Charlene was fifteen. You were thirty-four. You should have been imprisoned back then."

Randal's face reddened. From anger or embarrassment couldn't be told. Whatever it was, it was his first sign of genuine emotion. "I didn't know her age. I didn't even know who she was. It was dark. I'd had a lot to drink. She —" He stopped as they were all glaring at him. "I guess the end justifies the means," he mumbled and looked away from them.

"What does that mean?" Sara snapped. "You don't know what Charlene went through! She —"

Kate spoke up loudly. "I want the fighting to stop! Who was the man in the barn?"

They all looked at Randal.

"I have no idea."

It was obvious that no one believed him.

"Really," he said. "I don't know."

Sara said, "So who jumped on the desk,

then the reins rack, then went up into the loft?"

"Uh . . ." Randal began, then was silent.

They leaned forward.

"That might have been a guy named Lenny."

They waited for him to explain.

Randal shrugged. "His part in this is personal. It has nothing to do with Charlene. By the way, how is she? I hope she's happy. She deserves it. She . . ."

They were still waiting for him to answer the question.

"Lenny was hired by a man I know."

"Who you met on your island?" Kate was being sarcastic.

Randal smiled. "Yes, I did. Lovely man. Innocently incarcerated and —"

There was a collective groan.

"It does happen," Randal said. "Anyway, Mel wants me to do something for him so he sent Lenny to find me. I don't know who fell out of the barn."

"Mel?" Jack looked at Sara. "Didn't you mention a lawyer named Mel? He threatened Everett with a lawsuit?"

They looked back at Randal.

"One does what one must," he said.

Sara narrowed her eyes at her brother. "What happened to the loot from the Oliver job?"

Randal seemed surprised but quickly recovered. "I have no idea what you're talking about."

Kate looked at Sheriff Flynn, who had been silent. "I think you know something about that, don't you, Baby Driver?" She was referring to a movie where a young man drove the car in several robberies. "Or maybe I should call you Dan Fields."

The sheriff's answer was to turn a deep red.

"Okay," Jack said. "We need to talk to Lenny."

"And find the motorcycle guy," Kate said.

They looked at her. "Within minutes of being hoodwinked into a meeting with my father, we were attacked by a person on a motorcycle. He had a hidden knife that cut."

Randal held up his hand to show the bandage. He was grinning. "She called me her father. Do you know how long I've waited to hear her say that again?"

"I can tell you the exact number of days," Sara said while the others stared at him.

"Why am I being blamed for everything?"

Sheriff Flynn said, "Because it's all coming from *you*. Somehow, *you* have caused everything. This is why I tried to stay out of it."

Randal's face changed to sadness. "Maybe I should leave town. I just wanted to see my daughter after so many years away from her. What is so bad about that?"

Sara said, "Mother's not here to believe you, so cut out the poor-me act. And it's *very* bad if you bring murder with you."

Kate added, "And if you're trying to run away and leave us to deal with Mother *alone,* it's double bad."

Randal leaned forward to look across Sara to Sheriff Flynn. "Tough crowd."

The sheriff replied, "I think your daughter might be your match."

"She is glorious, isn't she?" He looked at Kate. "So what's your plan?"

They all turned to Kate. Her eyes were on her father. "First of all, *you* are to deal with Mother."

Randal lost his smile.

"We'll move them into the guesthouse." Sara at last sounded happy. "Just the two of you. You can answer all her questions about everything."

Kate nodded to her father. "You have to keep her from interfering in our investigation. And you must keep her from attacking Aunt Sara. She can bully me all she wants. I'll tell her myself that I am *not* moving anywhere. It's Aunt Sara who is to be protected."

Sara opened her mouth to protest that, but then smiled at the prospect of not having to deal with Ava's accusations. And it was nice to be taken care of. She gave her brother a very sweet smile.

Sheriff Flynn looked across to Randal. "Anybody else from prison owe you?"

Randal looked pleased at not being accused of something. "I believe in friendship." He plucked at his shirtsleeve — a fine, long-fiber cotton in pale green. "This is from the nephew of a man I met while I was, uh, away. And dear Kate and I had lunch at Hank Crestler's little restaurant. He goes by Henri now. Would you like the address? And some new clothes?"

If the circumstances had been different, it would have sounded like a considerate offer.

Sheriff Flynn opened his mouth to speak, but Kate covered him. "No, he doesn't want to get entangled in some prison obligations. And he and Jack like beef. By the pound."

Jack and Sheriff Flynn looked at each other and nodded.

Kate turned to Sara. "Where is my mother?"

"Maybe she's . . ." Sara began but stopped

at Kate's look. Sara's love of research was legendary. "Okay, so I made a few calls. She's at the Golden Palms Hotel."

"That's . . ." Kate didn't finish.

"Right. Mega expensive."

They looked at Randal. "It's not from me. I don't have a sou. A peso. It's not my doing."

"I'll pay for it," Sara said.

"No," Kate said. "She's my mother so I will pay." She looked at her father. "Jack will go with you to get Mother, and the two of you will move into Aunt Sara's guesthouse. Is that understood?"

Randal nodded.

"And don't let her buy anything, not a house, apartment, condo, nothing," Kate said.

Randal looked surprised, but again, he nodded in agreement.

"I'd like to talk to this guy Lenny," Jack said. "Where is he?"

Again, they looked at Randal.

"I'll ask Mel."

"That would be a good idea," Kate said. "What about the motorcycle guy?"

"No idea who that is."

"Who hates you?" Sara sounded as though it was a rhetorical question.

"Only you, my darling sister," Randal said

183

without concern. "Would anyone mind if I had something to eat? I'm a bit peckish."

"Sure," Kate said as she finally sat down. Now that she'd said what she meant to, she was deflating.

Jack leaned toward her, their heads together. The others were going after the food, and Sara joined the men. "Feeling better?" he asked quietly.

"Yes and no. It's been a traumatic few days."

"You've handled it well. Did you really have lunch with your father? Twice?"

"Yes, but I thought he was a rich client. And you knew about Sheriff Flynn."

"Beer and beef," he said, eyes sparkling. "You pegged us perfectly." He nodded toward the window. The three of them were holding plates of food and looking out at Sara's pretty garden and the big swimming pool. "They snip at each other, but at the bottom, they're old friends."

"What do you think this guy Mel wants my father to do for him?"

"Steal something. What do you think?"

"Did you know that Everett wrote a book about my father?"

Jack's look of surprise answered that.

"I read it last night. Your father was part

184

of their group. He —"

Jack groaned. "I'm not sure I want to hear what he did. But then, it couldn't have been too successful as he was never rich."

"Or he spent it all by gambling and buying a really big Harley."

Jack blinked a few times. He'd inherited his father's motorcycle and meticulously kept it in prime shape. He looked at the three standing by the window. "Why do I get the feeling the Medlar Three has just added members?"

"I sure would like to know what's inside their minds right now."

"Not me," Jack said. "Why don't you and I run away to the Highlands of Scotland and leave them to it?"

"I don't think —"

"I'll wear a kilt."

Kate sighed. "Get thee behind me, Satan."

Jack laughed.

It was 9:00 p.m. and Jack was sitting alone in the family room. After Kate's magnificent handling of the Randal-Flynn problem, she had retreated to her room — as had Sara. The two women were inside their bedrooms, speaking to no one. He'd tried to get them to come out, to talk about their worries, but he'd had no success. Frustrated, he'd

185

brought up Acorn TV and turned on *Mid-somer Murders.* He'd gone through the episodes and chosen one set in a medieval house that was possibly haunted. He'd turned up the sound quite loud. If that didn't lure them out, nothing would.

But even with this enticement, Kate and Sara hadn't left their rooms. Their bedroom doors, usually open and welcoming, were closed. *Might as well be barricaded,* he thought.

He put the TV on Mute and tried to think about what to do with "his" women. He'd rather deal with angry lions than two women who were . . . What? Angry? Hurt? Scared?

Truthfully, he wasn't sure what was going on with them. All he knew was that he couldn't take any more of it.

He got up and went to the door to Kate's quarters, gave a quick knock, then entered and marched down the hall to her bedroom.

She was sitting up in bed, wearing a beat-up old T-shirt, a book open on her lap, but she was staring at the wall in silence. She turned to him in surprise.

"Come on," he said. "Let's go."

"No. I've had enough today. I need quiet."

"You need to talk to Sara."

"Oh no." She pulled the cover up around her neck. "I said too much today."

186

"You said and did what was needed." He tightened his lips. "Remember how we said that a three-legged stool can't stand on just two legs? Right now it's trying to stand on just one leg. Mine. You two have to resolve this."

"I can't," Kate began. "Aunt Sara is . . ." She shrugged.

"Either get up or I will carry you." He opened the door to her closet and pulled a robe off the hook, then tossed it on her bed. "Three minutes . . . then I come and get you."

Kate knew he was right. She was going to have to face her aunt at some point. Better to get it over with and start packing.

She followed Jack out, her head bent, shoulders drooping.

As he'd done with Kate, he gave one quick knock, then opened Sara's door. A few steps to the left and he was facing her.

She was fully dressed and sitting on her all-white bed, notebook and pen in hand. As Kate had, she looked at Jack in surprise.

He stepped aside to reveal Kate. "You two need to tell each other the truth. Do one of those feeling things that women love so much." He looked from one to the other. "I'm going to bed."

The women watched him leave. When

187

they were alone, they looked at each other.

"I didn't mean to keep such a secret from you," Sara whispered.

"I guessed that."

For a moment, they looked at each other in silence, then Sara opened her arms and Kate ran to her.

"I didn't mean —"

"I should have —"

"I could have —"

"I'm so very sorry that I —"

Their words tumbled over each other.

They snuggled together. "Tell me what happened," Kate whispered.

Sara told her about the first years of Kate's life and how much they loved each other. "Randal and I even got along then." Sara told how she'd rented an apartment outside Chicago so she could be near her dear niece. "You and I chose all the furniture together." She paused. "Randal would go away for weeks at a time, but I didn't know where or why, and I never asked. Besides, between writing and publicity and you, I didn't have time to concern myself about anything else."

Kate knew she was hinting about the big jewel robbery that happened in Florida when Kate was just a year old.

"It was a hectic time," Sara said. "Before . . ." She took a breath. "I was subpoenaed to testify. I thought I'd be asked about some car. I wasn't in Florida when it happened so I wasn't concerned."

"But you were asked about childhood things."

"Yes." She paused. "The prosecuting attorney grilled me. He shot accusations at me. He quoted things I'd told other people. One of my books was about a thief, and yes, I used Randal as the basis of the character. The lawyer treated what I wrote as fact. I never meant —"

Kate hugged her aunt until she calmed.

Sara sat up. "What happens now?"

"We stand together." Kate pulled back to look at her aunt. "Are there any more big, huge secrets being kept from me? I don't think I can take much more."

"Not that I know of." Sara smiled. "You handled my brother well today. I was really proud of you."

"I wasn't kind to you."

Sara laughed. "I *loved* being told to stop paying Ava. She gets greedier every year. Oh! Sorry. She's your mother."

"Do you think my father will do what I told him to?"

"You mean will he go with Jack to get your mother, then move into the guesthouse where we can see what he's up to?"

Kate nodded.

"Not a chance." Sara shrugged. "Maybe all this is just as Cotilla said and the man falling out of the barn was an accident. Maybe we've been imagining problems where there aren't any."

"Possibly," Kate said, but she knew neither of them believed that. "Where do you think my father is now?"

"With Daryl. My brother could always hypnotize him. If it weren't for Evie, Daryl would have followed my brother to prison."

Kate frowned. "I just thought of something. Everett's book told how the other three men spent lavishly after the robbery, but he didn't say what Rowan Bletley, the ringleader, did with his share."

"Which would have been at least 60 percent," Sara said. "When he was a kid, Randal wouldn't even divide a candy bar in half. It was two-thirds for him and a third for anyone else."

For a moment, they looked at each other.

"Roy and Walter are dead," Sara said. "Which is the only way we're sure they aren't involved in this."

"However . . ." Kate said, "words live on. Maybe someone was told about what happened. Maybe . . ." She didn't finish the sentence.

They thought about that for a moment.

"You better go tell Jack we're fine," Sara said. "You know how he worries."

"But pretends he doesn't." She looked at Sara. "Thank you. Thank you for all of it. I don't believe your testimony put my father in prison. But thank you for taking care of Mother and me for all these years. If it hadn't been for you . . ." She didn't know what else to say.

Sara had tears in her eyes. "Go on. Check on the crown prince, then get some sleep. Let's try for normal tomorrow."

Kate got off the bed. "Normal? You mean Jack back to being deputy sheriff and constantly grumbling? Me back to selling houses and you to . . . ?"

"Hiding?" Sara's eyebrows were raised. "I'm still open to the house in Italy."

"If I marry Jack first."

Sara sighed. "I can see the wedding now. You in a lace dress and Jack in a tux. On a hillside by an old villa. There are flowers everywhere." She picked up her notebook. "I think I'll write this down. Who knows? I might be able to use it in a future book."

Smiling, Kate left the room, closing the door behind her.

ELEVEN

Curiosity is going to get me killed, Lenny thought. In spite of being told to back off after the man in the barn died, Lenny was still watching. The man who hired him had said, "I don't know what's going on. I never meant to cause that girl any problems."

Lenny was sure the man knew more than he was telling. A guy with a rifle just "happened" to be there? Lenny had reported how the whole family had been removed from the little farm. "The husband and kids were sent away. The place is now filled with gorillas. Or at least it's men the size of them. You wanta tell me what this is really about?"

The man hesitated. "It's just Randal. He's like the eye of a storm. Things happen around him. Where is he?"

"Slipping around town like an eel. He seems to know people."

"He should since he grew up there. How's Charlene handling all of this?"

Lenny wanted to say, *Since when did I become a therapist?* But he didn't. "She's with her sister." He didn't add that a guard was living with them. But then that guy didn't matter. He'd probably had two weeks of training somewhere. "Who do you want me to track?"

"No one," the man said quickly, then added, "Maybe Randal. If that's possible. He's good at hiding."

If Lenny were a confiding sort, he would have said that he'd seen a person on a motorcycle who used a concealed knife. *What was with youngsters today?* he wondered. *Hidden knives, bombs left in backpacks. Everything done in secret — except their personal lives. They videotaped and revealed those to the world. Or as they called it "sharing."*

"You want Medlar killed?"

"No! I want him kept alive, but I don't think everyone else does."

Lenny pulled the phone away from his ear to look at it. *You think?* he thought but didn't say.

"Just watch him. I'll be there soon. I have . . . things to take care of."

Yeah, Lenny thought. *Bet they involve lots of doctors.*

"Don't get too close," the man said. "Stay

in the background. Don't cause any problems. Maybe I should forget everything. It was a pipe dream, not real."

"Up to you," Lenny said. But the truth was, he was becoming curious — which was a very bad thing. Why had young Charlene's family been whisked away? And why was this Medlar guy skulking about? And what was all that about in the local bakery? The whole town was laughing. But he knew it wasn't good for him to ask why. *I'm getting older by the day,* he thought.

"Okay, follow him, just don't get too close."

"Sure thing." Lenny clicked off. He went straight to his car, one he'd "borrowed" from a long-term storage garage. Better that than filling out papers at a rental place. Leave No Trace was his motto.

It took hours to find Randal Medlar. But people always leave trails. Lenny had discovered that Medlar liked good food so he checked the best places near Lachlan. He found nothing.

The place Medlar had slept in the night before was empty.

It was only by chance that Lenny saw Medlar coming out of a fast-food joint. *Not his style,* Lenny thought. Which meant that Medlar was probably going to see someone who liked greasy burgers. Medlar got into a rental car — cheap against his quietly expensive clothes — and drove away. Lenny followed, then waited by the Dumpsters while Medlar stopped and bought three six-packs of beer.

Lenny followed him through the town and wasn't surprised when Medlar pulled into the driveway of the local sheriff. He parked where the rental car was hidden from the street. *But hadn't there been gossip at the tea shop — a place better than a police radio for local news — that the sheriff was out of town?*

Lenny left his car a quarter mile from the house, then jogged back. There was a big bush to the side and he practically melted into it. He was just in time to see Medlar carrying the food and drink to the back door. Even Lenny was impressed by how fast the man picked the lock.

Once Medlar was inside, all was quiet. For a few minutes, Lenny watched and waited. There was a blue light, probably a TV, on at the far end of the house. He could see a sliver through the drawn curtains. Looked like Medlar was making himself at home in the empty house. But if it was empty, who were the burgers for? Medlar didn't keep that flat belly on that diet!

Not my business, Lenny told himself, and

rolled over to get up. But just then he saw a movement. His first thought was that it was Florida so it could be any manner of creature. Gator, anaconda. They had roaches as big as plates.

Out of years of experience, Lenny froze in place. Only his eyes moved. They widened when he saw a figure moving through the plants. He could only see bits of black, the same outfit the person on the motorcycle had been wearing. Looked like he wasn't the only one spying on the sheriff's house.

Lenny didn't move and hardly breathed as the figure silently moved past him.

Only when he heard a step on the asphalt of the road did he let out his breath. In the next second he was on his knees and trying to see through the bushes.

He was astonished when he saw a motorcycle emerge from what looked like part of a damned jungle. *Probably grew up overnight,* he grumbled to himself.

When the bike left, Lenny ran to his car and started it. Thanks to a red light, he was able to catch up to the bike. He saw the rider look into the rearview mirror. Lenny put his hand up as though to shield his eyes from the morning sun but it was really to hide his face.

This isn't the same person, he thought.

Same bike, same clothes, but different bodies. This person was bigger than the one who'd lashed out at Medlar. *There are two of them,* he thought.

He was sure the person on the bike was the same one who had struck out at Medlar with a hidden knife.

The light changed, the bike went forward and Lenny followed. *This is too obvious,* he thought. *Too dangerous.*

He had driven only a short way when he realized that the bike was headed to Charlene's sister's house. Again, everything went back to Charlene.

For some odd reason, one of the birdhouses flashed across his mind. A woman who did nothing more than take care of her family and build pretty birdhouses didn't deserve to be attacked.

Soft, Lenny thought. *I've become a marshmallow.* He turned left and the bike continued going straight.

Lenny pulled to the side of the road. *I should stop. This isn't any of my business. It's not my fight.*

But even as he thought it, he made a U-turn and drove toward where Charlene was staying. There was no way the "guard" staying with her would see this person on the bike. Lenny hadn't seen it hidden at the side of the sheriff's house. And if Lenny didn't see it, then . . .

He stopped the car on the edge of the property, knowing that he was too close. He let up on the brake to move.

In the next second, he saw the rider, face hidden under the big helmet, appear at the passenger window. A gun was aimed at Lenny's head.

Lenny didn't react as fast as he would have twenty years ago, but he did move.

The bullet hit him on the side of his head.

The rider stepped back and watched the car roll forward until it bumped into a palm tree and stopped. With a nod of satisfaction, the rider slipped under the cover of a big ficus hedge.

TWELVE

The Medlar three were having breakfast together. They'd prepared the meal in near silence, then sat down to eat. They were quiet, heads down.

When Jack's phone played the first chords of the theme song to the movie *Jaws,* they knew it was Bea from the sheriff's office. Kate and Sara looked up as Jack answered the call.

"Yeah?" His face turned pale. "Yes, yes. I'll go. Yeah, I guess you better call them. Of course I know where Tayla lives! Send the coroner." He ended the call and looked at Sara. "Get your camera."

"Who?" Sara whispered.

"Some man. Shot in the head outside Tayla's house," Jack said. Seconds later, they were in Jack's patrol car. He didn't turn on the siren. When they got to her house, Tayla was standing by a black Toyota, her body hiding the driver's window.

Jack went to her, Kate behind him. Sara already had her camera out and had snapped a dozen photos of the car and the surroundings.

Tayla said nothing as she stepped aside. Inside the car was an older man who had been shot in the side of the head. His face was coated in great waves of blood.

"Who is he?" Jack asked.

"No idea." Tayla's voice was shaking.

Kate put her arm around her boss and steadied her. "Where is Charlene?"

"They're all inside. They don't know about this. Raye brought some papers for me to sign. Charlene offered her coffee, then Eddie got out some cookies, then . . . then . . . I went outside. I wanted to see if the iguanas had eaten my hibiscus flowers so I . . ." For a moment Tayla clasped onto Kate, then she stood up straight. She looked at Jack. "I called Bea and asked for you. I don't have your private number. I didn't know what to do. I . . ." She trailed off.

"You did everything right," he said. "Why don't you go back inside and keep everyone in there? Bea called Broward and they'll be here soon. I wish I could send you all away, but we'll need to ask questions."

Tayla was still shaking. "Who is he? Why is he here? Who would *do* this?"

"I don't know." Jack looked at Kate and nodded toward the house.

She understood. She guided Tayla to turn away, but as she did, the front door opened and Charlene came out. Behind her were Raye and Eddie, the guard. The three of them were laughing.

"There you are," Charlene said. "We were concerned about you and here you are having a party. Jack, you look great in that uniform. Whose car is that? Did . . . ?" She realized that they weren't smiling.

Jack took a step to block their view of the interior of the car.

"What is it?" Charlene asked. "What's happened?"

Tayla stepped forward and put her arm around her niece's shoulder. "Come on, honey, let's go back inside."

"I am *not* a child." She shrugged Tayla's arm away. Jack tried to block her but Charlene glared at him. He stepped away. At the sight of the man in the car, Charlene put her fist to her mouth.

"What is it?" Raye asked. She and Eddie were too far back to see in the car.

"Go back inside," Jack said. "We'll be there soon."

Raye nodded and went back into the house. As Eddie followed her, he took out his phone and put it to his ear.

Charlene looked like she was hypnotized as she stared at the man's bloody face. Tayla tried to pull her away, but Charlene moved out of her grasp. "I know him."

Everyone froze.

"Who is he?" Jack asked.

"No, I mean I saw him. He was leaning over the man on the ground." She looked at Jack. "I was going to my studio and I saw a man by the barn. I thought he was from the vet's office so I went toward him, but he sort of leaped out of sight. That's when I saw the man on the ground."

"And you tried to revive him," Kate said.

"I did. Then you arrived and called Jack. The others showed up, and I forgot about the first man. Him."

"You're sure it's the same man?" Jack asked.

"Yes. Tall man and that eyebrow. I remember it."

Sara took a half dozen photos of the bloody face, focusing on the left eyebrow that was scarred into two halves.

"You should go inside and wait," Jack said.

Charlene nodded and she and Tayla went back into the house.

Sara put down her camera. "The tall, thin person whose footprint was on the desk.

202

Wonder if he pushed the other man out the window?"

"Whose rifle was it?" Kate asked.

"You mean which dead guy owned the gun?" Sara asked.

Jack's phone rang and he answered it — and he turned even paler. He hung up and looked at Kate. "That was Flynn. Your father is on his way here. They heard about this on Flynn's radio. Damn him!"

"But Charlene is here," Kate said.

The Three looked at one another.

"Does she know he's alive or does she think he died?" Kate asked as she and Jack looked at Sara.

"I have no idea. Really. None. Whatever she knows, I don't think they've seen each other since . . ." She didn't finish.

Kate's teeth clenched. "Since my father impregnated her when she was a teenager?"

Sara gave a silent nod.

Jack ran his hand over his face. "Can one of you keep Charlene inside while I get rid of Randal?"

"You can try," Sara said. "But I warn you that I could *never* make my brother do anything he didn't want to do."

"What a lovely thing to say," Randal said from behind Sara.

Her fists clenched and her mouth formed

into a tight line. She didn't turn around to look at him.

"How's Mother?" Kate asked.

"Well, I assume." Randal was smiling.

"This is a crime scene," Jack said. "You need to leave."

Randal peered around Jack to see the bloodied man in the car. "Oh my! Quite unpleasant. My guess is that he's Lenny who my friend Mel hired." He looked at Jack. "But I bet you already know that." He smiled even brighter.

Jack glared at him.

The front door opened and Charlene came out. "Jack, we have coffee and —" She stopped when she saw Randal.

Sara took a step forward, as though to block the sight of her brother.

Jack and Kate didn't move. They were looking at Randal. His face seemed to dissolve into what could only be described as, well, love. His blue eyes filled with tears.

As for Charlene, she looked like she was about to faint.

Jack, who'd always had a crush on her, moved as though to protect her, but Randal got to her first. His arms opened and she fell into them in complete and total surrender. *I am yours* seemed to be her message.

They held each other in that way that only True Love can. It was submissive and joyous and very loving.

Charlene's face was pressed deep against Randal's chest. "I knew they lied to me," she said. "I knew you weren't gone. Not forever. But Grandmother and Captain Edison told me you died. It was while Walter was threatening Tayla and me and . . . I should have searched, but they said —"

"Shh." He caressed her hair away from her face and kissed her forehead. "It's all right." With his arm around her, he led her into the house.

The Three only breathed when the door closed behind the entwined couple.

Sara sat down hard on the curb. Her multipound camera and lens hit her in the chest but she paid no attention.

Kate was staring at the door. "I had no idea they were . . ."

"In love?" Sara asked. "That it wasn't just a one-nighter between them? As my brother said it was?" Her voice was rising. "That he lied all these years about what they were to each other?"

"Poor Leland," Jack said.

Sara stood up. "My lying, thieving brother is *not* going to break up a marriage. So help me, I'll murder him. I'll hire somebody like this guy" — she nodded toward the car — "to —" Abruptly, she stopped speaking and looked back through the car window.

"What is it?" Jack asked as he saw the coroner's van roll up. Behind it were three Broward County Police cars. Cotilla was in the first one. Jack looked at Sara in question. She was wide-eyed, staring.

"He's alive," she whispered. "He winked at me."

"Probably just a reflex. He couldn't be alive with a shot like that. He —" Jack broke off because the man's eye twitched. It wasn't an involuntary movement. Jack ran to the two men who were getting out of the van. In the next second an ambulance had been called.

"Suicide," Cotilla said to Sara as the EMTs took the man out of the car and put him on a stretcher.

Jack and Kate were in the distance, with the other police officers and answering questions. Sara had twisted her small body into an upside-down position on the passenger seat as she photographed every inch of the inside of the car. To make sure she got the details, she was using a macro lens, and she'd set up half a dozen Lume Cubes for extra light.

At Cotilla's word, she halted and looked at him as though he were stupid. "Suicide? Really? Where's his weapon? Or did he shoot himself in the head, then throw it away? Or maybe an iguana mistook the gun for a hibiscus and ate it."

Cotilla was unperturbed. His voice lowered. "If it's a murder I have to report it to the Broward brass. Maybe I should add that I believe the dead man at Mrs. Adams' barn is connected to this shooting. If I do that, they'll send lots and lots of men with big, shiny badges — and really big questions about everything."

Sara sat up straight and looked at him as she thought about what he was saying. It wasn't a good image.

"Just so you know," Detective Cotilla said, "if anybody does come, your Jack will be removed from the case. Anybody so dumb as to not check for life at first sight *should* be removed. And put on desk duty — where he should be anyway since he's been in law enforcement for what? Days? He's not qualified to lead a shoplifting investigation, much less a *murder.*" Cotilla leaned closer to Sara. "And what about your brother? I hear he's been released. Is he hanging out with Flynn?"

Sara's jaw dropped.

Cotilla gave a little smile. "You and your Scooby team may think I don't know what goes on in your secretive little town, but when an old salt like Flynn decides to dump his whole department onto the son of a criminal, I get suspicious. I did a little digging. Long ago, Randal Medlar and Daryl Flynn were great buddies. I bet you even know that ol' Captain Edison suspected them of stealing millions in jewels." He bent forward so his nose was almost touching Sara's. "Jewels that were *never recovered.*" He stood up straight. "This will be declared self-inflicted until the medical report tells me different. Got that?"

Sara swallowed. "Uh, yes. Uh . . . When will that be?"

"Week. Ten days. Unless there's no other explanation of what the hell is happening in this Den of Sin that is Lachlan, Florida. If there isn't one, we will take over. Do I make myself clear?"

Sara nodded.

Jack and Kate were walking toward them.

Cotilla said loudly, "Yes, I think this was an attempted suicide."

"Are you crazy?" Kate said. "He couldn't have done this to himself. He —"

Sara practically jumped out of the car and put herself in front of her niece. "Yes!

208

Suicide. I agree."

"What?" Kate said. "Are you kidding?"

Sara gave her niece a look to shut up.

Kate blinked. "Okay, suicide."

Cotilla turned to Jack. "Go write this up. I'm looking forward to reading why you didn't check for signs of life as soon as you saw him."

With a groan, Jack went toward the other officers. The ambulance drove away, sirens and lights blaring.

Cotilla turned to Sara. "Was your brother here when the man was found?"

"No." Sara sounded meek, subdued. "He arrived later."

"Then get him out of here. He complicates everything too much."

Sara looked at Kate.

"Sure," she said. "I'll get him."

Inside the house, Kate saw Raye and the guard, Eddie, in the kitchen. They were both on their cell phones. Eddie looked embarrassed and downcast, like he was being bawled out. *Probably is,* Kate thought.

Raye gave Kate a look of, *When can I go?*

Kate shrugged that she had no idea.

In the living room, Tayla was sitting on the edge of a chair. She was staring across the room at Randal and Charlene.

They were sitting on the couch, close

209

together, heads nearly touching, holding hands and talking so low they couldn't be heard.

Kate did *not* like what she was seeing. "We have to go," she said loudly.

Randal was twirling a strand of Charlene's hair around his hand. "I like it. It's nice."

She smiled at him as though she'd never heard anything so wonderful in her life.

Finally, Randal looked up at his daughter.

Kate gasped at his expression. Pure, unadulterated *love* — and the look made Kate angry. Furious, really. She clenched her fists and almost raised them to boxing position, ready to strike. "Up. Out. Now." She could hardly speak.

Randal turned back to Charlene. "I have to go." He kissed her cheek, then her forehead. "We have a lot to tell each other."

Kate gave a sound like a growl.

Randal stood up but he kissed Charlene's hands before he released them. He followed Kate out but he walked backward, his eyes never leaving Charlene's.

Once they were outside, Kate stopped at Jack's patrol car. She didn't dare start saying to her father what she wanted to. "Car. Now."

"How nice," Randal said. "It's been years since I've been in one of these."

When he put his hand on the front passenger door, Kate said, "Back seat!"

Randal opened the back door. "This certainly does bring back memories. Not fond ones, but they are there."

Only after Jack got behind the wheel and Sara and all her camera gear were next to him, did Kate get in the back beside her father.

"This is like family," Randal said cheerfully.

The pent-up anger inside Kate exploded. "You are *not* going to break up a marriage!" she shouted. "Charlene has two children. *Two* of them. And a wonderful husband. She has a good life. So help me, if you try to entice her, seduce her *again* I swear I'll . . . I'll do something horrible to you. I'll —"

"She showed me photos of them," Randal said calmly. "It's a lovely family."

"Yes, they are. And there is no place for *you.* You can*not* try to take away —"

Sara turned to look at her brother through the wire screen across the back of the seat. "Do you know what you did to her?"

Kate's anger increased. "You impregnated her! Then you abandoned her! She . . . She . . ." Kate's anger didn't override her sense of protection. She wasn't going to say what happened to Charlene afterward.

Randal lost his smile and his eyes were sad. "I didn't know," he said. "We agreed to separate. It was wrong between us. Her family. Mine. Our ages. It was all very wrong."

Sara nodded in understanding. "Tayla's mother was a snob to end all snobs. Even without the age difference, she wouldn't have allowed a marriage to a Medlar."

Randal looked away as he swallowed tears. "If I'd only known," he whispered.

As Jack drove, he'd been glancing in the rearview mirror. "The baby died," he said softly. "A little boy."

Randal kept fighting the tears.

Kate fell back against the seat. "Oh hell! *What* are you going to *do* to Charlene?"

Randal looked at her in surprise. "Nothing. It's too late. Charlene loves her family." His eyes, still full of tears, began to twinkle. "Is it my imagination or does her husband look a lot like *me*?"

It was such a vain statement — and so very true — that Kate almost laughed.

Sara rolled her eyes so hard, her head hit the back of the seat. "Narcissism at its essence. The reality of my brother."

"I'd like to see her little farm." Randal looked at Kate. "Is it true that you two build birdhouses? You get along? You work well

212

together?"

"We do. We —"

"Alert!" Jack said loudly. "At two o'clock."

They all turned to the right to look out the window. Sauntering down the street was Ava — and she was looking directly at the patrol car.

As though they were synchronized dancers — Sara in the front, and Randal and Kate in the back — they all hit the floor. They curled into the tiniest, most invisible balls they could physically manage. Medlars might tend to gain weight but they were quite agile.

From the outside, the car appeared to have only the driver, Jack in his uniform. He gave a smiling nod to Ava and kept driving. When he was past her, he said, "You cowards can come up now. The bogeyman isn't going to get you."

As Kate sat up on the seat, she glared at her father. "You *have* to see her! She's your wife. Or do you plan to ditch her for a young married woman who is half your age?"

For the first time, Randal looked angry. "Why haven't *you* sought her out? Invited her to build a damned birdhouse with you?"

"Leave me out of this! *All* of this is about *you.* You came back from the dead and people started dropping out of barns and getting shot. What have you done to cause all this?"

"Don't change the subject," he said. "I'm a master at that. The question is, when are you going to face Ava?"

"Not until you let her know that *you* are here and have been here for what? Weeks? You tried to con me into getting a furnished house for you. Was that for you and your wife to live in? Or was it a web to lure dear Charlene away from her family? And *I* would be left to dry Mother's tears from another of your abandonments."

"I wanted a place for you and me. Father and daughter. Now I'm stuck with Daryl and the rubbish he eats. I —"

Kate's voice rose. "You need to go to Mother. You owe her for all those years she visited you while you were in prison. You weren't a martyred dead man but a *criminal.*"

"And I was put there for something I didn't do," he yelled back.

Kate threw up her hands. "Of course you didn't. But now your crime is neglecting Mother. *Your* wife. She —"

In the front seat, Sara looked at Jack. The Kate they knew was a peacemaker, the one who smoothed away every argument. She'd often stepped between Jack and Sheriff Flynn, and had protected Sara from the entire town.

But now they were hearing a different Kate. She and her father were blasting each other at full volume.

Jack glanced at Sara. "Guess we better take the kids home and settle them down."

"Confiscated any drugs lately? Something we could use?"

"Just a few pounds of cocaine."

"Heavens no!" They were still shouting in the back seat. "Oh for the '70s and the abundance of marijuana."

Jack gave a one-sided grin. "We could always invite Ava for dinner. That should shut them up."

Sara didn't smile. "Do that and I leave."

"Can I go with you?" Jack asked, and they laughed.

When they reached the house, the shouting in the back was still going strong.

The four of them entered the house, Jack and Sara in front. Once they reached the living room with its two facing blue couches, Sara turned to the other two. "Sit," she said. It was a quiet order, but Kate and Randal obeyed. As they sat down beside each other on a couch, they stopped arguing.

Jack looked at his phone. "I can't stay. I have to go to the office and fill out papers. I have to write a whole story about what happened. I hope I can do it." He gave Sara a pleading look.

She knew what he wanted. "I'll write it for you, so sit down."

"Everyone will appreciate that." Smiling, Jack took the other couch.

Sara remained standing. "If we're to figure this out, we have to plan who does what." She looked at Kate and Randal. "The first order of business is Ava."

"She —"

"I think —"

Sara held up her hand. "If I know nothing else about my sister-in-law, it's that she can take care of herself. Ava knows where I live, but she hasn't shown up here. I don't believe we're supposed to know she's here — not until *she* tells *us.* That means she's not expecting either of you to appear at her hotel."

Kate and her father had identical facial expressions that said *I hadn't thought of that.*

Randal relaxed against the sofa, his arms extended across the back. He looked greatly relieved. "Have you checked your credit card statement?"

Sara grimaced. "I did in the car. And yes,

I have a brand-new charge for a five-star hotel and several room service meals." She shook her head. "How did she get my card number?"

Randal shrugged. "She often found out things about me and I never knew how she did it."

Jack spoke up. "Okay, we're done with Ava." He looked at Randal. "Who do you think is after you?"

Sara said, "He's asking who hates you enough to kill you."

"Other than my blood relatives?" Randal smiled at Kate and she glared back. "I'd say Captain Edison but he's dead. Then there's Mrs. Oliver's stepson, Derek. He was quite angry at me."

Sara nodded. "Don't forget Charlene's family. I'm sure they'd love to wipe you off the face of the earth."

"Didn't Charlene's grandmother die?" Jack asked.

"She did," Sara said. "But her parents are alive and the last I heard, still angry. And I'm sure Tayla would like a piece of him."

"Yes," Kate said. "Definitely Tayla. I don't think we should exclude the uncles back in Chicago. He hurt their little sister. In fact, I've wondered if it wasn't one of their sons on the motorcycle."

Jack shook his head. "I think this has to do with the jewel robbery. It comes up constantly. I believe that's why Captain Edison and the judge put him in jail."

"Not that anyone is asking me," Randal said, "but there are no jewels."

The Three looked at him, considered that for a second, dismissed it, then continued.

"I want to see Everett's research," Sara said.

"I read some of it," Kate replied.

"Is it any good?" Sara asked.

Randal spoke loudly. "Did he find out who betrayed me?"

Kate glared at her father. "He was more interested in who did the crime than who brought the criminal to justice."

"I did *not* —" Randal began.

"Yes, yes, we know," Sara said tiredly. "Even a Bentley is beneath your ambitious thievery. You're more into jewelry worth millions. But in fairness, Captain Edison was right to get you for anything that he could find. It's what happens on all the cop shows on TV."

Randal gave his sister a hard look. "I believe there was a time in your life when you were falsely accused of a crime. Did you get over it? Ever?"

Kate and Jack looked at Sara with inter-

218

est. They didn't know what Randal was talking about.

Color flooded Sara's face and the look she gave her brother was downright scary.

Randal smiled back at her.

Sara kept looking at her brother. "*Now* is what's important. Your job is to find out about the man who was in the barn. Who is he? Why was he there? Find out about the man who was shot."

"If he was after you, why was he at Tayla's house?"

"I can answer that one," Kate mumbled.

"If Cotilla sticks his nose into this, we'll be thrown off the case," Jack said.

"He's giving us time." Sara told them what the detective said, including his threats about Jack.

Jack ignored the threat part. "I'll be damned. All he does is belittle us and put us down. He calls us incompetent and interfering, yet he wants *us* to solve this."

"You expect praise from a detective?" Randal asked. "I helped with every fund-raiser, every —"

"We don't have time for male whining," Sara said. "Everyone has a job. I'm going with Jack to do the paperwork. And while I'm doing *his* work, he's going to see what he can find in his precious locked-away files, and he's going to tell me everything he finds." She didn't wait for Jack to agree. "Then I'm going to visit Everett and Arthur to see what they know." She looked at her brother. "*You* are going to stay here and contact your fellow criminals and talk to them in your very own prison jargon."

Randal grimaced. "You always judge me, don't you? Even as a child you never trusted me."

Sara narrowed her eyes. "If you mean I searched your pockets after every visit to every house, yes I did."

Randal didn't reply.

Sara looked at Kate. "You need to go to your office. Melissa can't do anything. There's no telling how long Tayla and Raye will be held for questioning. We need things to run as smoothly as possible." She looked at them all. "We'll meet back here this evening and compare notes. Got it?"

They nodded.

Sara turned to Jack. "I'll drive your truck so we can come home in it. I'm not fond of your patrol car."

"You and me both," he said.

"Nor I," Randal said in a way that made Jack laugh. Kate and Sara didn't so much as smile.

THIRTEEN

Kate gathered the paperwork she needed, got in her car and headed to her office. She was going to do exactly as she'd been told — but not really.

She parked a quarter of a mile away from the house, then walked back. As she'd anticipated, her father's feet were sticking out of the open door of Aunt Sara's car.

"Couldn't find these?" She was holding out the keys to the car.

He inched himself out of the car he'd been trying to hotwire and looked at his daughter. His expression was part annoyance and part pride. "I was just . . ." he began, then he grinned. "I want to know who betrayed me."

"So you've said a hundred times. How do you think you can find out after all this time?"

Randal wasn't fooled. He saw a tiny flicker of interest in his daughter's eyes. "I thought I'd start by talking to the Bentley owner."

"And you know where he lives? Oh wait! You stole his car, so of course you know where he lives."

Randal turned serious. "It was *his* drugs that were in the trunk of the car. Part of my very long sentence was for those drugs. I paid the price and he got off free. The man wisely saw what could happen to him so he changed his life. But no more drug dealing meant no more rich house. Certainly no more Bentleys."

For a few moments they stared at each other — and Kate felt herself caving. Go to the office and be bombarded with questions from Melissa or go searching for clues in a mystery?

Her father saw that he'd won. He walked around to the passenger side and opened the door for her. "Is this little car as fast as I've heard it is?"

"Better," she said as she handed him the keys and got in.

He knew the quirky way to start the car and he seemed to know exactly how to get to wherever he was taking them.

"Were you really friends with Mrs. Oliver?" Her insinuation was clear, that he'd stolen jewels from a woman who had befriended him.

"Want to hear a story?"

She gave him a look that was her answer. She wasn't Sara Medlar's niece for nothing.

"Once upon a time," he said, then smiled at Kate — and she couldn't help returning it. Storytelling was in her blood.

"Jefferson K. Oliver was the younger son of an old, rich Florida family. He was a nice young man who was overwhelmed by his father and older brother. They saw Jeff's youth and good looks as a tool to use as they conquered the world."

"I've met the type," Kate said.

"So have we all. Jeff wanted to please them, so when he was twenty-two he married a woman chosen by them. Of course she was the daughter of a very rich man. He didn't like her much, but she soon gave birth to twins, a boy and a girl."

"I bet his family liked that."

"I believe they thought it was a bit gaudy. After the birth, his wife felt she'd done her duty so she went off to see the world. Her children were cared for by nannies and the older brother and his wife."

"What about Jeff?"

"Interesting you should ask. He'd done what his family wanted so he was more or less free to live his life as he pleased."

"Wine, women and song?"

"No. Jeff went to business school. Gradu-

223

ated magna cum laude."

"Family impressed?"

"Not at all, which upset Jeff very much. Even after he got his degree, they still wouldn't let him in on their business deals. But Jeff didn't have long to think about it because his wife was killed in a plane crash — with her lover. Jeff flew to Italy to retrieve the body. On the private plane home, he met Selena, the young, beautiful flight attendant. It was instant love. They married not long after the funeral of his wife."

"And I bet the family welcomed her warmly," Kate said.

Randal smiled at her sarcasm. "They despised her. I don't want to repeat the nasty legalities of it all, and especially not what they said about dear Selena, but Jeff's brother and his overbearing wife took the twins from them. At the time, Jeff made himself believe that it was the best thing for all of them."

"So what happened to Prince Jeff and his working-class wife?"

Randal grinned. "They made money, lots of it. His business acumen and her street smarts covered it all. And since they were family outcasts, they didn't need to impress anyone. His father and brother felt they had to buy yachts and jets to keep their status.

Years later, when Jeff's brother was on the verge of bankruptcy, Jeff bought the family home. The ancestral castle, so to speak."

"I like this story," Kate said.

"There are sad bits. Jeff and Selena never had children and by the time they bought their way into the family, his kids were grown." Randal glanced at his daughter. "They'd been taught to hate Selena, to look down on her."

"The things children are taught! Like idolizing a ghost."

Randal shook his head at her reference to him, but he kept smiling. "When Jeff was dying, his children assumed that all he owned would go to them. They thought that since he'd bought the family's home, that made it family money."

"But he left it all to his wife, who was also his business partner," Kate said.

"Yes, he did. Jeff's daughter married a rich man and went away to live her life. But the son dedicated himself to . . ." He waited for Kate to fill in the story.

"To getting what he thought was rightfully his."

Randal was quiet, waiting for her to end the story.

"But you came along."

"Yes, Selena and I found each other. She

was older, widowed, lonely. And I was a misfit." He paused to let Kate comment, but she said nothing. "She educated me. She taught me the things she'd learned from Jeff when they were first married. How to properly use a knife and fork, how to carry myself. How to dress. She gave me clothes, watches, cuff links, even the shoes of her late husband. When my old car broke down, she gave me an ancient Mercedes. I truly loved that car."

Kate thought about saying something like, "And years later, you went back and stole from her." But she didn't. With her childhood, she knew all about loneliness. She thought about what would have happened next. "You saw her years later."

"Yes. Twenty-six years later, she and I met again. How the world had changed for me! I had a wife and a beloved child."

When he stopped at a red light, he gave Kate a look of such love that she turned away, her face flushed. *Please don't say you robbed someone for me,* she thought.

Her father seemed to read her mind. "None of this was your fault," he said softly. "You were innocent in all of it."

Kate looked out the side window and said nothing. When they entered an area of magnificent mansions, Randal pointed to one and said that was where the Bentley man used to live. He didn't stop but he did slow down.

When he spoke, his voice was earnest. "I didn't know you weren't told the truth about where I was. It was years before I found out and when I did, I was very angry. Ava said —"

Kate didn't want to be put in a position of siding with one parent over the other. "I don't want to get into this. The past is done." She suddenly jolted. "I know this place! I remember pink and purple balloons."

He smiled at her, glad she remembered.

They passed walled and gated mansions. Pulling to the side, Randal stopped the car in front of a sprawling white house. From what could be seen over the privacy wall, it was like the famous Flagler mansion that she and Jack had visited in Palm Beach.

"I know that roof." She thought for a moment. "There was a woman, older, and she had long hair. She was in bed and she gave me something good to eat."

"Eggs Benedict." Randal was smiling broadly. "What else do you remember?"

"A swing. I went very high. It was scary but exciting too. And there was a man." She paused. "Was that you?"

"Yes." For a moment, he looked out the car window. "When you were one, I came back to Florida. You and Ava stayed in Chicago."

She couldn't keep herself from saying, "That was the year of the Oliver jewel robbery."

"If that's how you want to think of it." He was stiff, as though he'd say no more, but then he exhaled and continued. "I returned because Roy called and told me that Mrs. Oliver was in the hospital and dying. I knew her stepkids wouldn't visit her so I flew back here to see her. And yes, I lied to the hospital staff and said I was her son. She welcomed me and backed up my story. I spent hours every day reading to her, just like I'd done when I was a teenager."

Kate felt herself softening. "And that's when she was robbed." Diplomatically, Kate didn't say that he'd done it.

"Yes. A couple of weeks after I arrived, she died. Her stepson, Derek, was furious that I'd been there. It was very unpleasant." Randal took a breath. "I had to return to Chicago because I had a job in a bank."

"Really?" There was disbelief in Kate's voice.

He ignored her tone. "I made very little money but even so, Ava gave a lot of it to her brothers. She called it 'a tithe.' "

"Like they were a church?" Kate was sneering.

"Exactly like that. Did you know that Sara had an apartment near us?"

"Yes, she told me."

"Anyway, by the time you were four, I was sick of everything in my life in that cold state. Ava and Sara fought constantly. Ava said Sara should also give the brothers money. Masses of it."

"Aunt Sara would refuse."

"She did, but that didn't keep Ava from making demands." Randal paused. "To be fair to my sister, she paid for our groceries and there was no limit to what she bought for you."

"But Mother wanted more," Kate said softly.

"Yes," Randal replied. "But worse was what the adult anger was doing to you. You were very young but I could see that you felt what was going on. Every day you got quieter. I saw you go from a laughing, happy child to playing alone with your toys and whispering to them. So I wrote a letter to Mrs. Augusta Lenore Meyers. She'd given me her card when I was visiting Mrs. Oliver in the hospital. She said that if I ever needed a job to call her."

"So you did."

"Yes, and right then, over the phone, she offered me a live-in position. I accepted and said we'd be there in a week."

"How did Mom take that?"

Randal shook his head in memory. "Not well. There were a lot of tears and great anger. The brothers said I was a Spawn of Satan and going to hell. I packed up you and Ava and we came here, to that house." He nodded toward the big place behind the security wall.

Kate well knew of her mother's wrath. Ava's temper could be ferocious.

"How did Aunt Sara take it?"

Randal's answer was a look that told of tears and anger and guilt.

Unfortunately, Kate could imagine it all. "What did you do for Mrs. Meyers?"

"I guess you'd say I was her butler."

He was in profile and she could see jaw muscles working. She didn't have to be told that being a butler was a job he'd consider beneath his dignity. But then, being in prison wasn't up to his standards either. *All for me,* she thought. "Aunt Sara didn't come back to Florida with you?"

"No. I asked her to but she couldn't bear seeing people in Lachlan again." Randal turned to Kate. "It was good. You were happy again. You and Mrs. Meyers adored each other. Every morning I delivered breakfast in bed to her. After just four days, curious little you sneaked in behind me. I'd tried to keep you in our rooms but you escaped. I'll never forget that morning. When Mrs. Meyers saw you, she patted the bed beside her. You got in with her and told her all about everything. I was shocked at how much you'd picked up. Mrs. Meyers loved hearing about the uncles. She said you were funnier than *Seinfeld.*"

Kate wondered what she'd revealed. "What about Mother? How did she take the move?"

"Not well. We had nice quarters, but you and I were in the house or the garden most of the day. Ava said that we had abandoned her. She really wanted to go back to her brothers."

"So Mother didn't have a job with Mrs. Meyers?" Kate sounded serious, without a hint of humor.

Randal started to respond in kind, but then they looked at each other. Ava work? It was impossible to imagine. Their faces, so alike, went from serious to amused, then to downright laughter. Hilarious, riotous laughter.

It took a while for them to calm their

laughter, then Randal started the car and pulled back onto the road.

"So what about the balloons?" Kate asked. "Why do I remember them so vividly? And they weren't here exactly. Did I go to a birthday party?"

"I don't think so, but you did go to a nursery school for a little while. Maybe they had balloons."

They didn't say any more. "For a little while" meant the time before he was led away to prison. *In handcuffs?* she wondered. *Did I see my daddy taken away?* She glanced at him and knew that he too was thinking of that day.

They were quiet as Randal drove from the richest part of Fort Lauderdale, away from the mansions that faced the water and had docks for their private yachts, to a normal suburban area. It was nice, but a long way from what they'd just seen.

Randal pulled onto the concrete drive of a house and turned off the engine.

"You told him we were coming, right?" Kate asked.

"Of course. I wanted to give him ample time to run away."

"We're showing up without warning?" she asked. "You should have —"

232

"Like you and Jack and my secretive sister always tell people when you're arriving?" Randal got out of the car and shut the door.

"Sometimes we do," Kate murmured and got out. Her father was already at the door and had pressed the bell. The door opened just as Kate got there.

A man was standing there, half-bald, wearing an old T-shirt and jeans. His belly swelled out. He wasn't what Kate had envisioned as "the Bentley man."

"We're not buyin' any," the man said, then his face drained of color. "It's you."

"I'd like to talk to you," Randal said.

"I don't want any trouble."

Randal stepped back so he could see Kate. "This is my daughter. I believe you met her when she was four."

If possible, the man's face grew even more pale. "I guess I do owe you." He opened the glass storm door and let them enter.

They followed him into a living room filled with furniture that looked to have been purchased from a discount catalog. It wasn't the highest quality. They sat down.

"My wife will be back soon and . . . and . . ."

"We won't stay long," Randal said. "I just want to hear the truth of what happened."

"I didn't lie on the stand. You did take my

233

car and I didn't give you permission."

"The drugs were *yours,*" Kate said.

When the man turned to look at her, she saw a flash of anger in his eyes.

He looked back at Randal. "No one asked me about the drugs. And I didn't volunteer to tell."

"But —" Kate began.

Randal gave her a look to be quiet. "I want to hear the whole story."

The man glanced at his watch. "That old guy, Edison, arranged everything. He told me what to do and what not to say."

Randal spoke in the tone of a therapist: caring, concerned, persuasive. "Would you tell us what you left out? Please?"

"I guess you deserve that." Again the man glanced at his watch. "I was in debt. My wife then — the one who left me — didn't know we were on the verge of bankruptcy. I went to the bank, to a VP, and begged him to give me more time. He asked how desperate I was. I made a joke and said I was ready to become a hit man if it got me out of debt. He didn't laugh, just told me to go home and wait."

"What was his name?" Randal asked.

"It doesn't matter. He died years ago. Anyway, I got a call. I was to go to a truck stop, leave the keys to my Bentley on the

234

left rear tire, then go in and eat. I figured my car would be taken but I was willing to pay that price."

"That's when the drugs were put in the trunk," Randal said.

"Yes. I was puzzled as to why my car was still there, so I opened the trunk and looked inside. When I saw the corner of a plastic bag, I slammed the trunk shut and I never looked again. From then on, I put my keys on the wheel and left the car where they told me to. I stayed out of it. I never saw anyone near my car. Never saw the packages being put inside or taken out."

"How many times did you do that?" Randal asked.

"Eight," he said. "After the sixth time, I received a letter from the bank saying my second mortgage had been paid off." The man looked at Randal. "When I saw you take the car away that morning, I didn't ask questions. The next thing I knew, the police were there and saying my car had been stolen and used to transport drugs. All I did was keep my mouth shut."

"And Sheriff Edison told you what to say at the trial," Kate said.

"He did." The man turned to Randal. "I'm really sorry that you . . ." He shrugged.

"Paid for *your* crime?" Kate shot at him.

"I too received a call." Randal's voice was calm, unperturbed. "Someone offered me a job driving your Bentley to Nashville. I was told where the keys were. Who called me?"

"I have no idea," the man said.

"You weren't curious?" Kate asked.

"Absolutely not! After the first day, I didn't want to know what was going on."

"Who else besides the bank VP contacted you?" Randal asked.

"No one. Ever. And he only called me twice. It was all very scheduled."

"What did the police do to the bank officer?" Kate asked.

The man looked at Randal. "Nothing. I was never asked about him. I was *told* what happened and *told* that if I deviated from that story I would be the one going to prison." He looked at Kate. "I saw you outside the courthouse. You were the cutest little girl and . . ." He looked back to Randal. "I really am sorry."

When Randal stood up, the other two stood. "I'd like to know who set me up. If you remember anything, please let me know." He handed the man a piece of paper with his name and Sara's address and three phone numbers on it. Kate knew they were hers, Jack's and Sara's. "Nothing will happen to you," Randal added. "I just want to know what I paid the time for."

The man took the paper. "I'll do everything I can to help you. I owe you."

"You do," Randal said, and he and Kate left.

In the car, Kate said, "Obviously, someone was watching him. Some law enforcement agency knew what he was doing with the keys and the drugs."

Randal backed out of the driveway. "And when I showed up, they dropped him and went after me."

"Because of the jewels."

Randal stopped the car and looked at her. "The jewels that Mrs. Oliver's stepson *said* were stolen? The ones he had appraised the very day after his stepmother was diagnosed with cancer? The jewels he had insured for 2.4 million, then collected the full amount on after she died? *Those* jewels?"

Kate was staring at him in openmouthed astonishment. No one had offered an alternate explanation of the robbery. Everyone had assumed that Randal was guilty. She didn't reply.

For a while, they didn't speak, then Randal said, "Home or office?"

Kate sighed. "Office. I better see what's

going on there. Melissa will be full of questions."

"Wouldn't she ask the other young woman? The one who was at Tayla's house?"

"Raye wouldn't answer them. She's smart enough to not put up with Melissa's invasions."

Randal pulled into the parking lot of Kirkwood Realty, but Kate didn't get out. He was looking at the park across the road. "I really like what Tayla has done with this town. It was rotting, decaying. Very sad."

"She and Charlene did it." Kate looked at her father. "What was Tayla's late husband like?"

"Difficult. You know, don't you, that he was one of the Magnificent Three? At least that's what they were called in high school."

"I heard that." Kate wasn't about to blurt out all she knew.

"Walter wasn't likable like Hamish Stewart was. He wasn't good-looking or as charismatic as Cal Wyatt."

"Smart?"

"Nope." Randal was smiling. "The other two beat him in every possible way, and the constant comparisons didn't make him a nice guy."

"But he got Tayla anyway."

"I think that was her mother's idea and

238

that woman always got her way." He sounded angry. But then, she was probably why Randal didn't marry Charlene.

"But Walter was your friend, with Roy and Sheriff Flynn."

Randal smiled. "Little Miss Detective. Always trying to find out everyone's secrets. Yes, I was friends with all of them. If you haven't noticed yet, I tend to get along with most people."

"Except Aunt Sara."

Randal laughed. "She and I have too much history, most of it bad." He looked at the office. "So you go back to work and I'll go to Daryl's house and watch his cop shows. That man refuses to eat anything but fast food. Pizza abounds. It would certainly be nice to be around people who go to a gym." He was looking at Kate with sad eyes.

It didn't take any work to know what he wanted. "It's not my house," she murmured.

Randal gave a deep, melodramatic sigh. "When Ava shows up at Sara's door, I hope you're prepared to be the referee between them. You'll need a very loud whistle. Or maybe those boxing gloves I saw at the house. Or —"

"Okay! I'll ask Aunt Sara." She was already tapping out the text asking if Randal could move in with them. Until when, she didn't know.

Sara texted back right away.

Put him in Jack's room. It's better to keep
enemies close.

"What did she say?" Randal asked.

"That she'd be glad to have you."

Randal grinned. "You have inherited my
ability to create a flexible truth."

As Kate sent Jack a text, she rolled her
eyes. *Flexible truth?* More like great whop-
ping lies.

Jack replied immediately.

I have to stay with you? Again?

Reading it, Kate smiled.

"My kingdom for a smile like that," Randal said. "Whatever did he say?"

"Nothing." She closed her phone. "He's
just welcoming you."

Randal looked at her. "You do know that
Jack is —"

She opened the car door. "Don't say it.
And stay out of my personal life."

"I'm just being a father."

She got out of the car. "Go pack your
things, then get Aunt Sara's car home."

"I know. We're all to meet to be interrogated by my dear sister. Shall I pick up some champagne? Or chocolate truffles? You and Mrs. Meyers used to eat boxes of them. Still like the soft chocolate centers?"

"Yes," Kate said, then shut the door and hurried into her office.

Melissa was waiting for her. "This place is hell. Everyone wants to know what happened. Where's Raye? Where's Tayla? Is it true that Charlene Adams is having an affair and her husband shot her lover? Will her place be put up for sale? I call dibs on the listing."

Kate watched her father pulling away and she was tempted to run after him. But she didn't. Feeling years older, she turned back to Melissa. "No, none of that is true." She began trying to answer all the questions.

By the time Kate got home, her mind was in turmoil. The afternoon meeting had been postponed because Sara was still at Arthur's house. Jack was at the sheriff's office doing the things that he'd been ignoring as he dealt with the two deaths. Her father hadn't yet arrived with his suitcases.

It was odd to be in the big house alone. She'd showered and put on a big T-shirt that she "borrowed" from Jack a year ago. It said Jack Wyatt Construction in big letters across the front. She'd told him she would return the shirt, but he'd said, "Keep it. I like my name so close to you."

She had a TV in her bedroom but she didn't turn it on. Neither did she pull a book from her to-be-read pile. All she wanted to do was be quiet and think. She needed to sort out what was going on in her life.

But as soon as she got into bed, she drew her knees to her chest and curled into a ball. Too much was happening too fast and she wasn't sure how to deal with it. She didn't know when the tears started but they began to seep out and run down her face.

She wasn't surprised when she felt Jack's arms around her. She was under the covers and he was on top of them. Turning to him, she buried her face in his shoulder.

They were quiet for a while, with Kate crying against him. Sara would say she was "weeping." Silent tears were coming from deep inside her. It was a while before she could speak. "I'm sorry. I . . ."

"There's no reason to be upset," he said. "Nothing has happened to you. Well, except your mother flaunting herself about town to make sure you know she's here — which is eating you with guilt. Sara's so angry that black mold is beginning to grow on the walls. And then there are a couple of dead bodies, but one's not dead. He's in a coma and may not ever wake up. And of course there's your not-dead father who's making you crazy by courting you like he's the Beast and you're Beauty. If he doesn't win you over to his side, he seems to think his life will be forfeit. And then there's —"

Kate's laugh cut him off.

He handed her a couple of tissues and she blew her nose.

"I told everyone off," she said. "I was awful."

He smoothed her hair back. "You were wonderful. You made Sara actually speak to her brother."

Kate sniffed. "I spent this afternoon with him."

"I know."

She pulled back to look at him.

He shrugged. "Being law enforcement does have some advantages."

"You have spy cameras everywhere?"

"I have Flynn calling me and being a tattletale."

"That makes sense." Kate put her head back down and snuggled against his shoulder. She fit perfectly. "We went to see the man whose car Dad stole."

"Dad, is it? Flynn said Randal would win

243

you. Looks like he was right."

"Maybe, but that's not important. The Bentley man was lying."

"About what?"

"I don't know. It just wasn't *real.* The house, him, none of it rang true. He said he went straight, no more drug dealing, so he'd lost his big house. Lost all his wealth. But I'm not sure."

"What made you think he was lying?"

"His watch was a Patek Philippe."

"Could have owned it for years."

"The house was furnished from one of those places where you buy it all in a lump — furniture, pictures, knickknacks. There were some really cheap ornaments. One doesn't go from a mansion and lose all taste." She sighed. "It didn't ring true. And something else. I think he *knew* we were coming."

"Maybe Randal told Flynn and he warned the guy."

"Think so?"

"No."

She looked up at him. "What do you think is going on?"

"No idea. None of it makes sense. I know you don't know your father well, but do you think he's being honest?"

Kate groaned. "He's so very *secretive.*

244

One minute he's a charming client, but he's lying about money. The next minute I find out he's my father and has spent the last twenty-plus years in prison. And he may not have committed the crime. I'm beginning to doubt that he stole the jewels. Maybe Everett made it all up."

"How was he with the drug guy?"

"I couldn't tell if he believed him or not. Dad's stories always cast him as an angel on earth."

"But Sara tells of a lying, sneaky brother," Jack said.

"How can he be both?"

"I don't know, but my instinct says we haven't even tapped into his secrets. He seems to be whatever the person he's with wants him to be."

"True," she said. "He got along with bad boys like your father and Tayla's husband. But he was also the darling of sweet little old ladies."

"Better not let Sara hear you use that term."

"Who is the *real* Randal Medlar?" Kate asked as she yawned.

He snuggled her to him, the coverlet separating their bodies. "I'm not sure we need to know. I just want to find out enough to keep more people from getting killed."

"It all has to do with my father, doesn't it?"

"That is the one thing I am absolutely *sure* is right."

He started to say more but she yawned again, so he kept quiet. When she fell asleep in his arms, he picked up the remote and turned on the TV. He put it on Mute and read the subtitles. He was exhausted from the last few days, but he couldn't allow himself to sleep. There was something else he was probably going to have to do today, and he didn't want to miss the opportunity.

FOURTEEN

When Jack's phone lit up and an image of the Batman logo appeared on the ceiling, he glanced at Kate, but she was sound asleep. Too bad, as he wanted to share with her what he'd done. After all, it had taken hours of work to rig. Yes, he'd agreed to Randal Medlar moving into his bedroom, but Jack well knew how easy it was to slip in and out of that room with no one knowing.

This afternoon, he and Gil had installed a silent alarm and synced it to Jack's phone. When either of the outside doors opened, Jack would be alerted. He and Gil laughed about the big bat that would show up. Given Randal's background, it seemed appropriate.

With a sigh of regret, Jack untangled himself from Kate, turned off the TV, then went out her bedroom door. There was a shortcut through the courtyard. Since he had all the car keys, he knew he had time before Randal got away.

Jack entered the garage through the side door, then halted. Randal was standing there, waiting for him. He was dressed head to foot in black. Kate had sent Jack a photo of the cover of Elliot's cat burglar book and Randal looked just like it.

"Nice alarm job," Randal said. "Take you long to install?"

Jack cursed his face. Kate loved to tell him that he tended to blush and he could feel his face turning red. "Only minutes. Going somewhere?"

"I want to do a follow-up visit to the man who put me in prison."

"I'm a deputy sheriff." Jack put his shoulders back. "I can't participate in revenge. I have to uphold —" He stopped. *Damn Sheriff Flynn! Damn oath taking. Damn —*

"I don't believe violence has ever been attributed to me, has it?"

Jack shook his head no. "Which car?"

"Sara's," Randal said. "Mind?" He held out his hand for the keys so he could drive.

Minutes later, they were headed to the east side of Fort Lauderdale. "What did Kate think of the man today?"

Jack wasn't about to betray a confidence, but at the same time he wanted to know

248

what Randal thought. "She liked his watch."

Randal smiled. "She saw that, did she?" He sounded proud. "There wasn't anything personal in the house. No photos. No mess of any kind."

"Think he actually lives there?"

"Maybe. And maybe he was told to clear out everything because we were on our way."

Jack frowned. "But why? The statute of limitations is past. Even if you find out who was behind it all, what can you do?"

"I'd like to know *why*," Randal said. "With all my heart and soul, I want to know why someone set me up."

Jack could understand that. Randal was certainly calmer than he would be if such a thing had been done to him. "Captain Edison hated all of you. He was good to me but he despised my father. And rightfully so."

Randal frowned. "I'm sorry you have such bad memories of Roy. He was proud of you."

"No!" Jack almost shouted. "Never!"

"Roy was afraid you were going to turn out like him. Daryl and I thought he divorced your mother to keep you safe from him."

"That's ridiculous. Roy Wyatt screwed half the women in town. He got drunk three nights a week. Gambled. Started fights. No one knew all of what he did."

"Except maybe you. When you were little, you adored him. You wanted to be just like him. You should have seen the two of you on his big Harley. You looked so much alike and you were never happier than when you were with your dad."

"I don't remember any of that. I just remember Granddad Cal and my *real* father."

"Ah yes. The man your mother married. Roy knew Henry Lowell was in love with her. When Roy was sober, he cursed Henry and threatened to hurt him. But when Roy was drunk, he'd say, 'Lowell's a better man than I am.' "

Jack gave a snort. "It's always amazed me that after someone is dead, people make them out to be saints. My father wasn't a good person."

"No, he wasn't," Randal said. "And I'm really glad that Roy released your mother to marry an upstanding and good man like Henry Lowell. And I'm especially glad that Cal told you to go to my sister if you ever needed help." Randal had entered a quiet residential area. He parked, turned off the engine and looked at Jack. "And look at you now. You have a good business, you've

250

stayed out of jail and you have true friends. It all worked out rather well, didn't it?"

"Not through any help from my father," Jack shot back.

"Except that none of it would have happened if Roy hadn't stepped aside. A handsome young buck like him could have persuaded your pretty mother away from an old guy like Henry Lowell. But Roy didn't even try." Randal got out of the car and shut the door.

Jack sat there for a moment. He didn't want to think about what Randal had said. It was better to stay on the problem at hand. When he got out, he looked Randal up and down. "Did you dress like a book cover or was it the other way around?"

Randal chuckled. "Take your pick." He quickly walked ahead of Jack and seemed to disappear into the darkness.

Jack wished he was wearing dark clothing. When he got to the house he saw there were no lights on. There were none by the front door or in the dark windows. There wasn't even a telltale TV light. Looking up, he saw that the streetlamp was out. It looked like the house had been darkened deliberately.

Jack waited, listening to see if he could hear Randal. But no, he had disappeared. *Kate will kill me for losing her father,* he thought. But then an idea hit him. Randal had seen the barren interior of the house. Maybe he'd skipped bedrooms and baths, but if the Bentley guy did clean out the place, he would have done those rooms too.

At the far end of the drive was a two-car garage, so dark he could hardly see it. Without a doubt, Jack knew that's where Randal went. He knew he was right when he found the side door unlocked. He went inside.

"Took you long enough." Randal handed Jack a tiny flashlight. Its beam was strong and pinpoint. From the outside it might look like the reflection of a headlamp.

Jack ran the light over the interior of the garage. Steel shelves lined the walls, all of them filled with labeled storage boxes. Christmas Decorations. Wool Sweaters. Hiking Boots. The boxes were new, with not so much as a scuff on them. It did indeed look as though they'd been filled recently.

In the center, where there was space for two cars, were neat piles of furniture. It didn't take much to see the good quality of it.

"Eastlake," Randal murmured. "Eames. Hepplewhite. Cheap house, rich insides."

"Could be leftovers from his drug dealing days."

Randal gave a one-sided smile. "But he says he was never involved in the drugs. He was innocent."

Jack smiled at the joke. He was running his light across the boxes. "We need the oldest thing we can find." As he stepped to the side, he saw a worn-out shoebox. It was the only old-looking thing on the shelves. "We —"

He broke off because a car pulled into the driveway. Jack and Randal turned off their lights, put their backs to the walls and waited. Would the Bentley guy open the garage door?

He didn't. They heard his car door shut, then the house door open and close.

"Bet he hates living with his cheap stuff," Randal said.

"Bet he hates *you* for making him have to do it," Jack replied.

"I'm sure he does." There was so much defeatism in Randal's tone that Jack grimaced. Had the man actually spent over twenty years in prison for a crime he didn't commit?

There was a sound outside, then they saw more headlights. It looked like Bentley had a late-night visitor.

"We have to go. Now," Randal whispered.

It was too dark for Jack to see clearly, but

he reached out, grabbed what he hoped was the old shoebox and started toward the door. As he made his way through the labyrinth of furniture, he cracked his shin on a heavy table leg. He had to clamp his mouth shut to keep from exclaiming in pain. As for Randal, he moved like liquid mercury, with not so much as a sound.

When Jack finally got outside, Randal relocked the door while Jack rubbed his shin.

"This way." Randal led them behind houses to emerge just feet from Sara's car.

"How did you know that way out?" Jack asked.

"Did a bit of recon this afternoon. How about a beer and let's see what you found?"

Jack was clutching the shoebox like it was a treasure chest. He knew he should go home and get some sleep. He had to be at the office early tomorrow. Besides, he shouldn't further involve himself in Randal's problems. But then, he'd just done a B and E. He sighed. "Yeah. A beer. Or three."

Randal opened the car door. "Roy's son to the core."

"Take that back!"

Laughing, Randal drove down the street.

It was late but the Brigade was still open. Firefighters and the police had odd hours, so the restaurant/bar needed long opening hours to accommodate their customers. That was the excuse, anyway. No one complained.

The place was fairly quiet and Jack and Randal took a booth. When the waitress came, Jack ordered fish and chips. "How about you?" he asked Randal.

"I gain weight just looking at food."

Jack told the waitress to bring two orders and she left. "Weight gain is Sara and Kate's biggest complaint in life. But Kate's mother never gains." He was staring hard at Randal, opening the way for him to share information.

But Randal didn't respond. He was gazing at the unopened shoebox Jack had set on the table.

"So why'd you marry her?" Jack asked.

Randal looked at him as though he had no idea who he was talking about.

"Ava? Remember? The wife you hid from when you saw her from the patrol car?"

The waitress put two frosty glasses of beer on the table, then went back to the bar.

Randal took a deep drink. "I missed this." He gestured at the handsome interior. There was a long antique oak bar with a mirrored wall behind it. Glass shelves held glittery bottles of booze. The opposite wall had booths and there were tables in the middle. At the end of the long room was a raised platform with a dance floor in front. "These people have chosen to be here. They chose the food they want to eat. Chose the people they want to share with. *Choice* is an under-appreciated part of life."

Jack had his hand over the shoebox. It was obvious that he wasn't going to release it until Randal answered his question about Ava.

Randal sipped his beer and sighed. "Has anyone ever worshipped you?"

"You mean like a rock star? Or are you talking religion?"

"Groupies who believe you are their religion."

"Never," Jack said. "Although, there is someone I wish felt that way about me. But she . . ." He trailed off, his eyes avoiding Randal's.

"I've had one — Ava. To her, I can do no wrong."

"I think Sara would say your mother thought that about you."

"No. Mother saw the truth about me and loved me anyway. But Ava sees all that I do as good." Randal looked at his beer for a moment, then back at Jack. "And there has always been Kate between us. I'd do *any-*

thing for my daughter."

"I agree with that." Jack raised his beer in a toast. "To *Anything for Kate.*"

"Yes. All for my beautiful, precious daughter." They clinked glasses.

Jack was thinking of his grandparents. They'd married because she was pregnant. Never mind that Granddad Cal was in love with Sara. Even as a child, Jack knew the marriage was an unhappy one. It looked like Randal had done the same thing. They'd all seen that he and Charlene were still in love. But he married the pregnant Ava — and he'd stayed with her. "You came back to Lachlan the same year that Charlene did," Jack said. "It took courage . . . and honor not to go to her."

Randal shook his head. "I'd like that accolade but I didn't know Charlene was here. My job with Mrs. Meyers was 24/7. And kids don't take the weekend off."

"What about your wife?"

Randal took his time answering. "Ava was depressed and homesick. She went to church a lot. It was something that soothed her, and Kate and I didn't mind her absence. Besides, Kate and Mrs. Meyers adored each other. It was a pleasant time for us. I was content."

What Randal said told a lot about his first

years with his daughter — and about his marriage. That he'd jeopardize what he had to drive a car full of drugs made no sense.

Their food came, then a local band showed up and started playing. With music, beer and fried food, neither man wanted to talk more.

They had just finished their meal when a young man came to stand by their table and stare in silence at Jack. A guitar was strapped across his back.

"I believe he wants something from you," Randal said.

"To sing. Do you mind?"

"Not at all. I shall enjoy listening. Know any Sinatra?"

"Every word of everything he ever sang."

Randal smiled. "Then I will definitely enjoy this."

Jack got out of the booth, then held out his hand. Randal put the car keys in it. Tucked under Jack's arm was the shoebox. He wasn't going to leave it or the keys with Randal.

Randal was on his second beer and enjoying it while he listened to Jack's rendition of "It Was a Very Good Year." The words were a bit old for Jack but Randal knew the song was for him. The whole evening of food, beer, music and freedom was so good that he closed his eyes in happiness.

A slight cough made him open them. Sitting across from him was a young woman. She was about Kate's age but her face didn't have the openness that Kate's did. *She has secrets,* Randal thought.

"Hi," she said. "I work for Tayla."

He motioned to the waitress. "Would you like something to drink? A cocktail, perhaps?"

"A beer would be nice."

He was watching her so intently that he barely turned to the waitress as he ordered. There was something about the young woman that made him wary. *She's had a hard life,* he thought. "And do you like your job, Miss . . . ?"

"Burgess. Call me Raye."

"How kind," Randal said with exaggerated courtesy.

"I don't know many people in Lachlan but I need to talk to someone."

Randal hesitated. He knew the last thing he needed was to get involved in anyone's personal problems. "Perhaps Tayla —"

"No! She's part of this. You see . . ." Raye looked down at her hands for a moment. "When I was growing up, I needed to keep on the lookout for things, to notice them."

259

"Or there were consequences," Randal said.

"Right. If I wasn't paying attention, day-dreaming as my father called it, I'd get a whack on the head. I learned to keep quiet and watch. It's made me see things that other people don't."

Randal couldn't help being intrigued. He waited to hear more.

"Kate's a good person but she's friends with everyone. I can't tell her what I know. She's part of . . . well, them."

"Rather like a gang," Randal said.

Raye nodded.

"And you've seen something about one of the gang members." When she nodded again, he held his breath. *Please don't let it be Kate. Please.* But she was his daughter so maybe she was too much like him. Maybe she had —

"It's Tayla."

Randal let out his breath. "What did you see?"

Raye took her time answering. "About a week ago I saw her talking to a man sitting on a motorcycle. She was frowning and looked angry, but they also looked like they were close. Later that day I mentioned it and she said she didn't know any man with a bike. I figured it was because the guy was

260

younger and she was embarrassed. I wouldn't have thought anything more about it, but then there was the basket."

"Tell me," he said softly.

"I saw you with Charlene. Kate was really angry with you, but I didn't think she was being fair. You see, I know Charlene doesn't have a happy marriage."

"Really?" Randal knew his tone revealed too much interest in what she was saying. "Why do you think that?"

"Charlene and her husband were at the office one morning and I heard them going after one another. It was about something that happened years ago. He said it was Charlene's fault and she should be behind bars now. I shouldn't say this but he sounded like he wished she *was* in prison."

Randal stared hard at her. "You're sure it was them?"

"Yes." She hesitated. "I guess you know that her husband looks like you. After I saw you two at Tayla's house, I don't think that was a coincidence. Maybe her husband is what she settled for, but now she wants the real thing."

Randal tried to keep his hope concealed. "Does Tayla know this?"

"I think so. I heard that a man died at Charlene's place so she was at Tayla's. Then you showed up, and Tayla went outside with that basket. The way you and Charlene looked at each other gave me chills. You two —"

"What about the basket?"

"We were all inside. Tayla and I had some work to do, but suddenly, she picked up a big basket. It wasn't one of those cheap things that you see everywhere. It was really nice — and it looked heavy, like something big was inside it." She paused. "When you grow up poor, you tend to notice things like that. You think, someday when I'm rich, I'll have things like that. You know what I mean?"

"To the bottom of my heart, I know all about that."

Raye smiled. "That was my guess about you. Anyway, I thought she was going to cut some flowers so I said I'd go with her. She said, 'No!' so loud that I stepped back and apologized. I'm just her employee, right? So Tayla went outside and we stayed in. About thirty minutes later, Charlene wondered where her aunt was, so we all went outside. That's when we saw that there was a man in a car and he'd been shot."

"Did you see Tayla's basket?"

"No." Raye leaned forward. "I looked for it. I was going to take it back inside, but it wasn't there. I wondered what happened to it."

"And you were curious about what was inside it," Randal said.

"I was."

Randal took out his phone and brought up the photo of the man who died at Charlene's barn. He handed his phone to Raye. "Ever see this man before?"

Her eyes widened. "That's him! He's the guy Tayla was talking to. He was on a bike. Not a big one like Jack's Harley, but smaller." She studied the photo. "I guess he's not sleeping, is he?"

"No, he's not."

Jack's song ended and the guitar player stood up. Time for a break.

"I'm afraid to tell Deputy Wyatt," Raye said quickly. "I don't know him well and I've seen his temper. I don't need more of that in my life."

Randal scowled. "Does he get angry at Kate?"

"Not that I've seen but there is some talk. Uh-oh. I've said too much." She slid out along the booth seat, then leaned toward Randal. "Please don't tell him what I told you. He and Tayla are friends, and that Wyatt temper . . . No thanks!" She stood up straight. Jack was just a few feet away.

"Thanks, Mr. Medlar," she said loudly. "Kate is a joy to work with. See you, Jack," she said, then hurried out of the bar.

Jack slid in across from Randal and put the shoebox on the seat beside him. "She works for Tayla, right?"

"Yes. Do you know her?"

"Not really. I've seen her. Kate says she does a good job so that's enough for me."

Randal said, "I think we should leave."

Jack didn't move. "You aren't asking me to open the box. Why not?"

Randal was standing at the end of the table. "I know you won't do it, so why bother?"

"What happened?"

"Nothing," Randal said. "I'm an old man and I need my sleep. That's all." Abruptly, he went to the door.

Jack stayed behind, watching him. All he knew for sure was that something had upset Randal Medlar. A call, an email? Something that girl said? He picked up the shoebox and followed Randal to the door.

FIFTEEN

Lenny woke up. Well, actually, his body didn't wake up but his mind did. It seemed that he was floating above his body and looking down. His first thought was, *When did I get so old?* He'd always prided himself on staying trim but now he thought he looked emaciated and fragile.

He was in a hospital room with machines beeping and needles in his arms. He'd never been one for drugs but he was glad of them now. From the look of the bandage on his head, he imagined there was a lot of pain. His eyes were open but he didn't blink. Now and then someone would put drops in his eyes, but Lenny didn't close them. He liked seeing what was happening.

Someone in the hall was talking. "We don't know if he can hear you or not." It was a woman's voice. "But do talk to him. Sometimes people come out of comas and they remember what was said to them."

The woman was no actress. Her tone said that there was no way anyone could live through his injury. "Just tell him what you're feeling about anything. Your life, whatever."

So now I'm a priest? Lenny thought. *My deathbed is a confessional?*

One by one, people came into the room.

The pretty young woman who had tried to revive the dead guy came first. *The birdhouse girl,* he thought. She said she was sorry for what happened to him, especially since he was probably protecting her.

That concept jolted him. *Protecting* was not a word anyone had ever applied to him.

The aunt came next. It was her house he'd been spying on when he was shot.

"I don't know what you were doing or why," Tayla whispered, "but if you hurt Charlene, I'll kill you."

If Lenny's hovering spirit had any eyebrows, he would have raised them. He believed the woman.

Pretty, red-haired Kate was next. She brought flowers and said she hoped he got well soon.

No one had ever given Lenny flowers.

An overweight guy he didn't know entered. He leaned over Lenny's body and spoke quickly. "I think maybe you are or have been a hit man. Please get well and please, please let me write your bio. I swear I'll keep your identity a secret." He paused. "Damn! They say I have to go. We'll share the profits. Eighty-twenty."

Lenny watched him leave. *Tell the world all I've done? Are you crazy? Share the profits? Does that mean share the bullets that would come my way if I ratted?*

Jack came in and sat down by the bed. "I don't know what you were doing in Charlene's barn or why you were at Tayla's house, but I plan to find out." He took a few breaths. "I'm sorry I didn't check to see if you were dead or not. You could have bled to death because of me. Maybe if I hadn't been so stupid you'd be alive now."

I am alive, Lenny wanted to shout. He tried to speak, tried to move a body part, but nothing happened.

The room darkened, and the quiet gave Lenny time to think. He wished he was the person they believed he was. He imagined retiring with grandkids and building birdhouses together. He had money in a few banks so he could buy a place. Then what? He'd watch TV all day? His job hadn't allowed him to make friends — at least not any that he'd turn his back on.

A man Lenny didn't recognize came in.

267

He was frowning and kept looking over his shoulder.

"I'm not supposed to be here," he said. "I should be on a cruise ship with my wife. But here I am." He took a breath. "Do you have anything to do with a jewel robbery back in '98? I was just a kid then. I mean, I was married and near thirty, but I was dumb enough to be a kid, so —" There was a sound in the hallway. "I have to go." He quickly left the room.

There was a bit of morning light coming from under the shades when another man came in. He was older and handsome. A silver fox, as the ladies say. The man Lenny followed.

At last, Lenny thought. *Up close with the elusive Randal Medlar.*

"I know Mel sent you. I'm sorry for this. I'm trying to find out who did this and why."

The man reached out and ran his hands over Lenny's eyes to close them. It was a struggle to get them open again, and when he did, the man was gone.

If Lenny could have laughed, he would have. Medlar didn't even allow what they all thought was a dead man to see what he was up to.

The light in the room grew stronger but it

268

was still so early that the shades were down. A person came into the room. He or she was so encased in blue hospital attire Lenny couldn't identify them. A mask and a low headpiece covered the mouth and nose. By the shape of the nose, it was the person who cut Randal.

Calmly, the person removed the oxygen tube from Lenny's nose, then slipped a wide piece of plastic across his face.

Lenny tried but he couldn't move. Couldn't fight. He tried holding his breath but couldn't control it. He felt himself fading. Where were all those people who'd been visiting?

He could feel himself going back into his body. He didn't want to because there was sure to be pain, but he was being sucked down into it.

When his spirit hit his body, he blinked. It wasn't much but it's what he'd done before to get attention. *I* am *alive,* he tried to convey.

On the bed by his hand was a cord with a button at the end. He used his last ounce of strength to push it. In the distance, he heard an alarm go off.

Immediately, the plastic was removed from his face. Lenny took a breath as he heard running footsteps. He saw the person in blue slip out in the chaos.

"Holy crap!" he heard a woman say. "Get the doctor. I think he's waking up."

When Lenny saw the woman cross herself, he did his best to smile. *A fellow catholic.* Feeling safe, he went to sleep and this time, his spirit stayed in his body.

SIXTEEN

The first time Jack woke, he heard a familiar sound: Sara and Kate were frantically straightening and cleaning the house. That meant it was Wednesday, and Dora, the housekeeper, was coming. The idea that they cleaned before the cleaning had puzzled him.

"We don't want her to think we're slobs," Kate snapped.

"Dora knows everyone in town. She'll tell them all about us," Sara said as she put dishes in the dishwasher.

"And we have to be sure that no signs of murder are where she can see them," Kate added.

In normal circumstances that would make no sense, but in their lives it was a good policy.

Jack lifted his head enough to see that the shoebox was still on the side table and the tape was intact. He should probably call the office, but at the moment he didn't care what happened. He went back to sleep.

When he awoke again it was nearly noon. He folded up Kate's couch, then took a long shower in her bathroom and used some of her shampoo. That it smelled like her made him smile. He pulled on jeans and started to grab a T-shirt but didn't. It was probably Randal's influence that made him put on a long-sleeve blue shirt. He rolled up the sleeves neatly.

When he left the apartment and entered the main house, he saw Kate and Sara busy in the kitchen and the house smelled great. Randal was in the formal living room looking at Sara's big iPad. Kate had told them about showing her father how to use his new iPhone, but they agreed that he obviously knew about electronics.

"Where's your uniform?" Sara asked.

"Bottom of the dung heap, I hope," Jack answered, then sighed in defeat. "Anybody call? Any major catastrophes?"

"Not at all," Randal said. "You see anything interesting?"

Jack knew he was talking about the shoebox. "Haven't looked inside yet."

When Sara said lunch was ready, they met at the big dining table. Jack started to sit down, then saw that Sara and Randal were

272

glaring at him. He'd never noticed that they looked alike. With Kate beside them, all of the Medlars were together. Their frowns were identical.

"You three sure look alike," he said. "Great family resemblance. What's for lunch?"

Randal and Sara gave him hard glares while Kate looked like she might start laughing.

"Did I miss something?" Jack asked innocently.

"They want to see the shoebox," Kate said.

"Oh? I'd forgotten all about that."

Kate gave a scoff of laughter.

"I'll go get it."

"Good idea." Sara pulled out a chair and sat down.

Jack took his time returning. It was interesting that Randal had told them about their nighttime rummage in the garage. Suddenly, Jack felt like an outsider. *They* were the Medlar Three. Linked by blood, not friendship.

When he got back to the dining room, they were seated and waiting. The table was loaded with a Florida feast of seafood and salads. There was even bread for the non-keto diners.

Jack put the heavily taped shoebox in the middle of the table, then sat down. "Crab cakes. My favorite."

Sara whipped out one of the little retractable, box cutter knives that she had all over the house and slit the tape all around. She looked at her brother. "You want to open it?"

"I'll give that honor to Kate."

Impatiently, Jack slid the lid up but the contents weren't revealed. He started eating.

Sara lifted the lid. "Ah," she said. "Photos."

Kate cleared an area on the table and dumped them out.

They were photos of unknown people. Some pictures were old and faded, some new. They were taken in front of houses or camping tents or picturesque landscapes. "Know anybody?"

The Medlars let out a collective sigh of disappointment.

"No one," Sara said.

It was Randal who found the two photos stuck together. His face lit up and he handed the faded black-and-white picture to Sara.

She drew in her breath. It was two women, one young, one older and a young man.

"Who are they?" Kate asked. "Wait! Isn't that Tayla when she was in her twenties? I love her dress. And those boots are great."

"The height of seventies fashion. She was always beautifully dressed." Sara looked across to Randal. "Walter, Tayla and dear old Inez."

Randal began filling his plate.

"Nothing to say about her?" Sara asked.

"I'm afraid that even saying her name will bring her back from the grave."

Kate was looking at her aunt to explain.

"The man is Tayla's late husband, Walter." Sara was grimacing. "And the older woman is Inez, Tayla's mother and Charlene's grandmother. She was a truly awful woman."

Jack studied the picture. "I wonder why this old photo is mixed in with the new ones? And what does it have to do with the Bentley guy?"

Randal looked at Sara, and when he spoke, his voice was soft. "I saw Inez with Kate at the trial. What happened?"

They could see Sara's discomfort at the memory. Had it really been her testimony that put her brother in prison for so many years? "She . . ." Sara took a deep breath. "Inez thanked me for helping put you where you belonged."

Randal didn't seem surprised. "How did she act toward Kate?"

"I'll never forget it," Sara said. "Inez stared at little Kate with almost a sneer. To a child!" She turned to her niece. "But you weren't intimidated by her. You glared back at her in exactly the same way. I thought you two were going to fight."

"Yes," Randal whispered. "That makes sense. Was Ava there?"

"No. As soon as she saw Inez, she ran to the restroom. I wanted to follow her."

"Exactly what did Inez say?" Randal asked.

"It was odd. She asked why you'd named her Kate. I said the first thing that came to my mind — *The Taming of the Shrew.* I didn't know and I never asked."

"What else?" Randal asked.

"Nothing. Inez stomped away and later Ava . . ." Sara couldn't finish.

"Right," Randal said. "Ava forbade you from ever seeing Kate again."

Sara could only nod at the horrible memory.

Kate clasped her aunt's hand. "I'm sorry that you and I missed out on so much time together."

"Me too," Sara said.

They were silent, haunted by those dreadful memories.

"Wow!" Jack said. "Get a bucket for the tears."

"You jerk," Kate murmured but there was no real anger in her voice. They needed the relief.

"Is there any more of the potato salad?" Jack looked at Randal. "You're being greatly honored. We don't get many carbs around this place. But I warn you that if you're ever served pasta it means you're about to die."

They smiled enough that the misery was broken.

When the doorbell rang, Kate went to answer it.

"It's probably someone from the office," Jack muttered. "No doubt they want to tell me there's been another murder."

"Maybe we should send Kate away," Randal said. "She doesn't deserve to —" He broke off when he saw Charlene walking beside Kate.

"I don't mean to intrude," Charlene said. "It's just that Tayla went to work and the guard is having confidence issues. I was told that I need to go somewhere safer so . . ." She shrugged, as though to say *So here I am.*

Randal stood up and offered his chair next to Sara.

Kate moved beside Jack. "We're very glad to see you. Have you eaten?"

"Not today," Charlene said.

In a husbandly way, Randal got a clean plate and began filling it. He didn't hesitate in choosing food for her, proving that he and Charlene knew each other far better than they said they did.

Randal set the full plate before Charlene.

Jack started to pour a glass of lemonade for her, but Randal said, "No. Too acidic. She drinks iced tea, unsweetened, no lemon."

With a silent nod, Jack put the pitcher down.

"How is Leland? And your children?" Kate said loudly.

Her implication was so pointed that Randal gave a one-sided smile.

"They're doing well, but we miss each other." Charlene gave Kate such a look of warning that she ducked her head.

Sara handed Charlene the black-and-white photo. "Do you know anything about this picture?"

"It's before my time. Tayla looks great, doesn't she?" She put the photo back on the table.

"And Walter?" Sara asked.

Charlene's lips went into a sneer. "Sorry. I

278

have no fond memories of him. He blamed me for Tayla leaving him."

"Then you should get an award," Sara said happily.

Charlene smiled.

"And your grandmother?" Kate asked.

Charlene started to speak but then looked away.

"It's all right." Randal put his arm around her shoulders, his hand over hers. "I'm glad Tayla got you away from her, and I'm sorry everything happened the way it did. If I'd known what was going on, I would have been there."

The silence in the room was heavy. They knew he was talking about when a young Charlene gave birth to their stillborn son.

The front door was thrown open so hard it hit the wall. It looked like Kate hadn't turned the lock when she let Charlene in. They all stopped and waited for whoever would appear.

Ava came into sight, then stood there glaring at them. She was a thin woman, quite plain, and she hadn't aged well. She looked older than Randal. Her expression was of hurt and sadness — until she saw Charlene. Then her face changed to rage.

Randal removed his arm from around Charlene's shoulders, looked at Jack and made a quick head gesture.

Jack understood. He quickly went around the table and protectively escorted Charlene out of the house.

Randal stayed in place, his face unreadable as he looked at his angry wife.

"Mother," Kate said. "How good to see you." She got up and went to Ava, arms extended for a hug.

But Ava stepped back. "You're with them," she said. "With them and against me. I'm your mother but you chose *her* over *me*." It wasn't clear if she meant Sara or Charlene.

"I didn't," Kate said. "Please sit down with us. How have you been?"

"You're acting like you didn't know I was here. You think I don't know that you've been avoiding me? Your own *mother*?"

Kate's face turned red with guilt.

Ava looked at Sara. "This is all *your* fault. You've always wanted what I have."

Jack came back into the room and gave a quick nod to Randal. Charlene was safely away. He went to stand near Kate, who was a few feet from her mother.

Ava was aiming her words at Sara. "It wasn't enough for you to put my husband in prison. You wanted more of what I had. You wanted it *all*. And you *took* it. Look at this!" Ava waved her hand to indicate the

280

house. "My daughter and I lived in a slum while you have all this. Now my husband lives with you too and —" Ava took a step toward Sara, seemingly with the intention of striking her.

Jack and Kate reacted at the same time. They put their bodies in front of Ava so she couldn't get to Sara.

Ava glared at her daughter. "So now you choose *him* over me? He's a criminal. Even I know that."

Behind them, Randal slowly dabbed at his mouth with a napkin, then stood up. He went to the end of the table and pulled out a chair. It was the traditional seat of the owner of the house. In a low, firm voice, he said, "Sit."

Ava tightened her thin lips, gave Jack a look of threat, then went to the chair and sat down. Her arms were folded tightly across her chest and she looked like she might explode.

Randal got a clean plate and put it on the table in front of her. "Eat," he said calmly.

With a look of curiosity, as though he wanted to see how this played out, Jack took the seat next to Ava.

Kate took her mother's plate and began to fill it.

Randal sat next to Ava so she was flanked

by the two men.

As Kate filled the plate for her mother, Jack looked at Sara, eyebrows raised. It was interesting that Randal didn't prepare a plate for his wife as he'd done for Charlene. Nor had he greeted his wife with any affection.

"When did you get here?" Randal asked Ava.

"You know when." She narrowed her eyes. "All of you were in that police car." She shot Jack a look of anger, then turned to Sara. "And you hid from me in the bakery."

Randal bent sideways to block Ava's view of Sara. "So why didn't you speak to us?"

"I knew I wasn't wanted." Ava's tone went from anger to misery. "My daughter and husband didn't *want* me. You could have found me. I was on her credit card."

"Her" was obviously Sara.

"It was good of you to leave a message via Aunt Sara's card," Kate said as she put a full plate in front of her mother. "We all wanted to see you, but we didn't want to involve you in a couple of dirty, nasty murders."

Ava gave Kate a hard look. "One accident and one shooting and he's not dead." She looked at Jack. "No thanks to *you.*"

Jack was unperturbed. "In spite of my

282

criminal past, I'm not used to bullet wounds. Next time I'll call *you* for assistance."

Kate gave him a look of *Don't antagonize her.* Randal almost smiled, while Sara looked like she wanted to run away and hide.

"So what brings you here today?" Randal asked.

"To see *my* daughter and *my* husband." Ava's mouth was full as she looked at Randal. "You have to go home with me. Both of you."

Randal stayed calm. "I'm not going to Chicago, and Kate seems perfectly happy here."

"Ha!" Ava said. "It's just the money. You can buy us a big house and —"

"Mother!" Kate said firmly. "I do like it here and it has nothing to do with money. I don't want to go back to the uncles. You know they were trying to marry me off."

"When did this come about?" Jack snapped.

Kate gave him a look to be quiet.

"It's time you married and Noah is a very nice young man. You've always loved him." Ava glared at Jack. "At least *he* hasn't been in prison."

"Kate likes jailbirds," Randal said, smiling. "She's even accepted me."

Ava pushed away her plate. "And *I* am left out."

Kate sat down in the chair beside Jack and looked around him to her mother. "You should have told me the truth about my father. You could have taken me on your visits to see him."

"I protected you!" Ava said. "If you'd known the truth, you would have been tortured in school. The daughter of a criminal! Your life would have been miserable. And you couldn't have kept a secret about something like that. I saved you from all that pain and misery."

There was enough truth in Ava's words that Kate looked away.

Ava turned back to her husband. "So you're going to leave me for *her*?"

No one questioned that she meant Charlene.

"She has her own family now." Randal was again using his therapist voice of exaggerated calm.

"She'll choose *you* over them." Ava sounded as though her life was over.

Randal gave a bit of a smile. "Thank you for the compliment, but she will not. She's quite happy where she is."

"But you are very unhappy." Ava's voice

was full of tears.

"Less now than I have been. I'm going to stay here in Lachlan — with my daughter. I'm not going to leave her again. You may stay with us or return to your brothers. It's your choice. I know you're angry at Sara, but she has a guesthouse. I'm going to stay in it until I find a job."

Sara, Jack and Kate looked at him with interest. It was the first they'd heard of him and a job.

"You're going to be a maid again?" Ava's use of the feminine was derogatory.

"I have some possibilities. Maybe I'll become a personal trainer."

"You'd go to women's houses and . . . and . . . ?"

"Yes, certainly." Anger came into Randal's voice. "I'll do whatever my clients ask of me. You know me, anything for money." He turned away from her.

The others looked at Ava. It was her move next.

"I don't want to live here." She was pleading. "There are big bugs and the trees have no leaves."

Randal shrugged. Not his concern.

Ava looked at Kate, her eyes begging.

Kate sighed as though helpless. "The man is the head of the household. Isn't that what the uncles always say? I *must* obey my father."

Randal gave her a quick glance of humor. Kate was certainly twisting things around.

"I guess . . ." Ava began. "But I —"

She didn't finish because Sheriff Flynn entered the room. He'd silently come in through the garage. He looked at the surprised faces, then fixed on Ava. "Here you are." He turned to Jack. "Hiding a fugitive is *not* part of your job. I hope you aren't locked up for this."

Jack stood up. "A fugitive? What the hell are you talking about?"

Randal looked at his wife, who had bent her head. "So that's why you came here today. What have you done?"

Ava bent lower and said nothing.

The others looked at Sheriff Flynn.

He was glaring at Ava. "DNA came back. The guy who so-called 'fell' out of Charlene's barn? There were traces of two different DNAs on him. Both were unknown and both were in his mouth. We know one was Charlene trying to save him, but the other one . . ." He looked at Jack. "The other one is from a close relative of Kate's, probably her mother. The Broward brass are looking for Mrs. Randal Medlar."

Randal turned to his wife. "You heard

286

about this on a police radio." When Ava didn't respond, Randal turned to the sheriff. "I'm sure this is all a misunderstanding."

They looked at the top of Ava's bowed head.

"You want to tell them the truth?" Randal asked softly.

"I did it." Ava lifted her head. "I told him it was over but he wouldn't leave me alone. We fought and I pushed him out of the barn. He died!"

There was a moment of silent shock from everyone except Randal. He poured himself more tea.

"Why were you in Charlene's barn?" Jack asked.

"Because I knew *he* would be *there*!" Ava shouted. "He's always there. With her. He went to *her* instead of to *me.*"

"What about the rifle?" Sara asked.

"That man was going to *kill* her for me," Ava said. "I'd be rid of her forever, then I'd have peace. Finally and at last, I'd get my husband and daughter back. Forever."

Jack's phone buzzed. It was the office. They're on their way was Bea's curt text. Jack read it to the others.

"This is your job," Sheriff Flynn said to Jack. "Just don't be a hero and let her get away."

As the sheriff left, all Jack could do was shake his head no, that he wouldn't.

Minutes later, Jack was in his uniform. Sara had cleared the table while Kate plundered Jack's supposedly secret stash of cookies and candy bars. She put a pile of them in front of her mother. Ava was still sitting at the head of the table, Randal beside her. Ava was talking incessantly, but her voice was so low only Randal could hear her.

Kate made a big mug of chocolate milk and set it before her mother.

"You have to protect me," Ava was saying to her husband. "Like I did for you all those years you were away. I gave up so much for you and I was always there. You never needed anything."

Kate didn't dare look at her father. Her sympathy would go to him. Being in prison was not "needing" anything?

"You okay?" Sara asked Kate when they were alone in the kitchen.

"No. Not at all. How about you?"

"The same. Sure you don't want to run away to Italy?"

"Not sure at all."

They smiled at each other.

In the next second there was a pounding on the front door and Jack opened it.

Detective Cotilla was standing there. "We meet again," he said. "How many dead bodies are piled up in here? What was used this time? Guns? Knives? Poison? Oh right. They've all been done. How about a piano falling on somebody? That would be an interesting variation."

Jack didn't reply, just stepped back and let the detective and two deputies enter.

Ava was standing in the living room, Randal and Kate at her sides.

"Ava Medlar," one of the deputies said, "I have a warrant for your arrest." He read her rights and put handcuffs on her.

"You know how I knew where to find her?" Cotilla asked Jack but didn't wait for an answer. "This house seems to be the hub of all evil that goes on in this little town. I hear the name *Lachlan* and I know where to go."

"And I bet you got an anonymous call," Jack said.

"And yeah, I got a phone call. That voice sure sounded familiar."

"You do know that several people touched the dead guy," Jack said.

"And we plan to get DNA from all of them. Right now only Kate's and yours and Sara's are in the system."

"Charlene gave him mouth-to-mouth."

Cotilla grew serious. "We assume the unknown DNA is hers. I'll send someone to get a sample from her to make sure."

Jack frowned. He didn't think there was anything to link Charlene to what happened when she was a kid, but maybe there was. "I'll do it. She's been traumatized enough by the last few days. She doesn't need strangers pushing her around."

Cotilla scoffed. "Pretty Kate isn't enough for you?" When Jack didn't answer, he nodded toward Randal, who was listening to Ava. "How's he doing? I was told to watch out for him, but he seems to be clean. Maybe he did this and put the blame on his wife."

Jack gave a snort. "Probably the other way around."

Cotilla didn't laugh. "Are you forgetting your oath to be on the side of the law? Do you know something?" Again, Jack didn't answer. "I was told you two are now drinking buddies, out late at the local tavern. Are you sucking up to Dad to get the daughter? Or is it something more devious than that?"

Jack gave the detective a look so like one of Roy Wyatt's threatening scowls that Cotilla took a step back.

"I'm just making sure you aren't taken in by a master thief. You can't lose your perspective." As he spoke, Cotilla kept stepping back until he turned and followed his men and the handcuffed Ava out the door.

When the house was quiet again, the four of them sat down on the blue couches. For a moment they stared into space.

Kate looked across at her father. "Is it possible that Mom is telling the truth?"

"That she hired a man to shoot Charlene? Yes, she's quite capable of doing that. She is a here-and-now person, who never considers the future. I've not been able to assure her that Charlene and I aren't . . ." He looked at Sara and Jack in helplessness.

"You mean you can't make Ava believe that you aren't madly, insanely, passionately, to-the-death in love with Charlene?" Sara sounded very matter-of-fact, but then she'd spent forty-plus years writing about mad, insane love. "I can't imagine why she doesn't believe you."

Randal shrugged.

"Why did no one *see* what was between you two?" Sara asked. "I consider myself a perceptive person, but I never knew about you two."

"You weren't *here.*" Randal's usually calm voice sounded angry. "You and Cal fought, then you ran away. You didn't come back."

"Yes I did," Sara said.

291

"Right. How could I forget? But by then Cal had impregnated someone other than you, so you went away to sulk. For the rest of your life. You —"

"Stop!" Kate said. "The problem is now, not who did something before TVs were invented."

"She —" Randal said.

"He —" Sara said.

Jack spoke up. "Did Ava kill somebody or not? Did she hire a hit man? Did she shoot the guy in the head?"

They looked at each other blankly.

"She could have, but did she?" Randal said. "That's the real question."

Sara stood up. "I want to know why that photo was in the Bentley man's garage."

"You could ask Tayla," Kate said. "She might know something, and she'd more likely tell you than me."

Randal snorted. "My sister doesn't speak to Tayla, remember? A million years ago, when people still wrote on stone tablets, the fight Sara had with Cal had something to do with Tayla."

"How the hell do you know that?" Sara shot at him.

"Unlike you, dear sister, *I* didn't run away. *I* didn't hide and sulk and therefore ruin my life."

"Half your life has been in prison and that didn't ruin it?" Sara shot back. "And why does your wife think you can afford to buy her a big house?"

Jack held out his hand to Kate. She took it and they went out the front door.

"I can't take much of that," Kate said.

"Me either." He held out his arms to her and she snuggled against him. The glorious Florida weather made it hard to imagine murder and death.

"I'm sure I should be angry and take sides," Jack said, "but as you once pointed out, if Sara had married Cal, then she'd be my grandmother."

"And you and I would be cousins. We'd have grown up together, side by side. Like brother and sister."

He kissed the top of her head. "Sorry for what they went through, but I'm glad we aren't relatives."

"Me too," Kate said.

They held each other for a while, then Jack pulled away. "When this is done, let's talk seriously about the future."

"About how you want to stay in law enforcement and someday have Cotilla's job?"

Jack groaned. "May the earth swallow me at the thought! Has Sara spoken to you about Italy?"

Kate was grinning. "Oh yes. A villa, a sunset and a wed —" She broke off.

"Yeah, one of those. Borrowed, blue, that sort of thing. Let's talk about that."

Kate could feel her face turning pink.

"Good color," he said. He got into his patrol car and, smiling broadly, he drove away.

SEVENTEEN

As soon as Jack and Kate left the house, Sara gave a sigh of relief. If she'd learned nothing else in her long life, it was that to get rid of young people, all you had to do was start an argument. She blamed this on the kids having a lifetime of being told that everyone is a winner. Everyone gets a trophy. They couldn't abide competition.

With their audience gone, Sara looked at her brother. She could see that he didn't want to pursue the "what you did to me" argument. Their look was the same as when they were kids: *Mother is gone so let's do what we want.*

One good thing about relatives — *if there was such a thing,* Sara thought — is that you don't have to explain yourself. "What do you know that you aren't telling anyone?" Her voice was that of the older sister, the one who often found stolen objects in her little brother's pockets. It was Sara's thankless job to return them and try to keep the kid from being caught.

"I'm beginning to think Tayla may have shot the man in the car."

"If Tayla did, it was because she was protecting Charlene. And it makes sense. The man was at her house. Scary."

"Of course she was. What do you know?"

"I made sure Flynn saw the photo of Walter and he turned pale." She was staring at her brother, waiting for an answer.

"If there's any truth to Everett's book, my guess is that Daryl is terrified he'll be named as your accomplice in a jewel robbery."

Randal's lips closed tightly and his eyes turned cold.

Sara knew from years of experience that when her brother gave that look, he'd tell no more. Even when he was five, he would shut down in exactly the same way. He was not going to reveal anything about the jewel robbery. "Does Daryl have a reason to be afraid of Tayla? She's the only one still alive."

Randal's face relaxed. "Not that I know of."

Sara thought for a moment, then looked at her brother. "What are you planning to do now?"

"Jack's office texted him that Lenny woke up. I'm going to visit him in the hospital."

She didn't ask how he knew of Jack's private text. "And what if he tells you that Tayla shot him?"

Randal gave a small smile. "Then she did it because he was about to hurt Charlene."

Sara glared at him. "Do *not* smother that man!"

Randal smiled broadly. "Wouldn't think of it. And what are your plans?"

"To find out why Daryl is so worried about all this. He's hiding something big."

"Besides his belly?"

Brother and sister looked at each other and smiled. People like them, who were genetically predisposed to easily gaining weight, had spent a lifetime in hunger. They envied people who could eat whatever they wanted, who didn't endlessly deny themselves the pleasure of food. But sometimes, that envy showed itself in smug self-satisfaction.

"I'm going to have to come up with something to occupy Everett. If I don't, he'll start asking questions about Charlene." She was watching her brother intensely. Like a predator. She wanted to know how much he knew about that.

When Randal didn't ask any questions,

Sara was sure he knew more than he was telling.

"Just so that writer stays away from me," Randal said.

Sara smiled. "What? No cat burglar interview? I'm sure Everett would love to do a follow-up book about you. Charlene, Ava, Inez, Tayla. All the women in your life could make a good addition. And what *did* happen to all those jewels you stole?"

Randal stood up. "How amusing you are. What do you think Kate is doing?"

They looked at each other. They knew the answer to that.

"Ava," Sara said.

Randal sighed. "Of course."

"You don't seem to be worried about your wife being taken off to prison."

He started down the hall toward Jack's bedroom. "I assume they'll need proof of her guilt. I'll take Jack's truck."

"Do you even have a driver's license?"

Randal's laugh echoed down the hall.

Minutes later, Dora showed up to clean, and Sara left.

Daryl paid the pizza delivery boy in cash. He'd ordered from a place in nearby Sunrise. He paid extra for the distance of the delivery, but that was better than ordering within Lachlan. He imagined some kid saying, "I know you. You arrested my dad." Then the kid would tell everyone that the sheriff was still in town.

Not that Daryl had been able to keep his presence totally secret. Every day someone else knew he was there. It didn't help that he'd driven to Sara's house to warn them that Kate's mother was about to be arrested. He could have texted, but the forced isolation was getting to him. Humans weren't meant to be locked up alone.

He grabbed a couple of cold beers, put the cans on top of the pizza box, then went down the hall. He was marathoning the *NCIS* episodes. Maybe the murder would be solved by the time he finished them.

When he saw Sara Medlar sitting in the other leather chair, he almost dropped everything. But he didn't. He was adjusting to surprises. He put the beer and pizza on the ottoman and sat down. "Should I ask how you got in here?"

"It's better if you don't," she said. "But I didn't think you'd answer the doorbell."

He popped open a beer, held it up in offer to her and motioned to the pizza.

"No thanks."

"Sure? I remember you used to pack it away."

"Don't remind me."

He settled back in the chair, hands full. "What do you want from me?"

"You nearly fainted when you saw the photo of Walter on the table. Why?"

"Who else noticed that?"

"Just me. Not even Randal."

Daryl finished a slice of pizza but didn't reach for another one. When his throat was clear, he said softly, "I was the one who sent Randal to prison."

Sara let out her breath. "So he wouldn't tell anyone that you were in the jewel robbery?"

"No! It wasn't like that. I was a deputy for Edison, and I knew he didn't trust me."

"Because of your friendship with my brother?"

"Maybe, but Edison was a bastard. Everyone had to prove himself. Sort of like in a gang."

"And you did so by ratting out your friend."

Daryl took a breath. "I didn't do it on purpose, just from stupidity. I was playing poker with some guys. Walter was one of them and he asked me what jobs I was working on. He was smirking at me. You know what Walter was like."

"Yes, I do," Sara said. "All put-downs and

degradations. He humiliated people to make himself seem bigger. More of a man. Better than —" She cut herself off.

"Right. I wanted to impress him, so I told him I'd been on a stakeout of a man who was involved in some high-end drug deals."

"A man who drove a Bentley."

"Yes," Daryl said.

Sara waited but he said no more. "What else did you do?"

"Nothing. That's it. But someone called Randal and gave him the job of driving the Bentley and . . ." He stopped talking.

"And my brother was arrested the moment he crossed the state line. He was right that it was a setup," Sara said. "Did you make the call?"

"No, I didn't, but I think Walter did. He was furious at Randal. Tayla had left him and he was going broke and he believed Randal had secretly kept the bulk of the jewels. Walter went after him in a big way."

"You *think* this is what happened? But you don't know for sure?"

"I base it on a lifetime of knowing Walter. Isn't that enough?"

"Maybe. I know my brother's reputation, but what made Walter so sure Randal hadn't divided the take?"

Daryl hesitated. He didn't like openly

301

talking about his one and only robbery, but he could see that Sara wasn't going to let up. "On that day of the . . . you know, Walter and Randal went upstairs. I stayed in the car and Roy was in the house but downstairs. Randal was afraid Mrs. Oliver's son would show up. You know that Randal never liked violence."

"So Roy was the muscle, while Walter and Randal were the actual thieves."

Daryl gave a bit of a smile that she'd left him out of the pack. "Mrs. Oliver had told Randal where things were so it was to be an easy job."

"I take it there were complications," Sara said.

"Yes. Walter came down with a black bag, not very big. The jewelry was mostly in cases and he was disappointed that there wasn't more. He thought Randal was behind him but he wasn't. Ten minutes later, Randal came downstairs. He was wearing tight black clothes and you could see that the only thing he had was a red leather book in his hand. He said he'd taken so long because Mrs. Oliver asked him to get her private journal and he'd had a hard time finding it."

"But Walter didn't believe that."

"No. When they got in the car, Walter

302

grabbed the book and opened it. He thought the insides had been cut out."

"My brother wouldn't be that dumb. But what about the jewels? I don't know that Randal ever had much money."

Daryl snorted. "That's because he's smart. He told us not to cash out. But we did. Thanks to Mrs. Oliver's son, every piece had been photographed for insurance. It was hard to sell hot items and we got rock-bottom prices. But Randal held on to his share."

Sara was thoughtful. "If my brother was holding on to jewels, why would he take a menial job years later? I paid the costs of his trial. If he'd had money hidden away, he would have spent it then."

"Unless he meant to save it for his daughter."

"That's possible. But all this is speculation. Did you and Roy also think Randal had some hidden away?"

"No. Roy smashed Walter in the mouth over it, but it made no difference. But then, Roy and I are simple people. I just wanted Evie, a nice house and for my boss to respect me."

"What did Roy get?"

"A good time, lots of beer and that Harley Jack rides around town on."

For a minute, they were quiet.

Sara stood up. "This has been interesting."

"You know, when Randal returned here years later, I thought it was because he and Tayla were having an affair."

Sara sat back down. "That's a joke, right? Randal likes sweet, complacent women. Tayla would rip him apart."

Daryl drank deeply. "I have no answers, but it did all fit together. Tayla returned to Lachlan at the same time Randal did. And of course Charlene was here too. Pretty big coincidences. I don't think anybody noticed this, but Walter got Tayla and Charlene to go back to California during the trial. But then, Inez kept that whole thing out of the papers."

"So Walter got Randal taken out of the picture by putting him in prison."

"Due to my big mouth," Daryl said. "Are you going to tell him?"

"I don't see any reason to tell my brother this. Randal paid the price. He doesn't need more hatred."

Daryl shook his head. "You love him, don't you?"

"I love Kate." Sara stood up again. "If Randal traces all this to Walter, it will be a literal dead end. He'll have to stop looking.

Do me a favor and don't confess to anyone else. Just keep your mouth shut, okay?"

"Gladly. So what's next?"

"We haven't come close to figuring out who pushed the man out of the barn or who shot the guy in the car. And there's Ava, who has confessed to hiring and kissing. If she's lying, I don't know why she's done it."

Daryl got up, went to the bookcase, opened the bottom drawer and took out the folder marked Randal Medlar. He handed it to Sara. "See what you can find in it."

"I will." She put her hand on the folder.

He didn't release it. "Please don't let Randal hate me."

Sara smiled. "Even if he finds out, all I have to do is get Kate to say 'Don't hate Sheriff Flynn' and you'll be forgiven everything."

Daryl laughed. "Thank you." He released the folder. "And use the door, will you?"

Sara started to leave but she turned back. "What happened between you and Edison after the trial?"

Daryl's face reddened. "He trusted me. From then on, I was his favorite. I could do no wrong. Ultimately, it all led to my being made sheriff."

Sara nodded. "It looks like Walter told

Edison who spilled the beans, so they were obviously working together. But who made the call to Randal?"

"Could have been anyone."

Sara nodded in agreement, then left the house. By the door.

EIGHTEEN

Kate pulled into the parking lot of Kirk-wood Realty. She had every intention of going to work. There were some contracts she needed to go over and there'd be clients who wanted to find their dream home. The husband would say he had to have a pool, and the wife would say she wouldn't buy a house with a pool. Those kinds of conversations were always lots of fun.

Along one side of the parking lot there were three cars: Tayla's silver Mercedes, Melissa's red Toyota and Raye's black Honda. There was an empty spot next to them. The four women always parked together.

If Tayla was there, Kate knew she should talk to her about the photo of the three people. She had a copy of it on her phone. But how could she do that? Yes, she and Tayla were friends, but still, the woman was her boss. Did she show her the picture and ask, "What do you have to do with a man who was running drugs? The man who got off free while my father was sent to prison — something my mother never told me about?"

Yeah, that would go over well.

Kate leaned back against the seat. She needed to go inside. Instead, she sat there.

Everything that was happening was so very personal. A dead father come to life. A mother confessing to attempted murder. An unidentified body, another man shot.

"I don't need to find a murderer," she said. "I need a therapist."

No, she thought. What she needed was some fun. Dancing with the Lachlan fire-fighters. Jack would sing and —

Her phone dinged. It was a text from Jack.

I can't find Charlene.

Kate looked at the text for nearly a minute, waiting to see if there'd be more. Nope. That was it.

"I'm fine," she said in answer to his unasked question. "My mother was taken away in handcuffs, but I should be used to that. It seems that I saw the same thing done to my father."

She knew that Jack wanted her to look for

Charlene. He was probably busy dealing with parking tickets or whatever, so it was Kate's job to run around town searching for one of Jack's many crushes.

"Maybe Charlene and I will build a birdhouse together," she said to the phone. "And while we're gluing down tiny roof tiles, I'll casually ask her if she's planning to destroy her family and run off with my father. I'm sure she won't mind a question like that."

Kate glared at Jack's short text. Is this all he had to say after what happened between them? "Borrowed and blue," he'd said. Now all he could think of was Charlene?

When Jack said that about Italy and the sunset, she'd thought it was cute. But now she was annoyed. Maybe she was supposed to consider herself engaged. Why not? Everything else in her life had been done without fanfare. Dead father? Oh no. He's just been in prison for twenty-some years. Her loving mother? No, she might be a murderer.

After those announcements, what did a "Hey, let's go to Italy and do the borrowed and blue thing" matter?

But, Jack said they should talk about it. What exactly did that mean? Where and when? What happened to "Will you marry me?"

Kate put her hands on the steering wheel and rested her head on them. She knew that her real problem was that she should go see her mother. But Kate dreaded it with all her being.

It had been years since she'd lived with her mother. Phone calls, video chats and emails could be manipulated. One time when Ava was telling Kate that she absolutely *had* to return home immediately, Kate gave a little scream and said there was a fire. She'd closed her laptop before Ava could say another word.

But now the safety of distance was gone — and Kate deeply dreaded what was coming. She was going to postpone it as long as possible.

She left the parking lot and drove on Fort Lauderdale's wide streets to Southwest Ranches. She passed Flamingo Road, her favorite place for plant nurseries, then continued on Stirling to Charlene's little farm.

She punched in the gate code and drove in. The last time she'd been there, Charlene was French-kissing some dead guy.

Be nice, she told herself.

Gil came out of the house, and the sight of him made her smile. He was big and cuddly and very cute.

"What a treat," he said. "Two beautiful women here in one day."

"So Jack's been here?"

Gil gave a laugh that came from his belly. "What's he done now?"

"Nothing really. He just asked me to check on Charlene. I have things to do, but Charlene is more important. At least she is to Jack. And to my father."

Gil put his big, strong arm around Kate's shoulders. "If it helps, I like *you* the best."

It was silly, but he made her feel better. When she leaned her head against his chest, he put his other arm around her.

"Can we share?" came a deep, male voice.

Kate looked up to see Gil's two cousins, big bears of men, so masculine they made shotguns seem girlie.

She couldn't help herself as she hugged them too. It was nice to be female and surrounded by so much rampant masculinity.

"You need us for anything?"

Gil's question brought her back to reality. "Has Charlene been here?"

"Yeah, about an hour ago. She said she forgot something, went into the house for a few minutes, then came back out and drove away."

"She didn't have a suitcase, did she?"

"No. Just one of those big bags you ladies like."

"What did she take?" Kate asked.

The men looked at her blankly.

"I think I better go see." She turned away, but then looked back. "Anyone want to help me search?"

"Yeah," they said, and followed her inside.

It took only minutes to find what they wanted. The bottom drawer on one of the bedside tables was open slightly. Inside was an empty metal box.

Kate sat down on the side of the bed. "What do you think?"

"She got money and probably a passport," Gil said, and the cousins nodded. He sat down beside her. "We could check the airport."

"She won't do that," a cousin said. "That would leave a trail. If she wants to disappear, she won't use her name. Is it possible that she has a car hidden somewhere? One that's not registered to anyone in her family?"

Kate knew there were many storage places in Fort Lauderdale where you could leave a car. The snowbirds, people who came only for the winter, stored vehicles in them during the hot summers. "I think there's a strong chance that Charlene's husband arranged such a car."

"Then they probably have a place for her to hide," the other cousin said.

"At least she hasn't run away with my father," Kate muttered as she stood up. "I have to go. My mother's in jail."

"She's what?" Gil asked.

"My mother confessed to . . ." Kate started out of the room, the men behind her. "I don't know. Attempted murder? She says she paid the dead guy to have Charlene *killed.*"

When Kate stopped at the front door, the men were looking at her in shock. "And Mother seems to have paid him in kisses. Big, fat DNA-loaded kisses. Thanks for everything. Tell Quinn hello for me." She looked at Gil. "Would you call Jack and tell him what we found and that I'll be at his office soon?"

"You and Jack aren't speaking?" Gil sounded hopeful.

Kate opened the door. "I'm not sure but we might be engaged."

"Kate," Gil said, "I think you need to step back from all this."

"It's okay. It's just been a traumatic day.

313

And it's going to get worse when I see my mother. Bye." She got into her car and left.

When Kate got there, Jack was entering the sheriff's office. "Where have you been?" He held the door open for her.

She nodded hello to Bea, then smiled broadly at Dave and Pete.

Jack gave an exaggerated sigh. "Finished yet?"

"Just saying hello." She looked back at him. "Didn't Gil tell you that I was at Charlene's place? She showed up there, and we think she took her passport and some cash."

Jack nodded. "That fits. I found her car in a Publix parking lot. Wherever she went, it wasn't by public transport. No company has a record of picking her up."

Kate gave Bea a thumbs-up. She was great at finding out things like that. Kate turned back to Jack. "I need to see Mother. Is she at the station downtown?"

"No," Jack said. "She's here. I think Cotilla wants *us* to get a confession out of her."

"But she already . . ." Kate trailed off. She knew he meant an *honest* confession. "Have you talked to her?"

"Nope. I've been out looking for a car and asking about alibis. Where was Ava when?"

"What did you find out?"

"That your mother isn't someone people

pay much attention to. Only one person at the hotel remembered her, but nothing specific. No one could say for sure where she was when."

"I guess I better go talk to her." Kate's voice was full of dread.

"While I was out, she made a phone call and a lawyer came to see her."

Kate showed her surprise. "Who did she call? Who got her the lawyer? Did Dad do it?"

"I don't know. Dave checked him in. He signed in as James Hamilton, Esquire, and showed an ID but Bea can't find him. It was fake. He was in there for about fifteen minutes, then left. Bea said that when he left he was smiling like he'd won a bet."

Kate held out her hands. "I didn't bring any gifts for Mother. I was going to stop somewhere on the way downtown and get something."

Jack put his hands on her shoulders, his face close to hers. "I'd go in with you but I think she'll tell more without me there."

Kate nodded, knowing what he said was true. But oh how she dreaded it!

"Find out what you can so we can disprove this idiocy."

"You don't think she tried to kill Charlene?"

315

"No, I don't. And I can't imagine your mother passionately *kissing* that young man who was lying dead on the ground."

Kate understood his meaning. "Of course. She was doing mouth-to-mouth. Like Charlene."

"Probably so, which might mean that she knows who the guy is. See if you can find out."

Kate nodded, then Jack led her down the hall to the first of their two barred cells.

Ava was sitting on a hard wooden bench. She glanced at her daughter, then turned away, her face angry.

Jack gave Kate a look of encouragement, unlocked the door, let her in, locked it, then hurried out of the room.

"Coward!" Kate said under her breath. "Mother, are you all right?" she asked louder.

Ava didn't respond.

Kate let out her breath. "You need to talk to me."

"Where is my husband?"

"I have no idea, but I'm sure he'll be here soon."

"He's with *her*," Ava muttered.

Kate straightened her back. "Charlene has disappeared. We think she's gone into hiding. She is not and never will be with my father. Now that we have that out of the way, tell me who you called."

"Ebb."

With a groan, Kate sat down at the far end of the bench. Ebenezer was the oldest of her mother's brothers. The patriarch. The one most rigid, most judgmental. "You called *him*?"

"Of course. I need a *friend.*" Ava gave Kate a pointed look.

"Did Uncle Ebb get you the lawyer?"

"What do they know of lawyers? Ebb is coming here to be on my side since no one else is."

"What is the real name of the lawyer who came to see you?"

"I don't remember."

"Did he leave a card?"

Ava made no reply.

"How can I help you if you don't tell me anything?"

"I don't need help. I just need my husband. He really is with her, isn't he?"

"No, he's not! Mother, this is serious. You said you tried to kill Charlene."

"Didn't succeed, did I? They can't prosecute me for thoughts."

Kate took a moment to get back on track. "So what really happened with the dead man? Were you hanging around Charlene's

317

place and saw him lying there? Did you try to revive him?" She paused. "Do you *know* him?"

Ava folded her arms across her chest. "I'm not going to say any more until I see my husband." Her eyes softened. "I went to him when he was in prison. Why am I here alone?"

"You're not alone. I'm here, and if you'd give Jack a chance, he'd help you."

"Ha! When Ebb gets here, he'll fix it all. He'll find Randal and everything will be fine." Ava turned away, her back to her daughter.

"Did you tell Uncle Ebb who the dead man is? Did you tell the lawyer?" When Ava said nothing, Kate knew she was going to get no more out of her mother. Kate felt her body deflate. She got up and went to the cell door, but then she turned back. Her mother had on what Kate called her "bull-dog look." Nothing on earth was going to move her.

Kate spoke softly. "Every time you went to New York, I baked dozens of cookies and you took them with you. Did you give them to my father?"

When Ava looked at her daughter, her eyes were sparkling. "Yes I did! All those men loved them."

"Men? What men?"

"Mel and Buster and . . ." Ava shrugged. "Them. You know." The bulldog look returned.

Kate called for Jack to let her out. She was realizing that her mother had a whole life that Kate knew nothing about. How many times had she heard her mother say, *"My daughter and I have no secrets"*?

Kate was learning that everything in her life had been a secret.

As soon as she was in the office, Kate took her phone out. Her thumbs flew over the letters as she texted her father.

Mother won't talk to me. She wants YOU. She called Uncle Ebb and he's coming here. A lawyer has been to see her but she won't tell me his name. Charlene has disappeared.

She sent the text, then added another one.

So help me if you ran off with Charlene, I'll find you. I'll tell Mother AND the uncles where you are.

She sent it, then handed her phone to Jack to read.

"That last one is a bit harsh, isn't it?" He

was teasing.

Kate didn't smile. "What in the world has my mother gotten herself into? Did the lawyer say anything? What did he look like?"

"Middle-aged, dark hair, trim build. Nothing notable."

"Expensive suit," Bea said. She was pretending to use the file cabinet nearby as she listened. She didn't trust computers so she kept hard copies of everything.

Kate turned to her. "You didn't happen to take a photo of him, did you?"

"My camera is at home."

"You could have —" Kate cut herself off from saying Bea could have used her phone. Too modern for her. She looked at Dave. "Did you guys see or hear anything?"

"Just words of courtesy," Dave said. "Nice man."

"I let him out," Pete said. "The only thing I heard him say to Mrs. Medlar was, 'Balloons.' Is it her birthday?"

"That doesn't help," Jack said. "You should have —"

"What color of balloons?" Kate asked.

Everyone looked at her in question.

"Now that you mention it, he said, 'Purple balloons.' "

Jack was still holding Kate's phone, and she grabbed it from him. She sent another text to her father.

Lawyer said purple balloons. Meet us at your old house at four.

She sent a text to Sara.

What do purple and pink balloons have to do with any of this? Try 1988. Everyone is meeting at your old house at four.

Jack read the texts. "Sara will love a research problem like that."

"That's what I'm hoping. How's the man in the hospital?"

"Doing better. They text me about his condition and who visits him."

She waited for him to say more but he didn't. "I have to go. See you at the meeting?"

"Definitely."

NINETEEN

Kate knew she'd have to hurry to make it to the Medlar house by four. When she got to the office, she almost cried in relief that Tayla wasn't there. That meant Kate got out of having to ask her if she knew where Charlene was. And why did the Bentley guy have an old photo of her in his garage?

Kate did what she could to get the contracts ready for next week's closing. Melissa was there, and she wasn't happy that Kate was out of the office so much of the time.

"You leave the work for the rest of us while you go out playing with Jack," Melissa said.

Raye, at her desk, rolled her eyes and said, "I'll take care of it."

With a smile of thanks, Kate ran to her car.

When she got to the house, she counted the vehicles and saw that everyone was already there. She opened the door of Sara's house and gasped at the sight. The ceiling had lots of pink and purple balloons gently bouncing on it.

Below the balloons, a makeshift table had been set on a couple of sawhorses, then draped in blue silk that was covered by an exquisite cloth of Irish lace. A silver bucket held ice and a bottle of champagne with flutes of etched glass beside it.

Sara, Jack and her father were waiting for her reaction.

"This is pretty," she said, but they were still staring at her. "What?"

"We were hoping to jog your memory," Randal said. "Any luck?"

"No, nothing. I've seen that lace before."

Sara grimaced. "He cleaned out my cabinets. I bought that on my first trip to Ireland."

"And have never used it since," Randal said. "Or the flutes or the silver or the Herend dishes or —"

"I get it," Sara said, but she didn't seem as angry at her brother as she usually did. In fact, her eyes were sparkling.

Randal opened the champagne and filled the glasses. "My sister is dying to tell us a story."

Jack stepped forward, his eyes on Randal. "Before that, tell us how the guy in the hospital is."

Randal showed only the slightest surprise that Jack knew where he'd been. "Awake." He lifted a white linen napkin to reveal a plate full of cookies. "Keto from Bessie."

Jack was still staring at him, wanting more information.

Randal gestured to the balloons. "Memory is such a funny thing. Kate remembers the balloons but not why. And the man in the hospital remembers his name but nothing else. Not his past and not the present. He says he has no idea why he was at Tayla's house or who shot him. Quite convenient."

"Yes, very." Jack took a handful of cookies.

"Mother wants to see you," Kate said to her father.

"I imagine she does," Randal said.

"What does she want from you?" Jack asked.

"Bail money?" Randal said it as a joke.

Sara was looking at her brother intensely. "Ava always has a purpose for what she does. Why is she demanding to see *you*?"

Randal didn't answer. He looked at Jack. "Any word on Charlene?"

"So help me," Kate said, "if you go after her, I'll —"

"I'm not going to!" Randal said. "I swear

it. I'm curious about the DNA. I'm sure hers could be obtained from something in her house."

"No!" Sara, Jack and Kate said in unison.

If Randal was surprised by their fierceness, he didn't show it. "Did Charlene murder someone?" he asked calmly.

"Of course not," Sara snapped.

"Unless it's murder, the statute of limitations for the crime covers it. Whatever she did long ago doesn't matter now."

"Her reputation would be ruined," Sara said.

"Dear sister, today criminals are glorified. Especially if they got away with the crime."

"So what went wrong with you?" Sara said under her breath.

"Charlene isn't like that," Kate said quickly and loudly. "To be found out would hurt her irreparably."

"That's true," Sara said. "Charlene would —"

Randal stepped away from the women to go to Jack. "Roy used to look at me like you are now. For all that most people thought your father was an insensitive lout, he could see to the inside of a person."

Jack gave a little smile. "Are you implying that I can see that you're withholding something? What do you know that we don't? And why are you refusing to go see your wife?"

Randal gave a quick glance over his shoulder to make sure the women weren't listening. "She believes she can persuade me to not reveal a secret."

"And can she?"

Randal smiled. "No. She can only postpone it."

"Then tell me what it is."

Sara and Kate had stopped talking and were looking at them.

"There's more to Charlene than you think," Randal said so only Jack could hear. He went back to the table and turned to his sister. "It's time for one of your stories."

Sara laughed. "That's what you always said when we were kids and Mother was in one of her tirades against me."

"Your stories calmed her down."

"I never understood why. I created evil witches who said the exact same things she did."

"And short, beautiful princesses who overcame all evil."

For a moment, brother and sister looked at each other in fond memory. Kate thought it was nice that there was no anger from her or defiance from him.

Sara began. "In 1988 in Fort Lauderdale —"

"When I was working for Mrs. Meyers," Randal said.

"Did she have a big, new black Mercedes?" Sara asked.

"She did." Randal raised his eyebrows in interest.

Sara continued. "Mr. Theodore Ingles was giving a third birthday party for his adored granddaughter. The child's favorite colors were pink and purple, so he hired a decorator to put up a huge arch of pink and purple balloons over his driveway."

"And Kate saw them," Randal said. "I had an idea it was something like that."

"There's more to this," Sara said. "A woman — described only as 'very thin' — was sitting in a big black Mercedes parked across the road from Mr. Ingles's house. In the back was a pretty little red-haired girl."

Everyone looked at Kate, but her eyes were on her aunt.

"The thin woman got out and used cuticle scissors to cut away two balloons."

"A pink one and a purple one," Kate said. "One from each end of the arch."

"Yes. She handed them through the window to the child."

So far this didn't seem like much of a crime.

Like all good storytellers, Sara waited until she had their full attention. "Unfortunately, the balloons weren't secured very well. The whole arch rose from the ground and flew up into the sky." Sara paused. "And in a rage, Mr. Ingles called the police."

Sara stepped aside and picked up her favorite red leather portfolio — the one she'd bought in Venice — and pulled out photocopies of a newspaper article. "Note the writer," she added as she handed them out.

Kate scanned the article in disgust. "Yet another attempt at humor by your girlfriend."

Jack read the paper. It was written by Elliot Hughes, a woman he'd had a very brief liaison with. It was written in her style of making fun of the whole incident. To her, the man's anger over losing the balloons was a great joke. Her sympathy was on the side of the woman who'd cut the balloons away and given them to the little red-haired girl, who was sitting all alone in the back of the big, empty car.

The police took Mr. Ingles's statement. One of them told the reporter they didn't have a file for "Balloon Crimes." They left grinning.

There was no identification of the car, the driver, or the little red-haired thief. They had driven away when the balloon arch disappeared into the sky.

Jack looked at Kate. "I think we can agree that it was your mother and you in Mrs. Meyers's car." He didn't wait for a reply. "So now we know why you remember the balloons. Hundreds floating up into the sky must have been a sight that a child would remember forever. And then there was probably a man trying to catch them."

"And no doubt yelling in anger," Sara added.

"I guess so." Kate was frowning.

Randal was still staring at the paper. "Look at the photo."

Jack looked back at his paper. There was a picture of an angry man, his house in the background. To the left, barely visible, was a garage. "I'd know that door anywhere."

It was the garage that he and Randal had sneaked into and found the box of photos.

Randal folded the paper and put it in his shirt pocket. "I must go."

Before any of them could speak, Randal was gone.

Jack and Kate looked at Sara, and she shrugged. "He's always been like that. Silent and secretive."

"Was this a coincidence?" Kate asked. "My mother cutting balloons next door to the man who ended up putting my father in prison?"

Sara and Jack didn't answer, but their faces said it most certainly wasn't a coincidence.

Jack spoke first. "I vote we go to the Brigade and talk about everything we know." He glanced at the door. "Somewhere we can be sure we're not overheard."

They'd had years of working together and it took them only minutes to clear the place. They left the balloons on the ceiling. They'd started out as a fun gesture but now seemed to hide some darker undertone.

They put everything in the trunk of Kate's car. Randal had taken Sara's MINI. They didn't mention that he'd not asked permission. They'd learned that it was better not to know exactly what Randal was up to.

Jack opened the passenger door of his truck. "I guess we're together."

They all smiled.

Jack drove, Kate in the middle and Sara was by the door. They didn't speak until they got to the bar and took one of the booths.

The waitress came immediately, smiling at Jack. "You going to sing today?"

"Only if you ask me to," he said in a low voice.

Kate and Sara groaned.

Laughing, Jack ordered a big bowl of guacamole, and a vodka and soda with lime for Sara.

She smiled. It was a low carb drink.

Jack had carried a jacket for Sara and he picked it up to show a box of crackers made of cauliflower, something she could eat with the guac. She smiled adoringly at him. Kate ordered a margarita with salt on the rim and Jack had a beer.

When they were alone, Kate said, "I miss us. I miss the three of us. I feel like I haven't seen you two in years."

Jack sighed. "I hate the sheriff's job."

Sara said, "I hate finding out things, then having to tell you two. I like it when we see and hear things together."

Kate grimaced. "I like when murder doesn't make *me* the center of attention. Father, Mother here and an uncle who has a god complex soon to arrive."

Jack looked at Sara. "What else did you find out in your excellent research job?"

Kate narrowed her eyes at him. "You mean besides that your girlfriend was the

331

one who caused all the problems? And how old is she anyway? I was four and she was writing for the newspaper. But then, you two are probably the same age."

Jack gave a one-sided grin. "I do love your jealousy." He waited for Sara to answer his question.

Sara said, "Nothing really." The looks on their faces said they didn't believe her. "I knew that was Bentley's house next door. It's how I found the balloon article. The date and his address minus the house number. This means that Ava was outside the Bentley guy's house."

"She could have been driving by, saw the balloons and stopped," Jack said.

"My mother hates driving. She only does it when necessary," Kate said. She looked at Sara. "What else?"

They had to wait for their drinks to be served along with the guacamole. Jack and Kate dipped in with the warm tortilla chips, while Sara used the cauliflower crackers.

"I got a photo of Bentley." Sara dusted her hands and swiped her phone. "It's from a company site and he's young." She handed them her phone.

Kate and Jack had their heads together as they looked.

"When Dad and I saw him, he had a

belly," Kate said.

"It could have been a disguise," Jack said. "Mind if I send this to Bea? She knows a lot of people."

Sara and Kate knew what he was really saying. Today a man had mentioned purple balloons to Ava. Who was he?

Bea's answer came right away.

That's the lawyer who visited Ava.

Jack and Sara looked at Kate.

"Go on," she said. "Say it. My mother is deeply connected to all of this."

Sara's voice was soft. "Maybe even to what happened in the past."

"You mean . . . ?" Kate asked.

"The trial," Sara said. "Of course Bentley was there. He was the key to it all."

Jack spoke before Kate could. "Let's not jump to conclusions. From what I've seen of your mother she tends to speak before she thinks. Let's find out more."

Sara said, "Let's not forget what everyone loves — the jewels. My bet is that Ava told people she knows all about them. She wouldn't want anyone to think her husband doesn't confide in her."

Jack nodded. "It always seems to lead back to those damned jewels."

333

"But not to the stepson who was paid 2.4 million in insurance," Kate said.

Sara and Jack looked at her.

"Dad told me. I'm not sure there is any great treasure hidden away somewhere. X marks the spot, that sort of thing."

"Maybe Randal isn't actually a thief," Sara said. "He's so very charming, isn't he?" There was no mistaking her sarcasm. It was imbued with a lifetime of dealing with her brother.

Kate's face closed up in a way that looked remarkably like her father. She said nothing, just glared at her aunt.

"Oh goody," Jack said. "A girl fight."

"Shut up," Kate said.

"Shut up," Sara said, but both women were smiling. "It seems that we have too many mysteries."

Jack raised an eyebrow. "You mean the mystery of the jewel robbery? Was it or wasn't it? Then Randal being sent to prison for what I've come to believe was a setup? Or the mystery of the guy with a rifle falling out of a barn? And we can't forget the man hired by some jailbird, then he was shot in the head. Am I missing anything?"

"The balloons," Sara said.

"And the Bentley guy — the *real* thief — posing as a lawyer to see my mother."

"And talking to her about those balloons," Sara added. "Why? You can't blackmail someone for cutting a string."

"Unless it's connected to a parachute," Kate said.

"Or to a life raft," Sara said.

"Or a —"

Jack spoke up. "It seems that we have pieces of several puzzles. So how do we solve them?"

"If it were one of my books," Sara said, "I'd spend half a day outlining just one of the puzzles, then working on it. The others can wait."

"I think they will all eventually link," Kate said. "It's like a chess game played on four levels, but in the end, it's just one game."

"So which one first?" Jack asked.

"Dead man," Kate said quickly. "My mother's DNA was on him, and I'd like to do what I can to get her out of jail."

Sara and Jack were looking at each other.

Kate sighed. "Okay, Sherlock and Watson. What do you two propose?"

"Going back," Sara said. "In time, that is. It's too weird that the balloons and the Bentley guy and Ava are linked. We need to find out how they go together."

"Think she was having an affair with Bentley?" Jack asked solemnly.

335

That was such an absurd concept that the three of them burst out laughing, then ordered another round of drinks and placed three orders for fajitas.

When they got home, the women were drowsy from food and alcohol, so Jack took care of them. He sent them to their bedrooms to do the "comfort thing" they so loved: fuzzy slippers and soft, ugly clothes with cartoon characters on the front. He led them to the big couch in the family room and turned on the TV.

When they were settled, he went outside and punched in Randal's number. He answered right away. "Where the hell are you?"

"Enjoying the Florida weather." Randal was good at telling nothing. "How are the girls?"

"Half-drunk and happy. What are you up to? Have you seen Ava?"

"Lord, no!" Randal said with passion.

"So you're leaving her to make *us* miserable?"

Randal chuckled. "How clever you are. Roy would be proud. Did you find out anything?"

"That's my question for you," Jack said. "Again, I ask you. Where are you?"

"I want to find out what Bentley knows. Did you figure out who the lawyer that visited my wife is?"

"I think you know the answer."

Randal laughed. "Yeah. Our own Bentley guy. My guess is that he's holding something over her and I want to know what it is."

"Why don't you visit her and ask?"

Randal snorted. "She wouldn't tell me. Her only concern in life is that I don't —" He quit talking.

"That you don't what? Run off with Charlene?"

"Tell what I know. I have to go. Bentley is on the move."

"Do you think Ava — ?" Jack began, but Randal had clicked off. He frowned at his phone. It looked like Randal was wherever Bentley was. Following him. Jack knew he should get in his truck and try to find Randal. Get him home before he got into trouble.

But Jack didn't want to. He wanted time with his "girls." He put the phone in his pocket and went into the family room. The two women were stretched out, heads on opposite couch arms, and sleepily watching some costume drama. If a show had a British accent and historical clothes, they'd watch it in utter fascination, even if they'd seen it a dozen times.

He lifted both sets of feet, sat down, removed slippers and pulled their sock-clad feet onto his lap. He almost sneezed when a bit of pink fuzz hit his nose. He pulled the lap robe off the back of the sofa and covered their feet. Somehow, both women always managed to have cold feet.

"There's a football game on tonight," he said. "We could —"

"Not if you value your life," Kate murmured.

Sara shook her head but didn't take her eyes off the screen.

Jack smiled. He was utterly and completely content.

TWENTY

"Your dad," Jack said the next morning. Sara was cooking eggs and bacon.

"What's he done now?" Kate yawned. "Other than stealing Aunt Sara's car, that is?"

"It's back." Sara slid scrambled eggs into a bowl. "My brother is nowhere to be seen, but my car is here."

"He's by the pool," Jack said.

"Getting ready to go see Mother?" Kate meant it as a joke. "He really does need to go see her."

"That's only going to happen if I arrest him, put him in handcuffs and carry him into her cell," Jack said.

The women looked at him with hopeful eyes.

"No," Jack said, "I can't do that. I think we should find out who set up your dad and sent him to prison. That's my vote for the first mystery to solve."

"This is before we figure out about the dead guy?" Sara asked. "And has anyone besides Randal talked to the poor man in the hospital?"

"Captain Edison sent my dad away," Kate said. "I thought that was established."

"Edison used something he was told," Jack said. "I want to know who did the telling."

"I believe it was Walter Kirkwood," Sara said. When they looked at her, she told them what Sheriff Flynn had told her about opening his big mouth to Walter at a poker game. "Walter wanted revenge and he got it."

"Was he the one who called my father and gave him the job of driving the Bentley?" Kate asked.

"Probably," Sara said. "Or he paid someone to do it."

"Does Randal know this?" Jack asked.

"I have no idea what my brother does or doesn't know," Sara answered. "But finding the photo of Walter in the Bentley guy's garage seems to verify everything. I'd believe any bad thing said about Walter Kirkwood."

"That sounds plausible to me," Kate said. "We should tell Dad."

"So he'll stop stalking people and finally go see your mother and everyone will calm down?" Jack asked.

Kate shrugged. "Pretty much, yes."

"So why did Bentley pose as a lawyer, visit your mother and talk to her about balloons?" Sara asked.

"Friendship?" Kate said.

Sara and Jack laughed.

"Right. Exactly." Jack stood up. "I'm going to pay a visit to the man who hung up the balloons. Either of you want to go with me?"

Neither woman answered, just ran with lightning speed to their bedrooms to dress quickly.

Jack was in his truck, the engine running, when Kate and Sara jumped in. Sara had her camera bag.

As he pulled onto the road, Sara asked, "You called ahead? Made sure he'll talk to us?"

"Oh yeah," Jack said. "Mr. Ingles is dying to talk to anyone on the planet except Elliot Hughes."

"Smart man," Kate muttered. "Although by now she's pretty old." She smiled innocently at Jack.

He shook his head, with a rueful grin.

The man greeted them at the front door. He was older than the grainy news photo showed him and he'd added a few pounds, but he looked healthy. He wasn't smiling.

He led them to the living room. As they

sat on the couch, the man took a big leather chair across from them. Glasses and a pitcher of iced tea were on the marble coffee table. There was a plate of chocolate chip cookies. Jack filled four glasses, took cookies for himself and leaned back, ready to listen.

"It was one of the worst things in my life," Mr. Ingles said. "I was publicly humiliated by all of them. Everyone I knew laughed at me. People in the grocery saw me and —" He broke off as he stared at Kate. "Who are you?"

Kate brought up a photo of her and her mother when Kate was a child. She handed her phone to him. He nodded and gave it back to her.

"I thought that's who you were. I had just walked out of the house so I saw the whole thing. Little red-haired girl in the back of a big black Mercedes and the woman cutting away my balloons. She's your mother?"

"Yes."

"You don't look like her," Mr. Ingles said. He tightened his lips. "I tried to tell those two policemen that it wasn't just about the balloons, but every time I said anything, that reporter woman made a joke out of it. No one listened to me!"

"We're listening now," Sara said.

342

"I'd seen her before. Many times."

"Ava?" Sara asked.

"If that's the skinny woman, yes. She used to sit there with the engine running, and until that day, she was always by herself."

They were looking at him in surprise.

"Why was she there?" Kate asked.

"To tell you the truth, I thought she was with the police or the FBI. Maybe I watch too much TV, but I knew the guy next door was involved in something illegal."

"What made you think that?" Jack asked.

"At first, things only happened during the night. Men came by. I'm a light sleeper and they had loud motors. Or very quiet ones. Whatever, their headlights lit up my bedroom."

"What were they doing?" Jack asked.

"They put bags in his car, then they'd drive away. But they got bolder and started coming during the day."

"What about him?" Sara asked. "What did the man do about all this?"

"Not much. He was a bad neighbor. I'd say good morning and he'd run inside like some frightened rabbit. One time I did catch him out and I told him he ought to put his car in his garage. I was trying to warn him. If I saw what was going on, so did other people. But he didn't take the hint. He said his trunk was full of stuff his wife bought and she needed access. I knew that was a lie. She had her own car. Besides, she'd told my wife she hated that big Bentley."

"How many times did this happen?" Jack asked.

"Dozens. It went on for months."

"Was the woman in the Mercedes ever there during the transfers?" Sara asked.

"Yes. Often. One time I was getting the mail and I heard men tell her to move her car. They weren't polite about it."

"Did she move it?" Kate asked.

"Yes, but only a few feet. It was like watching a cop show where she was on a stakeout. I told all this to the reporter, but she paid no attention to me. She had her mind made up before she got here. And later, she wrote it all like it was a joke. Something to laugh at. Worse was that her jokes made the police laugh at me too. They wouldn't listen about what I'd seen at the house next door."

"Elliot Hughes tends to do that," Sara said. "She ruins people with her words."

"And she loves to get revenge," Kate added.

"I guess she did get it," Jack said. "The man lost his house, his wife, everything."

Mr. Ingles snorted. "Who told you that?

344

His wife and mine were friends. They moved to Boca and bought a mansion. Whatever he was doing, he made a fortune from it."

"Well!" Sara said when they were back in Jack's truck. "Talk about lies! Each one bigger than the last."

Jack glanced at Kate who was silent. "You okay?"

"Not really," she said. "What was my mother doing there? Was she involved in something illegal? Is that why the Bentley guy showed up to visit her in jail? He was going to tell on her?"

"If you want us to stop investigating," Sara said, "we will."

"I'll turn it over to Cotilla and Broward County and that'll stop everything," Jack said. "They'll say the guy in the barn was an accident and the man shot in the head didn't die, so there's no murder. Case closed."

"And forgetting someone attacked my dad and me," Kate said. "I guess that was a random mugging."

Jack and Sara didn't reply since they agreed.

"Let's go home and talk about what we're going to do," Sara said.

They were quiet until they reached home — then Sara let out a sound like a trapped animal. There were three cars parked in front of her door. It was an introvert's nightmare. She started sliding down in the seat, hiding from them all.

Kate took her aunt's hand and didn't let her get to the floor. Sara was so small she could fit in the space between the seat and the dashboard. "I'll take care of this."

"At least there are no police cars," Jack mumbled as he got out.

One of the cars was Sara's, which meant Randal had returned. But instead of parking at the side, out of the way, he was front and center. It looked like he had something to say.

Beside it was Arthur's big old sedan. In its day, it had been the height of fashion. When Arthur could no longer drive, he couldn't bear to part with his last vestiges of independence. He'd left it in the garage. When Everett moved in, he'd loved the car. "It reeks of old money," he'd told them, and he proudly drove it everywhere.

The last vehicle was Dora's, a cute red SUV.

All three of them were inside the house, sitting in the living room. Randal, always the host, was serving fruit punch laced with vodka. There was a tray of cheeses with four kinds of crackers.

Everett was eating like he was starving, all while staring at Randal with the wide eyes of an avid fan. After all, he'd written a book about the man but had never met him.

Dora was sitting so far forward on the edge of her seat that she looked like she might tip forward and fall facedown on the rug.

"What can I get for you?" Randal cheerfully asked them as they stood there staring.

Sara answered. "It's my house. I will do the asking."

Randal smiled. "Then I'll let you be hostess. I'd like a brandy, please. And could you put some olives out? I'm sure everyone would enjoy them." He sat down on the couch across from Everett — who hadn't blinked since they'd arrived.

If there was anything an introvert hated more than hosting a party, it would be hard to find. Sara, lips tight, took a seat next to Dora. She sat as far back as possible, her feet not even close to touching the floor. She and Dora looked like kids at opposite ends of a seesaw.

"Crap!" Jack muttered.

Kate stepped forward. She was used to being the bridge in their little family. She spoke first to Everett. "Why are you here?"

He didn't stop staring at Randal.

"Everett!" Kate said. "What do you need? Do you have something to tell us?"

Reluctantly, he looked at her. "Does anybody mind if I interview the man in the hospital?"

Randal stood up quickly. "I think that's a brilliant idea." He extended his arm, meant to usher Everett out. "Find out everything he knows. Befriend him. I bet you can get a bestseller out of him. It'll beat my sister's books by millions."

"You think so?" As he walked close beside Randal to the door, he looked as though he'd been hypnotized.

The others waited in silence until the door closed, the lock clicked and Randal returned. "One down," he said softly to Kate, then took his seat.

Everyone looked at Dora, who hadn't said a word, and waited.

She took a sip of her drink. "I wasn't snooping," she began. "And the truth is that I didn't pay attention to any of it. I never liked Walter Kirkwood. It's Tayla who I like."

She had everyone's attention. Sara quit sulking and slid forward on the couch.

"Herbert told me to tell you." She waited

for any replies to that. Herbert was Dora's deceased husband.

Nobody spoke. Kate, between Jack and her father, smiled in encouragement.

"It was your mother," Dora said to Kate.

Everyone's eyes widened, but Dora said no more.

Jack spoke. "You cleaned the sheriff's office. And the cells. You're so quiet and efficient and good at your job that I never really thought about it, but you must see a lot."

"Thank you," she said. "I appreciate that." She looked back at Kate. "I saw your mother there, locked up. She looked very angry. I thought she looked like she needed a friend so I told her I'd met her before, but she said I hadn't. It was only later that I remembered the photos I saw on the table here."

Sara and Kate looked at each other. They had forgotten to put away the photos from Jack's box.

Jack got the old photo of the three people and put in on the coffee table. Dora nodded that that was the one she meant.

"Herbert reminded me of it all by making me dream about it." She turned to Sara. "Remember the old Hendricks house?"

Sara nodded. "It was turned into a B and

349

B, wasn't it?"

"Yes. Mrs. Hendricks was a lovely woman. I was a waitress there, but I didn't like the job. People are too picky about their food." She looked at Kate. "That's where I saw her."

"My mother was there?"

Dora nodded. "She didn't have a room, just a meal."

"When was this?" Randal asked.

"Nineteen ninety-eight," Dora said. "Herbert and I were celebrating ten years of marriage. We had the most wonderful second honeymoon. We went to —" She looked at them, all waiting to hear her story. "I noted her because she was so skinny but she ordered a big steak and ate it all."

"She does," Kate said.

"I wouldn't have remembered it if Walter Kirkwood hadn't joined her."

There was a collective gasp from the others.

"You see," Dora said, "my mother had a crush on Walter. She said that in high school he was one of the Magnificent Three."

"He was," Randal said impatiently. "An undeserved accolade but given to him all the same. He and Ava were together?"

"Not like that," Dora said. "They didn't act like lovers but like friends. Close friends considering that what she said made Mr. Kirkwood cry."

Sara picked up the photo and pointed. "She made him cry? *This* man cried? How? Why?"

"Well, yes, but I wasn't really listening. I'd never do that."

"Of course not," Kate said.

"It was just that he was so angry and so very hurt." Dora hesitated.

"Angry about what?" Sara's impatience exactly matched her brother's.

Dora looked at her hands. "The woman was telling Mr. Kirkwood that their spouses were having an affair. His wife and her husband were lovers."

The others looked at Randal.

"I've heard this before but I didn't believe it," Sara said.

Randal shook his head. "Never happened."

"Why would Ava tell Walter you were having an affair with his wife?" Jack asked him.

Randal held his hands palms up. "I have no idea. Back then, Ava had one goal in life. She wanted Kate and me to return to Chicago so we'd be near her brothers. The doom prophets. I had no idea she had any other thoughts in her mind. If so, she never mentioned them to me."

351

Sara was frowning at her brother. "So she got Walter riled up so he'd . . . what? Threaten you?"

"I can't imagine what he planned to do," Randal said.

Jack spoke up. "We can't discount that Walter believed you'd ripped him off at the —" With a glance at Dora, he stopped. He wasn't going to mention the jewel robbery. "Walter would probably believe anything if it meant getting revenge on you."

Dora said, "I heard her say, 'They plan to take my child away from me.' It was so sad that I remember it all these years later."

Randal groaned. "Charlene. With Ava, it's always about Charlene. She was living with Tayla and Walter then, but I didn't know they were back in Florida. Later, I was told they left abruptly. I think we just heard why."

"Clever of Ava." Sara's voice held both admiration and disgust. "She got Charlene out of the way and no one knew the reason it happened."

"Until now." Unusual for Randal, there was venom in his voice.

"Poor Mother," Kate said. "She must have been near hysteria."

Dora stood up. "I have to go. I hope I haven't caused any problems."

"No," Sara said. "You've helped us a lot." She walked her to the door, then returned to the others.

Randal was glowering. "Ava told me she was going to church. I let her use the Mercedes. But she was meeting Walter and telling him lies about me."

"We know it's not the only place she went," Sara said.

"What does that mean?" Randal asked.

Jack told Mr. Ingles's story of the balloons and how Ava had been there often.

Randal was stunned. "Why?" he whispered.

"I suggest you go and ask her," Sara said forcibly. "In person. Now."

Jack's phone buzzed and he read the text. "Well! Here's a turn of events. Ava has been released. One of her relatives showed up to Cotilla with proof of Ava's alibi. On the morning the man fell out of Charlene's barn, Ava was on a plane back from Chicago. She didn't get back to Florida until about one thirty."

"But the DNA they found was hers," Sara said.

"No," Randal said to his sister. "It was that of a close relative of Kate's. It could have been *you*." He looked at Jack. "Any suggestion that my sister is about to be arrested for murder?"

"No. She wasn't there. She was . . ." He looked at Sara.

"I was home alone," Sara said. "Kissing no one. Alas." She wasn't taking Randal's idea seriously.

Kate had been quiet. "Which of her relatives came here?"

"They didn't say. Didn't she call one of your uncles?" Jack was tapping a return text.

"Ebenezer." Sara was grim. "He'll demand to stay in my house for free and we are to wait on him. And he'll tell of his latest glorious scheme that I should pay for." She looked at her brother. "He'll stay in the guesthouse with you."

"Oh no you don't. I'd be afraid to sleep."

"Since when do *you* sleep?" Sara shot back. "Everett says you tiptoe across roofs and —"

Jack cut in. "It's some guy named Noah."

"Noah?" Kate said, then smiled. "Noah." She grinned broadly. "It's Noah!" she yelled joyfully. "Oh no! I look awful." She ran into her bedroom and loudly closed the door behind her.

"Who the hell is Noah?" Jack half shouted.

Randal and Sara shrugged. They had no idea.

TWENTY-ONE

Thirty minutes later, Kate was still hidden away in her bedroom. Randal was in a chair by the window in the living room, reading. He said he had a lot to catch up on in the modern world. Jack knew he should go to the office, but he'd called Bea and said he was dealing with something else, then quickly hung up. Theoretically, since he was the newest at the job, he was the least important person. They all knew that wasn't true. But after the way Kate had acted about some guy named Noah, Jack wasn't about to leave.

Sara had photos to edit and she usually did that in her bedroom, laptop across her legs, big TV on. But today she was in the kitchen, wiping down spice jars in the tall rack. She too was waiting to find out about Kate.

"Why don't you call someone?" Jack was sitting on a stool at the kitchen island. He didn't need to say that he wanted her to find out who Noah was.

"And who would I call?" Sara asked.

"Ava. Ask her how she's feeling."

"And then she'd tell me," Sara said. "I'd have hours of hearing how miserable she is and it's all my fault. Randal didn't go see her so I must have kept him away. I sent her husband to prison so now I have to —"

"Okay," Jack said. "I get it. I thought Ebenezer was coming."

Sara put down her cloth and glared at him. "Yet again, I'll tell you that I don't know anyone named Noah — unless heroes in my books count. I had a father and son, both named Noah, who were really wonderful. True salt of the earth. Everyone else was going bonkers about some killer on the loose, but my two Noahs stayed cool. They were a joy to write about. They —" Jack's look was not friendly. "Anyway, I do not know a human Noah."

"Why would Ava call him?"

"I have never understood anything that my sister-in-law said or did. Why don't you go to work and ask questions? I bet Bea knows something."

"She'll think my concern is self-interest," he said gloomily.

"Based on your insane jealousy over any

356

male Kate so much as looks at? Yet you never make a positive move toward her? If you were in one of my books, the *real* hero — the Noah — would show up on a black stallion and take her away."

"That's unfair," Jack said. "I am very respectful of Kate. I —" The doorbell rang. "Who the hell is that?" He got off the stool and went to the door.

Sara followed him. "There is respect and there's laziness. It's past time for you to pick up the pace."

"Kate deserves only the best." He opened the door but kept looking at Sara. "Kate is too fine to —" He broke off at Sara's wide-eyed look and turned.

Standing in the doorway was a young man. He was beautiful. Tall, very muscular, honey-colored hair, blue eyes.

Sara thought about the heroes in her books. Jack was handsome with his dark features and sharp cheekbones, but there was a daredevil look about him. He was a man women lusted after and would risk everything for a night of wild pleasure.

But the man in the doorway was the guy a woman married, had children with, sat beside in church and grew old with.

"Hello," he said. "I'm Noah Preston. Does Kate Medlar live here?"

Great voice, beautiful teeth, perfect elocution.

"No," Jack said. "Try the next town over."

He started to shut the door, but Sara recovered her shock in time to put herself between the two men. "Yes, she does. Please come in. Can I get you something to drink? To eat?"

Jack followed them into the living room. "What?" he muttered. "No free car? A free place to live?"

Sara gave him a look to shut him up.

"No, ma'am," Noah said as he sat down. Sara sat across from him. "I just came to see Kate. Is she all right? All this with Aunt Ava must be hard on her."

Jack was standing at the end of the two sofas, never taking his eyes off Noah and not saying a word. Randal was silent. It was as though he was an audience of one and watching a fascinating movie.

"I think she'll be better now that you got Ava released," Sara said. "It was you who did that, wasn't it?"

"I did what I could. My father sent me here with dated photos and a boarding pass Aunt Ava had left behind. And there was a dated ticket to a prayer meeting."

"All of this on the day Ava said she was here?" Sara asked.

"Yes. The twenty-four hours before was a traumatic time. Aunt Ava and Dad and the uncles spent hours locked away and talking. We all heard her crying. I don't understand why she said she was here in Florida that morning, and certainly not why she said she hurt someone."

"How convenient." Jack took a seat next to Sara. He sat so close to her that they were like one person. It appeared to be two versus one. Randal was the silent audience.

Sara gave Jack a look and he moved a foot away. "I don't mean to be nosy but who are you?"

"Oh." Noah sounded disappointed. "I hoped Kate would have told you about me."

"She told us about her uncles," Jack said. "And the aunts and her first cousins. All her close blood relatives. I assume you're one of them, a close relation."

"Yes and no." When Noah smiled, Sara smiled back.

Jack was stoic. Randal watched with great interest.

"I guess I better explain. My father was a soldier who was killed in combat. He left behind my mother and me, a three-month-old baby."

"I'm sorry," Sara said.

"Thank you. For years, it was just Mom

and me. But then, Dad came into our lives. They married soon after meeting and we moved to Chicago."

"Dad?" Sara asked.

"Jedidiah Overby." Noah looked at Jack. "He's the youngest of the brothers. He's only a year older than Aunt Ava."

"I know who he is," Jack said tersely.

"How old were you when they married?" Sara asked.

"Six and Kate was almost five. She was the flower girl and I was the ring bearer at their wedding. We —"

Jack cut in. "Kate was still four? That means her uncle showed up with a new stepson just weeks after her father was hauled off to prison."

"I guess so," Noah said. "I was told that Kate's daddy had died and if I said anything about it, Kate would cry. I never asked." He turned to Sara. "I have photos of the wedding if you'd like to see them. Kate is really cute."

"I would love to see them," Sara said. "I guess you know that I was there until Kate was four."

"I do now, but I knew nothing about you or that Kate's father was alive until a few days ago. It's been a shock to me and I can't imagine what Kate has been through." He looked at Randal. "You're Mr. Medlar?"

"I am," Randal said. "But I can assure you that I'm not to be addressed as 'Uncle Randal.' "

"I understand," Noah said politely.

If possible, Jack's frown deepened. "Kate has us to help her. We're always here with her. We can —"

When the door to Kate's bedroom opened, they all turned to see her. She looked great. Her hair was so shiny it was like little slivers of mirror. Her makeup was subtle and perfect, and her sparkling eyes showed no evidence of the stress of the last few days.

Jack did his best to get to her first, but getting past Noah was like trying to go through a concrete wall.

Neither Kate nor Noah spoke. He just opened his big strong arms and she went to him. Her head seemed to fit exactly in the curve of his shoulder — and it certainly appeared to be a place she was familiar with.

Kate had been trying to stay strong but Noah's heart beating against her cheek took away her strength. "Mother won't talk to anyone, and now I have a father. And a man was shot in the head and —"

"Shhh," Noah said as he stroked her hair. "It's all going to be okay. Aunt Ava will talk to me and I'll find out what's going on. Come on and sit down and I'll tell you everything I know." He led her to the couches and they sat.

Noah kept his arm around Kate as he looked up at Jack, who was staring at them in shock. "Could you get her some water, please?"

Jack didn't move so Sara hurried to get two glasses of iced water and set them on the coffee table. She took a seat across from them, staring with undisguised curiosity. Had it been anyone else, she would have given them privacy, but nothing less than a bomb would have taken her away from Kate. Sara made a head jerk movement to Jack and he sat beside her, his arms crossed over his chest. His face was a mix of rage and an emotion so strong there was no word for it.

Like he was dealing with a child, Noah held the glass to Kate's lips so she could drink. "Mom died last year."

"No!" Kate said. "I loved her so much."

"And she loved you. You were her sanity among the girls."

Kate groaned. "Why didn't Mother tell me about her passing?"

Noah smoothed Kate's hair away from her face. "Because Aunt Ava is consumed with the fear of losing you. There is nothing and no one else on her mind."

"I know," Kate whispered. "I should have gone back to visit her, to visit all of you."

"It's okay. We've looked after Aunt Ava for years. She practically moved in with Dad and me after Mom died."

Kate's shoulders slumped in guilt. "I didn't know. I've been too absorbed in my own life here. I should have —"

Noah's arm tightened around her. "Your mother is the *worst* houseguest! Dad and I do all the cooking. And the chores. You should see Dad and me in the grocery. Did you know there are half a dozen different kinds of onions? We got one of each but your mother still said we didn't get the kind she likes best."

Kate sniffed. "She likes leeks and shallots. The expensive items."

"So we found out."

Sara handed Noah some tissues, he mouthed thanks and gave them to Kate.

She sat up straight and blew her nose. "What are you going to do now?"

"I got a job in Arizona."

Kate paused in blotting her eyes. "Arizona? Are they all going to move down there with you?"

"No. I'm going on my own. Just me."

"Oh," Kate said. "Oh."

"I wish you'd go with me. We could —"

Jack stood up so fast he nearly knocked over the heavy coffee table. "We need to leave. All of us. Now."

No one moved.

"You go," Sara said. "I'm sure you're needed at the office."

Jack wasn't used to Sara being on anyone's side except his and Kate's. He sat back down beside her.

Kate continued as though Jack hadn't interrupted. "You got a job? A real one?"

"As what?" Jack muttered. "A bouncer?"

Kate looked at him. "Noah is a theoretical physicist. It's not easy to find work in his line of expertise."

Jack, Sara and Randal blinked at the young man.

Noah looked at Sara. "I must say that you're not like I was told you were. In the last few days I've heard so much about you that I expected horns and a tail."

Sara didn't smile. "They're always with me. I just cover them with clothes and makeup."

Noah turned to Randal, who raised an eyebrow. "Did you expect me in an orange suit and handcuffs?"

Noah laughed. "I see where Kate gets her

sense of humor." He looked around the house. "This isn't the prison I was told it was."

Kate knew what he'd been told. Her mother often spoke of her daughter being held prisoner. "I'm free to come and go whenever and wherever. You'll have to see my office and I'll drive you around town and show you all the houses I've sold."

"I brought photos of when we were kids. Remember the wedding and the rose petals I put in your hair?"

"I remember how we stole chocolates and hid under a table and ate them all. We —"

Jack interrupted. "You remember that but not your father being taken away in handcuffs?"

Kate turned on him. "Ever hear of blocking out traumatic events? PTSD?"

Jack stood up abruptly. "Could I see you alone?"

"Noah just got here," she said. "We haven't seen each other in ages."

Noah put his hand on her arm. "Go ahead. I'll be fine."

"She doesn't need your permission to leave," Jack said. "She can —"

Kate glared at him, then went to her bedroom, Jack close behind her. She closed the door, but the others could hear every word they said. Noah politely excused himself from the room, but Sara and Randal listened as though unable to get away.

In the bedroom, Jack spoke first. "Your father was taken away to prison and just months later your uncle brings home an unrelated boy? I think maybe your uncle went out and found a future husband for you. It's like something out of a book about arranged marriages."

"That's disgusting," Kate said.

"You two look chummy enough, so why didn't you marry him?"

"And move in with the uncles, aunts and my weird cousins? No thanks. Noah couldn't leave his mother and she refused to leave Uncle Jed."

"So he *did* ask you."

"Not that it's any of your business, but yes he did."

Jack took a step back and lowered his voice. "He should have done anything to get you."

"Noah thinks of people other than himself. He couldn't leave. His mother had no income and Noah had no job. The uncles paid for his years at school so he owes them."

"You've kept all these secrets for years."

Kate grimaced. "That I didn't tell you

everything in my life before you came into it does not qualify as 'keeping secrets.' Have you told me about every woman you've been to bed with? Every crime you've committed? I don't even know the extent of your juvenile record."

"It's not the same," Jack said. "But right now that doesn't matter."

"Why? Because I'm female and you're a big strong male? You know what? Under your façade of being a modern man, you're just like my uncles. You're the rogue and I'm supposed to be a virgin."

"Virgin? What are you talking about? I'm saying that none of this is a coincidence. Your father was sent to prison and suddenly you're paired up with a noncousin. Your father reappears and suddenly that pseudo cousin shows up. It's all too neat and tidy."

"You make me sound like a very valuable commodity. That's absurd."

Jack's voice lowered more. "But Sara supports everyone, doesn't she? They wouldn't want to lose that."

"You are horrible!" Kate yelled at him, but the doubt could be heard in her voice. Her tone and her words didn't match. She left the sitting room and went outside to the garden.

Jack knew better than to follow her. He got in his truck and went to his office.

TWENTY-TWO

Sara couldn't take hearing anymore. She didn't like seeing Jack or Kate upset, and worse was that Kate's obvious affection for Noah seemed to hold too much possibility. The idea that her and Jack's secure little world could turn upside down was something Sara couldn't handle.

She went to her bedroom, closed the double doors behind her, grabbed her big iPad and went into her tiny private garden. When Jack was remodeling the old house, he'd called it Sara's Safe Room. She put birdseed out every morning and sometimes the squawking got very loud. But Sara loved it. There were many nonindigenous, flamboyantly colored birds in Florida. People bought the exotic birds, tired of taking care of them, then released them — or they escaped. They thrived in Florida's tropical climate. Sara scattered seed around her big, heavy Tommy Bahama chair, then settled down with a movie on her iPad. She needed all the distraction she could create.

Randal left when Sara did. He couldn't bear hearing what was being said. That Jack was probably right about everything hurt him deeply. It didn't help that he knew none of this would have happened to Kate if he'd been there.

Sara had left her extra set of car keys in a pretty African basket by the door. "So you can stop hot-wiring my car," she'd said. She'd tried to sound like he was a burden but he knew that inside her was great generosity. Part of the problem now was that she'd supported Kate and Ava for all those years and a lot of those funds had gone to the brothers. Those men didn't want to give that up.

Once he was in Sara's car, he knew where he was going. He needed privacy and time to think about all he'd learned.

Kate was the last to escape the turmoil. When she went back into the house and saw that everyone was gone, she grabbed her bag and left. She wanted to take Sara's car. She'd like to go fast and whip around corners, but she had to take her sedate four door.

She didn't consciously think about where

she was going, but it was like her car was on autopilot. She ended up at Sara's old house. She wondered if the balloons were still inside, the ones meant to help her remember the past. Jack had been right when he said it was odd that she remembered being a flower girl in a wedding but didn't remember her father being taken away to prison.

She didn't want to park where someone could see her car, so she drove to the back. She wasn't surprised to see Sara's MINI. It looked like her father was also trying to escape the past.

Randal wasn't in sight but she had an idea where he was. When Sara was growing up, the Wyatts lived next door. Jack's grandfather, Cal, and Sara had been best friends and eventually lovers. There was a place between the two houses where they met.

Kate walked down the old path. Cal, whose father had an auto repair shop, had laid the way with flattened hubcaps. Now they were nearly hidden beneath Florida's abundant growth, but they were still there.

Between the houses was a level place with remnants of a concrete floor. To the side she saw her father, shirtsleeves rolled up and digging with a shiny shovel. It was an amusing sight. As always, Randal was exquisitely dressed. It wasn't what a ditchdigger wore.

She sat down on what was left of a rusty bench.

Randal didn't look up. "How did you get away?"

"Walked out."

He nodded. "Medlars aren't ones for confrontation if it can be avoided."

"Aunt Sara's sarcasm can kill most arguments."

Randal smiled. "That it can. But today was too much for all of us. Jack sounded just like his father."

"He said some things that I didn't like hearing."

"I know. He made all of us think."

They were silent for a moment, then Kate said, "Is that Aunt Sara's shovel? The expensive one she ordered from England?"

Smiling, he looked at her. "It is. Will you turn me in?"

She looked around at the palm trees and the undergrowth. "Are you digging up the jewels you and Walter and the sheriff and Jack's dad stole?"

Randal laughed. "I wish I were. When I was a child, I buried four boxes full of loot." The shovel hit metal. "Here's the first one." He pulled a clean white handkerchief out of his pocket, bent and tugged a metal box from the earth. "Shall we look inside?"

"I'd love to."

There was an old step to the side and they sat on it, the box between them.

"I guess I'm to pry it open, dirt and all." She picked up the box and began working at the lid. "I certainly didn't inherit your fastidiousness."

"Your mother loves to garden," he said softly.

Kate halted. "Does she? I never saw her plant anything. The uncles have huge gardens but —" The top came loose. "We should have a drumroll." She lifted the rusty lid. Inside was a nest of cheap old jewelry: necklaces of plastic beads, earrings with the gold paint flaked off, bracelets with colored glass stones. It was a sad little hoard, full of things a child would think were pretty, maybe even valuable. But they weren't. They were just sparkly trash. She set the box down between them and looked at the plants moving in the breeze. "Why?" she asked. "What made you steal things?"

"I could say poverty. That's the usual poor-little-me answer. It gets lots of sympathy from rich do-gooders. But it was deeper than that. I think it had to do with my mother. And Sara."

Kate turned fierce eyes to him. "You are *not* going to blame her."

Randal smiled. "The Medlar bond is alive and well. No. That's not what I meant. It was the war between Sara and our mother."

Kate pulled her legs up, put her arms around them and rested her chin on her knees. "Tell me."

"I guess you've realized that Sara isn't like other people. She was always smart and quick-witted. Never at a loss for a fast comeback. It was like being with Dorothy Parker. But Sara's flaw has always been that she can't bear boring or stupid people. If my sister met a serial killer, she'd be fascinated and would ask him a lot of questions."

"Not like her mother," Kate said.

"Far from it. Mother was socially awkward, not smart or creative and always complaining."

"Just like — !" Kate cut herself off, but they both knew what she had almost said. *Just like my mother!*

"Anyway," Randal said, "Sara just plain wasn't interested in our mother."

"Then you came along."

Randal gave a chuckle. "I've always been able to quickly assess a situation. From a very young age I knew that being nice to Mother got me *anything*. By the third grade,

I was experimenting. Was there anything I could do that would make my mother not defend me? No! I never found a single thing."

"And she blamed Sara for everything."

Randal nodded. "Yes, she did. Whatever wrong thing I did, Mother said it was because of Sara." He paused for a moment. "Sara never realized it, but I adored her. I envied her so much. She never gave in to baser urges, never forgot who she was. And she and Cal had each other. I used to fantasize about finding someone like that."

"What about your father?"

Randal gave a snort of derision. "He was terrified of his wife. Today they would have divorced but back then, no. He escaped with hobbies and reading crime novels. He couldn't handle the war between Sara and Mother."

"Did Aunt Sara and your mother ever reconcile? Even a bit?"

Randal shook his head. "Sara tried once. It was just before she left for college. Left us forever. Something had happened between her and Cal. It had to do with Walter Kirkwood, but I'm not sure what. Sara was . . . Well, I've never seen her so low."

"What happened?"

"She told Mother that she was in pain and

needed a friend. Mother . . ." Randal took a breath. "I shouldn't have heard this and I wish I hadn't. Mother told Sara that she'd always been a terrible child and no parent could have stood her. She said Sara had hurt her every day since her birth. Mother concluded by saying that she had only one child. If that wasn't enough, years later, at the trial, Mother told Sara that her jealousy had put me in prison."

"That's not true," Kate said. "None of it."

"Of course it's not."

She looked at him. "Who did send you to prison?"

Randal took a moment before answering. "I think it was Ava's brothers."

Kate was surprised. "How? Why?"

"Jack seems to be coming to the same conclusion. Control over me and thereby over Sara's wealth. It's all connected. If they got rid of me, I'm sure they thought they'd be able to control Sara."

"Like they rule Mother."

"Yes, like that. They really are an evil bunch."

Kate looked at her father, her feelings showing in her eyes. What would her life have been like if he'd always been there? She wouldn't have had to deal with her mother's debilitating depressions by herself.

For sure, they wouldn't have lived near the uncles. Aunt Sara would have always been in her life.

Randal put his arm out and she went to him, placing her head on his shoulder. "I'm so sorry," he said. "I'm just now hearing what you had to go through while I was away. Sara told me about Ava's depression. You were left to take care of yourself. And I know why you couldn't ask for help."

"The authorities would have given custody of me to the uncles."

"Yes. I'm sorry I wasn't there. Sorry for all of it."

She heard the tears in his voice and for a while they sat there, holding on to each other.

Randal broke the spell as he became alert. He released her.

"What is it?"

"Nothing. I thought I heard someone. Prison makes a person vigilant — and paranoid." He looked at her. "We left your two young men alone. Do you think they've killed each other yet?"

"I can only hope so," Kate said.

"Which one of them are you planning to choose?"

"Aunt Sara and I are going to run away to Scotland and have mad love affairs with men who wear kilts."

"I'll go with you and be the laird of a castle. I think a kilt would suit me."

She stood up. "I better go back. I'm going to have to face Mother." She gave him a pointed look.

Randal sighed. "Yes, I must find her and talk to her."

She nodded at the box. "Do we take it or rebury it?"

He picked it up with his handkerchief. "I think I'll wash all of it, then have everything appraised. Who knows? Maybe I accidently borrowed something valuable."

Kate narrowed her eyes. "If you did, we'll find the true owner and return it."

"Oh yes. Of course we will."

His tone was so insincere that she laughed. "Come on, Mr. Cat Burglar. Let's go stand up to the Wrath of Ava." She was parodying *Star Trek II: The Wrath of Khan*. It was funny, but comparing Ava to the overlord Khan was so real that they both groaned.

Against her father's protest, Kate put the box of jewelry in her car.

TWENTY-THREE

Just as Kate was about to get into her car, her phone dinged. It was a text from Sara.

> Sent the boys to the gym to fight it out.
> Ava is here. Please save me.

She added emojis of praying hands and a crying face.

Kate started to tell her father but thought better of it. He might run away and hide. To be sure he went home, she followed close behind him. She didn't even allow him to park at the end of the drive by the guesthouse. Too easy to escape.

"Ava's here, isn't she?" Randal asked as he got to the front door. "She's waiting for us."

Kate's silence was the reply.

"My darling daughter, whatever happens, know that I love you. Always have and always will."

379

Before she could say anything, Randal went inside the house, with Kate close behind him.

Sara and Ava were sitting across from each other — and Ava was doing all the talking. "None of this would have happened if it hadn't been for you. You could have prevented it, but you kept on and on. You would *not* stop."

Sara's face was like a stone mask. If she was hearing her sister-in-law, she gave no sign of it.

"Stop." Randal's voice was quiet but held authority. He sat down beside Sara, and Kate sat on the other side of her.

"I'm alone!" Ava said. "By myself." She stood up. "I don't have to take this. I'm leaving."

This time, Randal didn't speak. He made a gesture for her to sit and she obeyed.

"Mother," Kate said, "why did the man who owned the Bentley visit you in jail?"

Ava crossed her thin arms across her chest. "I have no idea what you mean, and I don't like your attitude. You have changed. Did she teach you to talk to me like this? With no respect?"

Randal leaned forward. "Did your brothers ask you to talk to Walter?"

"Tayla's husband?" Ava asked. "She's as

380

bad as your sister. She —"

"Mother, please," Kate said. "We'd like you to answer our questions. There are some things we don't understand. Remember the pink and purple balloons? You cut two of them for me."

Ava smiled. "Imagine you remembering that! I've always done everything for you. It was just us for so many years." She glared at Sara. "Until *you* came back into our lives."

For a second, Kate closed her eyes. "Why were you there?"

When Ava said nothing, Sara spoke. "Why did you tell Walter that Randal and Tayla were having an affair?"

Ava sneered at her. "I had to get rid of all of them. She was there! She was going to take what was mine."

Sara pieced that together. "All of them" was the Kirkwood family. "You mean Charlene was in Lachlan and Randal would leave you for her."

Ava didn't answer.

"My father didn't know Charlene was here," Kate said.

Ava snorted. "He would have found her. He always did." She glared at Randal. "I only did what I had to."

Randal had been quiet, but said, "What

381

does the Bentley man know about you?"

"Lies. All lies," Ava said. "He has no proof. I told him that. Edison said —" She closed her mouth.

"Edison said what?" Randal asked.

"Nothing." Ava looked at her daughter. "Did you see Noah? Isn't he handsome? Jed always said he would be. Now that his mother is gone, you can have him. She was always too possessive. I told Noah that if he played his cards right, you and he would be together. You two could —"

"Ava!" Randal snapped. "What do you have to do with the Bentley man and Captain Edison?"

"And Walter Kirkwood?" Sara added. "Why were you watching the man next door to the balloons?"

Ava's body tightened. "I'm not going to do this." She stood up. "I did what I had to. What I was forced to do." She looked at Kate. "You don't understand how serious it all was. My husband, your father, was going to leave us for her. For that baby stealer."

"No," Kate said. "I told you! Dad didn't know Charlene was here." Kate's temper was rising. She stood up, face-to-face with her mother, something she'd never before had the courage to do. "Dad had a job and he was taking care of us. You were doing nothing but riding around in a borrowed Mercedes and stealing balloons."

"Nothing?" Ava shouted. "Is that the appreciation I get? I fixed our lives. Do you think he would have taken you with him when he left with her? I arranged it all. Walter took that harlot away. Then I had your father removed from all temptation by putting him safely away. And I got your rich aunt to pay for everything. Why am I not appreciated — thanked! — for what I did? I saved everyone."

There was silence in the room. The air felt heavy and thick. It was the quiet that comes before a storm that will devastate the country.

Kate sat down hard on the couch, her eyes never leaving her mother's.

Sara and Randal stared, their minds trying to understand what they'd just heard.

"You . . ." Kate whispered. "It was *you* who sent my father to prison? Is that what you call 'keeping him from temptation'? 'Putting him away?' "

Ava looked at her husband, her face defiant. "There was no other way. And it all worked out. You weren't unhappy in that place. You made lots of friends, and I helped by bringing you all those cookies. Now we just need to be a family again. Away from *her."*

Randal's handsome face showed no emotion. He was utterly calm as he stood up, straightened the crease in his trousers, then looked at his wife. "Of course I would have taken Kate with me since Charlene gave birth to her."

Ava looked like she'd been hit. She nearly choked as she said, "You promised you would never tell."

Randal said nothing, just went to the front door and walked out.

TWENTY-FOUR

Jack was nearly knocked over by Randal as he hurried out of Sara's house. "Did something happen?" he asked, but Randal kept his head down and didn't answer.

Noah had to step aside to let Randal pass. "Hello, Mr. Medlar. Are you all right?"

Randal went past the two men, got into Sara's car and sped away. By the time he reached the road, he was doing at least ninety.

"Do you think someone was hurt?" Noah asked. He and Jack had done some male bonding over the weights. Noah was better at the bench press, and a squat rack was his second home. While Noah was a feet-in-place lifter, Jack was more versatile. He kept boxing gear in his truck and suggested using it. Noah instantly learned that if he didn't want to get hit by Jack's big black gloves, he had to move quickly.

After a couple of hours of pounding and

grunting, they weren't friends but they were less enemies. During the entire time, they hadn't spoken one word about their rivalry.

As soon as the men entered the house, they heard a woman's loud, frantic voice. "You do understand, don't you, Kate? I had to do what I did. There was no other choice."

"Aunt Ava sounds upset," Noah said.

Sara and Kate were sitting close together, holding hands like first graders. Standing in front of them, bent and hovering, was Ava, and she was talking loud and fast.

"He was always getting into trouble with the law. You don't know this but your father *stole* things! He robbed people's houses. He was with old Mrs. Meyers just so he could steal from her, but I knew Captain Edison was after him. The sheriff was going to *shoot* him. Is that what you wanted, Kate? For your father to be killed? I kept him *alive.* Handcuffs were better than bullets. Why does no one see that? Why is no one thanking me? Why — ?"

When Sara saw the men, she looked at Noah. Very calmly, she said, "Take her away or I will kill her."

Noah hesitated, but Jack reacted. "Get her out of here!"

Noah went to Ava and gently started to

386

lead her away, but she pushed at his hands.

"I can't go. I have to make Kate see the truth. Our life was good, wasn't it? We had everything. Love and happiness were ours. You had a big, happy family with uncles and cousins. And a mother who loves you. We all love you." She reached out to Kate, who twisted out of reach. "I gave up my husband for you," Ava pleaded. "The man I love! What mother makes a sacrifice like that for anyone? I did it just for you. Everything was for you."

Sara looked at Jack. He put his hands on Ava's narrow shoulders and turned her toward Noah. "Take her out. Now."

"Come on, Aunt Ava," Noah said. "Let's go get something to eat."

She tried to get out of his grasp but he held on and led her to the door. "No! This is important. I don't think Kate understands. She's been brainwashed by all of them. She can't think clearly. I have to explain until she understands that I'm the good person. I have to —"

Noah closed the door behind them.

Jack was looking down at Kate. She was staring straight ahead but didn't seem to be seeing anything.

Kneeling, he held out his arms to her. It took her a moment but she slid into them.

He carried her into her bedroom and put her on the bed. As he pulled the sheet over her, he saw Sara in the doorway.

"What caused this?" he asked softly.

Sara let out her breath. "Ava put Randal in prison and Charlene is Kate's biological mother."

Jack had no words.

"Stay with her. I'm going to find my brother." Sara held out her hand and Jack put his truck keys in it.

After Sara left, Jack went back to Kate. As he'd done before, he held her in his arms, their bodies separated only by the bed linens. "When you're ready to talk, I'm here," he said. "I won't leave you. Ever."

Kate said nothing.

Between a couple of hours at the gym and the comfort of holding Kate, Jack fell asleep. He awoke when the front door slammed shut. His first sense was panic. Kate was nowhere to be seen. His mind flooded with possibilities of what the trauma she'd just experienced would make her do. Seek out Ava? Have it out with her? It had always bothered him that Kate was so ruled by the little woman. That it had all been a lie might push Kate over the edge.

The double doors to the bedroom were

thrown open by Sara. "Where is she?"

"I'm here." Kate came out of her bathroom. Her hair was in a ponytail and she had on black leggings and a red tunic. It was her at-home clothes. "How's Dad?"

"I dumped him on Daryl. They can cry together. Oh, the unfairness of the world."

The women were staring at each other. Jack thought they looked so much alike that they were almost the same person. "What am I missing?"

"Guilt!" the women said in unison.

Jack got off the bed. "As I was told today, I'm just a clueless male so please explain things to me."

"Kate and I no longer have to carry around a backbreaking amount of guilt. My testimony did *not* put my brother in prison."

"The uncles," Kate said. "I never have to deal with them again."

"You know," Jack said, "you only feel guilt if you accept it."

Both women turned identical looks of such ferocity on him that he put up his hands in protection. "Sorry," he whispered.

"Oh! Dad said, 'Your mother loves to garden.' He meant Charlene." Kate looked at her aunt. "Has she been told?"

Before Sara could answer, Jack crooked

both his arms, the women took them, and he led them to the kitchen. When they were seated on the stools, he began preparing a drink he hated but they loved: matcha lattes. He dissolved the dark green tea in hot water.

"Randal called Tayla," Sara said. "Of course she and Leland know where Charlene is."

"Never doubted it. Oh no! Dad won't think that now he and Charlene can . . . you know. Get together?"

"Absolutely not!" Sara said. "In fact . . ." She paused to give drama to her story. "I called Stefan, my dear travel agent, and I booked Randal on a four-month-long cruise."

Smiling, Kate nodded. "Good idea. Brilliant, really. Let him see the world."

"And get him away from Charlene," Jack mumbled as he heated a pot of almond milk.

"Charlene's boys," Kate said. "They're my half brothers."

"And my grandchildren," Sara said.

Jack frowned. "Since their father is Leland and not your brother, I don't think they're related to —"

The women gave him hard looks.

"I'm sure they'd love to have more grandmothers." He put the frother in the milk, then poured it all together, filled two tall

390

mugs and set them before the women. "The DNA on the dead guy. Since it was from your mother, we assumed it was Ava's."

"There's still an unknown person's DNA on the dead man," Sara said.

Jack nodded. "Actually, there are still several unsolved mysteries. Did Randal say anything about the, uh, handover? You know, when Kate was a baby?"

Sara looked at her niece. "He'll tell you more later, but I got the basics of the story from him. Tayla's mother showed up at Randal's door with a newborn baby girl. She threatened him with imprisonment if he didn't take his daughter — you — and leave Lachlan immediately — and keep his mouth shut forever. She said he had twenty-four hours to come up with names of parents and a name for the kid to be put on the birth certificate. It was a private clinic and they were paid to overlook indiscretions."

Kate sipped her hot drink and nodded. "And Mother — I mean Ava — was close by. I've always had the idea that when they lived in Lachlan she stalked him."

"That's the gossip I heard," Sara said. "She and her brothers were here for some conference. She saw Randal and went after him."

"Like a groupie after a rock star," Jack said. When the women looked at him, he shrugged. "That's what Randal told me."

"Need and supply," Kate said. "Dad had no idea what to do with an infant and Mother had grown up surrounded by babies."

Sara continued. "Ava wouldn't agree to help — or keep the secret — unless he legally married her. Randal didn't elaborate, but I think that since he'd told her the truth, Ava hinted that she might tell the secret. That could have caused him to lose custody of you."

Kate and Jack nodded at that. It sounded like Ava.

"Anyway," Sara said, "Ava's name was put on the birth certificate as the mother. They immediately left for Chicago and were married in Tennessee."

"And Charlene was left behind, believing that her child was stillborn," Kate said.

"Tayla was shouting on the phone about that. Her mother let Charlene hold a . . ."

"Yeah," Kate said. "Her stillborn son. Only the child wasn't hers."

The women sipped their drinks in silence.

"So now what?" Jack asked. He was leaning on the counter.

"I don't ever, ever have to go back to

Chicago," Kate said.

Sara sighed. "All these years we could have been together. If I'd known, I would have fought for custody of you. I would have . . ." She put down her drink. "I'm still having trouble comprehending all of it. Ava sent Randal to prison."

"How did she do it?" Jack asked.

"Randal figured out what she did. He said it was like a game of dominoes." Sara was shaking her head in disbelief. "Ava used bits from everyone to make it all happen. Daryl told Walter about the Bentley guy. Meanwhile, Ava was lying to Walter, trying to get him to take Charlene away. When Walter told her about Bentley being investigated, she looked into it."

"Mother watched the Bentley guy so she knew exactly what was going on."

"Yes," Sara said. "But then, Ava was experienced at stalking. All she had to do was make it look like Randal was involved. She called him and offered him a job. It was all quite clever of her."

They took a moment to think about the depth of Ava's manipulations and lies. She'd played everyone against each other. Used their anger and feelings of injustice to get what she wanted. Her husband was put far away from "temptation."

"I bet she told Walter that Randal still had lots of jewels hidden away," Jack said.

"Probably," Sara said. "The worst thing is that I don't think Ava can be prosecuted for what she did. Other than gossiping lies, all she did was make a call to Randal. She falsely offered him a job, then she made all the evidence of that offer disappear. Randal had no proof of innocence. Sheriff Edison did the rest."

"They're dead," Jack said. "Edison, Walter. I don't think the Bentley guy is going to stand up and do the honorable thing of telling the truth."

"Certainly not!" Sara said. "Daryl found out that the house where Bentley met you two belonged to his late mother-in-law."

"Bet it'll be put up for sale now," Kate said.

Sara and Jack looked at her.

"Just saying. I still have to earn a living." Kate got off her stool. "This changes everything. My entire life changed in just minutes."

Sara was looking at her niece. "What will you do about her?"

They knew she meant Ava.

"I don't know. I guess I should be angry."

"Anger eats at you," Jack said. "It destroys everything inside and around you. You begin to see the world through a fog of pure hatred." He spoke from experience.

Kate sat down on the arm of the big sofa in the family room. "I want to think that Mother meant well."

"She seems to believe that you had a good childhood," Jack said softly.

They were thinking of what Kate had been through: her mother's depressions when she left everything to her young daughter, years of trying to elude the uncles and their self-righteousness. There'd been a lifetime of lies to Kate about her father. It wasn't easy to fully comprehend that her mother's jealousy had not only taken him away, but had imprisoned him.

"If I started to hate," Kate said, "I'd never be able to stop. I want to go forward, not backward."

Sara looked serious. "Whatever happened in the past, it's made you into a kind, caring, smart, creative person. Maybe we *should* thank Ava."

That was so ridiculous that they burst into laughter.

TWENTY-FIVE

Lenny's head hurt and he could barely move parts of his body. The doctor said he'd recover, but Lenny knew his career was over. There'd be no more climbing up the side of a barn and propelling himself into a loft. The doctor said it was a miracle he was alive. All Lenny knew for sure was that he very much wanted to continue living.

It was early morning, but Everett was already there. He had three tall paper cups full of hot chocolate and a big bag of pastries. "I didn't buy any of that keto stuff Sara likes," he was saying. "She may tell herself that it's the same as real food but it's not. I can hardly bring myself to eat it. So how are you feeling today?"

Even when Lenny could talk, he'd never been one to socialize. As a kid he'd stayed away from people. He was content to live with his father in the old hunting cabin, going for days without saying a word. Today they would be called survivalists, but back then they were just people who wanted to be left alone. Lenny blinked once to let Everett know he was all right.

"So where was I?" Everett began, his mouth full. "I think I should recap because I have a lot to tell you. Ava! That woman!" Everett gave a little shudder. "I never told you about when I met her, did I?" But of course he had. "She sicced her odious brothers on me. I was just asking about her husband. You'd think she'd want to tell me everything. Maybe I could help get him out of prison. But no. She threatened my life. My *life*!"

Lenny, floating in and out of hearing and understanding, did his best to smile. He wanted to do all he could to encourage Everett to stay with him. His presence was keeping Lenny from being killed by whoever shot him, then later tried to smother him. Lenny tried to nod at Everett's retelling of Ava's relatives as he watched everyone. Lenny knew that something had made someone want to kill him, but he didn't know what it was. He assumed it was from this job. The others were clean. So what happened this time? Was it about the guy who fell out of the barn window? Or did Lenny see someone? Hear something?

He blacked out for a moment and came back to Everett's voice.

"So you can imagine my shock when I heard all that! No wonder Ava wouldn't tell me about Randal."

Everett had moved his chair closer to Lenny's bed, which meant that he was telling him something he didn't want the hospital staff to hear.

Whatever anyone thought of Everett, Lenny knew the man was the best snoop in the world. The CIA should use him. Scotland Yard. INTERPOL. But whatever he spoke of, if it had anything to do with the Medlars, the foundation of the story was about jewels. Jewels on top of jewels. He realized that Everett was still talking. Lenny blinked rapidly. His eyelids were the only thing he could fully control.

"Oh!" Everett said. "You didn't hear?"

They had a code: twice for no; once for yes. Rapid for "heard nothing, please repeat."

Everett looked around to assure himself that no one was near. He lowered his voice. "Ava isn't Kate's biological mother. Charlene is. Charlene had her when she was a teenager."

Lenny's eyes opened wider. Charlene was the woman he'd been hired to watch. She was the one the guy with the rifle was watching. Was seeing this what got him shot?

"And . . ." Everett paused dramatically. He did so love a good drama. "Ava was the one who sent Randal to prison."

This time Lenny's blinks were in genuine surprise. How was all of this related? How did this go from some kid born over twenty years ago to Lenny sitting in a car and being shot?

Everett was talking again, only this time it was about himself and how he planned to put everything in a book — or several of them — and make millions. "Arthur wants us to wait until Sara figures out who is killing people this time, then she'll plot our next book for us. Of course I admire her greatly — we're practically besties — but I want to write about *you.* All about what you've done and seen. And any, uh, crimes. It would be anonymous, of course. Just our secret. But Arthur is balking. He says Sara plotted our first book and she can do the second one."

Everett took his last eclair out of the bag. "I want to hear about *you.*"

His fantasy of being told of Lenny's life was a twice daily plea. The first time Lenny woke and heard the plan, he'd tried to get out of the bed and run away. When his body wouldn't move, he had to face the reality that was now his life.

In the days since he was shot, and since surviving a second murder attempt, Lenny had changed. He realized he'd never considered retirement. But then he'd never imagined living to the age he was now. Never thought he'd live long enough to be called "old man." Long enough that kids wanted to say they took out a "legend."

But here he was, in a hospital, head bandaged, arms full of tubes, and he very much wanted to live. The life Everett told him about, of living with grumpy old Arthur in his wheelchair and telling Everett about his business was beginning to appeal to him. Of course the truth was boring. Sitting in cheap motels and waiting was most of it. But he'd heard some stories! He'd just tell them all to Everett and say he'd done everything himself.

Lenny drifted off to sleep, and when he woke there were other people in the room. When he fluttered his eyes, Everett recognized the fear and told them to go away. Lenny had never had anyone mother him and he was beginning to like it. He had no idea what happened to his own mother. He'd asked his father about her once but he'd received no answer. He didn't ask again.

At sixteen, Lenny left the cabin. What education he had was self-taught. It hadn't taken long to find out that his lack of government-recorded identity and his ability to handle any firearm were valuable assets.

It was in the late afternoon that Lenny saw someone he recognized. But no, the voice was wrong. So was the body. It was the eyes that he remembered.

Lenny's emotion, his fear, made the machine he was hooked up to begin to beep loudly and nurses came quickly. When the doctor got there, he told Everett to leave, but Lenny squeezed the man's hand. One thing about drama queens is that they can be turned on like high-powered floodlights. Everett's loud, flamboyant hysterics were like a stadium at night. He reminded the medical people that an unknown person had tried to kill Lenny. If it happened again, did they want to be responsible? The word *malpractice* flooded the room. They let him stay. "Don't worry," Everett said loudly to Lenny so everyone could hear. "I won't leave you." A cot was put in the room.

For the first time since he'd been shot, Lenny slept in peace.

"How are you?" Sara asked Kate the next morning. They'd had hours to let yesterday's news sink in. The initial euphoria of escaping guilt was buried under the question of *Now what do we do?* There were still problems to be solved, and Ava was at the top of the list.

"Surprisingly well," Kate answered.

Jack was in his uniform and sitting on a stool at the kitchen island. "I think you should stay with me today. I'll be at the office. You can read or watch videos. Something."

"I'm fine. Really," she assured them.

"You —" Jack began but stopped at a look from Sara.

"Mother — I mean Ava — wants to see me."

"I'll be ready in minutes," Sara said. "I'll —"

"No!" Kate lowered her voice. "I need to do this on my own."

"You won't let her talk you into leaving, will you?" Jack asked.

"Far from it." She looked at Sara. "I heard your phone ringing last night. Any news?"

"Tayla called me."

402

Jack and Kate raised their eyebrows. Those two weren't friends.

Sara ignored their looks. "She's angry. Leland told Charlene."

"And?" Kate asked.

"Charlene collapsed. I got a text a few minutes ago and Charlene has been crying for hours."

"Don't tell Randal," Jack said.

"I have no intention of telling my brother anything about Charlene," Sara said. "Daryl texted me that Randal is with him, and they've had visitors. I think everyone knows Daryl is still in town."

"Good," Jack said. "I can get out of this thing." He motioned to his uniform.

"Daryl won't let you," Sara said. "Not until this crime has been solved."

"Randal being sent to prison for a crime he didn't commit isn't enough?" The Wyatt temper was rising. "What was done to Charlene wasn't enough? If Tayla's mother was alive I'd arrest her. Slam her into a cell and leave her there to rot."

"And what would you charge her with?" Sara asked. "Ruining lives isn't a crime."

"Should be," Kate said softly.

They turned to her.

She put up her hands. "My life was not ruined. Look at me. I'm happy. I'm . . ."

She glared at them. "If anyone feels sorry for me, I'll start screaming. Got it?"

They nodded.

"So now I'm going to see the person who caused all this."

"We —" Sara said.

"I —" Jack said.

"No! Absolutely not." Kate calmed herself. "Jack, go see Gil and tell him what's going on. All of it."

"Sure you want more people to know?" he asked.

Sara grimaced. "By now, probably everyone at Bessie's is talking about it. I wouldn't be surprised if they're planning a baby shower for Charlene. They can shoot pink glitter out of a cannon."

"And use real gunpowder and kill someone," Jack said gloomily.

Kate almost laughed. "Think they make onesies to fit me?"

Jack and Sara didn't smile.

Kate looked at her watch. "I have to go. I'm meeting Mother —" She took a breath. "This is hard. What do I call her? Anyway, I'll be at the old Medlar house."

"Right," Sara said. "Meant to evoke memories. To remind you of the poverty you got away from by growing up near glamorous Chicago."

"I assume so," Kate said. "Whatever the reason, I'm to meet her there."

They followed Kate to the door, and she picked up her bag.

Sara and Jack acted like she was leaving for a long trip. Sara kissed her cheek and for a moment Jack held her so tightly she could hardly breathe. Kate didn't protest.

Minutes later, she was at the old house and Ava was standing at the back, waiting for her.

"Someone has been digging here," Ava said as a greeting. Her eyes had a feral look, like an animal trying to get out of a trap.

"Dad was looking for boxes that he buried when he was a child." Kate remembered that one of them was still on the floor of her car.

"Will you listen to me?" Ava asked.

"Of course." Kate sat down on the old bench.

"Everything will be fine. It'll all work out," Ava said with exaggerated patience. "You'll marry Noah and you two will buy a house. I'll live with you and help with everything so you can keep your job. It's unfair that the regular money will stop but Walter always said that Randal has millions. People don't know this, but Walter was a very angry man and he blamed Randal for everything bad in his life. I protected my husband from him."

"By putting him in prison?"

"Well, yes, actually. He was safe there."

"And he had the cookies I baked so that made everything okay."

"How you twist things around!" Ava said angrily.

Kate was calm. "It's not going to be like that. I'm not going to marry Noah. And I am definitely not going to move back to Chicago. I'm never going to put myself back under the rule of the uncles."

"But what about me?" Ava's voice was rising. "I'm to be left *alone*?"

Kate took a deep breath. "Nor am I ever again going to subject myself to your tantrums."

"Tantrums!" Ava said in anger. "They are depressions. They're medical. I need help."

"Yes, I think you do need help, but I'm not a therapist or a doctor. I don't know how to take care of you. I release myself from that responsibility."

"What does that mean?" Ava snapped. "After our whole lifetime together, you're going to abandon me? Is that what I get after all we've been to each other?"

"Yes," Kate said. "I need to stand on my

own two feet and so do you."

"*She* did this, didn't she? My sister-in-law. That evil witch has poisoned you against me. Changed you. Her money —"

Kate was less calm. "That's the last one. There'll be no more of your tirades. Do you understand me? Aunt Sara has been nothing but kind to me while you have —" She couldn't say what she wanted to for fear her anger would consume her. Spontaneous combustion.

Ava sat down on the old step. Her body seemed to fall into a puddle. "The hotel said my card has been canceled and I have to leave. I'll have to stay with you. At her house. How I'll hate that!"

"No," Kate said. "You can't stay with us. You're not nice to Aunt Sara."

"Randal will have to take care of me."

"I truly doubt that Dad will take you in."

Ava stood up. "Well, what am I supposed to do? Where do I stay?"

"I haven't a clue. I'm sure your brothers will support you."

Ava's eyes widened in fear as she whispered, "No. You don't understand. I have to contribute. It's always been that way. You will have to —"

Kate wasn't sympathetic. "Get a job and rent an apartment would be my suggestion.

407

Like the rest of us have to do." She spun around on her heel and went back to her car, got in and slammed the door. She went to start the engine, but she was shaking too much. She put her hands on the steering wheel, her head down.

When she'd been told that Ava wasn't her biological mother, her first thought had been of getting away from the uncles. No more pressure to do, be, say whatever they demanded.

Second was realizing that she no longer had to deal with her mother's depressions. No more of those fits where Kate had to take care of her mother as well as herself. At six years old, Kate had had to feed herself. Had to —

She leaned back in the seat. "Therein lies madness," she whispered. She mustn't allow herself to dwell on the past. She refused to be one of those people who excused their bad behavior due to a rotten childhood. *If my mother had loved me more I wouldn't have murdered twenty people.* Or whatever.

The question was what to do *now.* Did she really plan to turn her back on the woman who'd always been her mother? Was she now supposed to call Charlene "Mom?" Charlene was her friend, only sixteen years older, and Kate had always considered her a contemporary.

Kate closed her eyes for a moment. When she opened them, she noticed the dirty metal box on the floor. Maybe she should blame her father. It was his thievery and his passion for a teenager that had caused all the problems.

But then, maybe it was her paternal grandmother who'd loved her son but not her daughter. Or was it Sara's wimpy father who was the problem? On the other hand, if Sara had loved her mother, maybe everything would have been different.

And what about Charlene's mother? She had put someone's stillborn baby into Charlene's arms, then handed baby Kate over to Randal. All done in secret.

Or maybe —

Kate stopped trying to figure out who to blame and looked out the window, expecting to see her mother. Ava wasn't a person who gave up. If she wanted something, she figured out how to get it, consequences be damned — which is why she'd felt justified in sending her husband to prison. But she wasn't there.

So where was she? Why wasn't she telling Kate that she had to take care of her true mother? Heaping guilt onto Kate without conscience?

As Kate looked about the overgrown area, she wondered how her mother got there. There was no other car. Knowing Ava, she probably got someone to drop her at the house and said, "My daughter will give me a ride back."

Ava always believed Kate would take care of her. "Even to baking cookies for a dad I didn't know I had," she muttered.

Had Ava collapsed in one of her fits of depression? Was she lying on the damp ground and waiting for Kate to rescue her? Were iguanas crawling across her?

Kate put her hand out to start the car, but she didn't do it. "Damn, damn, damn," she said. So much for vows of leaving Ava on her own.

Thinking how Sara and Jack were going to be disappointed in her, Kate got out of the car. It was very quiet, just the sound of Florida birds. She started to call out but was stymied by what to say. Mother? Ava?

Annoyed, she pushed her way past the crumbling concrete pad. Past the shallow hole her father had dug to get the box. *Wonder if he returned Aunt Sara's shovel?*

There was no sign of Ava, but maybe she'd left on the far side of the house. That wasn't right. Ava loved great emotion and having people pay attention to her. When Kate was a child, if too much attention was given to Kate's good grades, her likability, or even to her red hair, Ava would do something to put the attention back on herself.

Kate saw Aunt Sara's stainless steel shovel on the ground and covered in dirt. That wasn't the way her father would use it, and he certainly wouldn't leave it like that.

When Kate picked it up, she saw that someone had dug half a dozen small holes. Since her father had been busy dealing with life crises, she didn't think it was him.

Kate gritted her teeth. She had no doubt that someone was looking for Randal's loot boxes. Who? Were her uncles here? One of her father's jail friends? What about the Bentley guy? He sure seemed to know a lot about what was going on.

Kate was wiping dirt off her hands, holding the shovel at arm's length, when she saw the edge of another hole. When she took a step forward, she saw that it was the size of a grave. "This is ridiculous," she muttered, and pushed aside short, thick areca palms to get closer.

Lying in the hole was Ava and she seemed to be passed out cold. Beside her was the Bentley man — and he looked to be dead.

The hole was several feet deep and Kate

jumped down into it. "Mother!" she said loudly.

Ava opened her eyes in a dreamy way. "Oh, Kate," she said happily. "I knew you'd wait for me. Everything will be all right. I told you it would be. Where's Randal?"

Kate bent forward to put her hand on the neck of the man that Ava was lying beside. His skin was cold.

"Ah, hugs," Ava said, seeming to think that's why Kate had leaned down so near her. "I knew you'd come to understand."

Kate was doing her best to remain calm. "Get up carefully and don't disturb anything. You have to get out of this hole."

Ava groaned. "Not again! You're back to that cold attitude. As your mother, your *real* mother, I demand that you —"

"Up!" Kate shouted.

"Do not speak to me in that way. I am your —" Ava turned her head. She was face-to-face with a corpse. She opened her mouth wide.

"Don't you dare scream," Kate ordered. "I have enough to deal with without your hysterics. Get out of this hole and go sit down somewhere and wait. Do not leave this place. Got it?"

Ava nodded. Her thin body was easy to maneuver. She put her foot on a tree root and catapulted herself up and over. Turning, she looked down at Kate. "I thought I was dreaming. After you were so cruel to me, I just wanted to disappear, to never live again. Death was preferable to what I was facing, so I —"

"Stop," Kate said in the same tone her father had used. She took her phone out of her pocket. "I don't have time for this now. Go sit down and wait. The sheriff will be here soon and he'll want to talk to you."

Ava looked shocked. "Did you forget what they put me through? I think I better go —"

"So help me, if you leave here now I'll not find a bed for you tonight. You'll sleep in the open and you'll probably be eaten by alligators. Do I make myself clear?"

Ava gave her a hard look. "You didn't use to be like this. Your aunt has made you just like she is. She —" At Kate's glare, Ava left the site.

Kate called Jack first. "I'm at the Medlar house and the Bentley man is here. He's dead."

She heard Jack's gasp. "Text Sara. Tell her to bring her camera," he said, then hung up. She knew he would call Daryl, who would tell Randal. *Soon it will be a Medlar family reunion,* Kate thought. *Again.*

■ ■ ■ ■

Sara arrived first. Last night Jack had seen
to it that her car was returned, so she'd sped
through Lachlan at full speed. At the Medlar house, she made her way through the
thick growth. Ava was sitting on the old
bench, the one Sara had often shared with
Cal.

Ava jumped to her feet. "You have to talk
to her. You have to make her understand
that it was all for the good of everyone. Kate
must —"

Sara ignored her sister-in-law as she
pushed through the thicket to find Kate
standing at the side of a big hole. Sara
barely glanced at the body as she set her
heavy bag down and began taking photos.
"How are you doing?" Sara moved her head
in Ava's direction.

"Okay. I'm holding out against a return to
Chicago, but I said I'd find her a place to
stay."

"I can come up with a suitable motel."
Sara's tone sent visions of rats and cock-
roaches.

Kate smiled. "How's Dad?"

"Daryl said that last night he was catatonic. Wouldn't speak. Just drank beer and

414

watched TV."

"Poor guy," Kate said. "She has a lot to be held accountable for."

"Understatement," Sara muttered. "Ava —" She stopped when they heard Daryl's voice on the other side of the foliage.

"Evie is still having the time of her life," Daryl was saying. "She's booked more cruises. She said that if she signs up while on board, she gets a big discount. I'm not sure she booked me to go with her."

Randal said, "Sara is sending me around the world. You could share a cabin with me and we'll split the cost."

"But Evie will miss me."

"Are you sure?"

Sara and Kate looked at each other. Randal sounded far from "catatonic." He certainly didn't seem to be brooding over the life-altering injustice that had been done to him. The two men were talking about the future, not the past.

No one seemed to be the least interested in yet another murder.

Sara and Kate, still looking at each other, were waiting to see what happened when the two men reached the clearing and saw Ava.

"Randal!" Ava sounded greatly relieved to

see him, like now all her problems would be solved.

The women couldn't see what was happening, but they heard no response from Randal. He stepped through the junglelike growth. Behind him, they could hear the soft rumble of Daryl's voice as he talked to Ava.

"Good morning," Randal said cheerfully. "My two beautiful ladies. And what have you found today?" He looked around the site at the little excavations, but not down into the big hole. "There certainly seems to have been an industrious lot of digging. Sara, I apologize for the state of your shovel. I should have returned it."

Sara narrowed her eyes at him. "Cut out the Charming Bandit act. What do you know about this?"

Randal stepped forward and only briefly glanced into the hole. "The man who helped send me away to prison is now dead. Such a shame." Obviously, he wasn't the least bit sad.

"You didn't . . . ?" Kate asked.

Randal looked at her. "I just steal and lie, remember? No murder."

"Where's Jack?" Sara asked.

"Daryl gave him a list of things to do. Broward people will be here soon. I better leave now."

"No," Sara said firmly. "You have to answer questions." She gestured to the many small holes. "We know what the diggers were searching for. Did they find anything?"

Randal looked about the place. "No." He turned to his daughter. "What happened to the box I retrieved?"

"It's in my car."

"Perhaps I should get it."

Sara groaned. "What's in it that you don't want anyone to see?"

Randal's face seemed to lose some color. "I, uh . . ." He took a breath. "There might be a pair of earrings in the bottom. From Mrs. Henderson."

"She — !" Sara clenched her teeth. "Mrs. Henderson was ninety years old. You stole from her?"

Randal shrugged. "She liked me. She gave me a gift."

"Right!" Sara said. "I guess everyone 'gave' you everything. You never stole anything or —"

"Ah, the sweet sound of my family," Jack said loudly. "What did I miss?" He'd hardly finished speaking when they heard sirens. It sounded like half of the Broward County police force was arriving.

"Cotilla," Jack said in such a fatalistic way that Sara and Kate looked at him in sympathy.

Daryl pushed through the palms. "Go," he said. "Now. All of you. I'll take care of this, and yes, I'm officially back."

Jack looked as if he could cry tears of gratitude.

"Might as well go back to work," Daryl said. "I wanted to escape Randal but it didn't work. Where is he?"

Randal had disappeared.

"Randal!" Daryl said loudly. "Come out or I'll send Ava after you."

Silently, Randal slipped out of the foliage. "Just checking the area for clues."

The sirens were sounding in front of the house.

"Go!" Daryl said. "Figure this out."

Jack grabbed Sara's heavy camera bag and they all ran.

Sara's car was a two-door so Kate and Randal got in the wide backseat first. To their chagrin, skinny Ava slid through the gap between the front seats and jammed herself between them. She smiled happily. "I am home."

Randal started to tell her to get out, but Jack tossed Sara's pillows to her seat, got in

418

and sent the seat flying back to make room for his legs. Sara took the other bucket seat and was still closing the door as Jack sped away. He was familiar with the property so he drove across grass and between trees before he got onto the road. He could see the police cars in his rearview mirror.

"Where to?" he asked Sara.

"Cracker Barrel. Pembroke Pines. That should be far enough away." She turned to look at the three in the back. "I think we need to talk."

Kate and her father were looking out the side windows, ignoring Ava squashed in the middle.

She was smiling. "Ah yes, biscuits and gravy. And bacon. And conversation with the people I love the most. I so look forward to it. I've missed my husband and daughter very much."

Sara looked at her sister-in-law. "If you don't stop pretending you're innocent, we'll set you out on the highway."

Ava started to reply but said nothing. She continued to smile broadly.

At the restaurant, the five of them sat at a table in front of the big, wide windows. They didn't say so, but they wanted to keep lookout.

Kate tried to sit by her father, but Ava

nearly knocked over a chair as she sat between them. Wisely, she said nothing other than to give her order to the waitress.

Sara spoke up. "If anyone is concealing any information, this is the time to reveal it." She looked directly at Ava.

For a full minute, they were all silent.

"Tayla," Randal said. "I think she knows more than she's told anyone. She . . ." He hesitated. "As I told my sister, I think she may have shot the man in the car."

If he'd expected shock, he didn't get it. Sara, Jack and Kate nodded. Ava just kept smiling.

"She'd do anything to protect Charlene," Jack said.

"Just what I said," Sara added.

"What makes you think she needed to?" Jack asked.

Randal looked at Ava. "Who killed the man we found today?"

Ava shrugged. "Walter talked to him, not me."

Kate looked like she might explode. "*You* sat outside that man's house day after day. You were watching him!"

"And I gave you balloons." Ava continued to smile.

"But you —" Kate began.

Randal interrupted. "On the day the man

in the hospital was shot, Tayla went outside with a big, heavy basket. When she was seen later, she didn't have the basket."

"What are you saying?" Jack asked.

"Tayla may have been concealing a gun," Randal said.

"Makes sense, considering that two men were hiding in her barn, and one of them was armed," Sara said.

"We assume the rifle belonged to the dead man," Jack said. "What if the other man, Lenny, had it?"

"Lenny was there because of me, not Charlene," Randal stated.

"Isn't everything about you?" Sara snapped, then paused as their food was served. When the waitress was gone, she leaned forward. "Where are you getting your information about Tayla and this guy Lenny? From your prison buddies?"

"About Lenny, yes. But the basket information came from that girl who works with you." He looked across Ava to Kate.

"Melissa? She told you about Tayla? They aren't friends, but you two are. You gave Melissa a thousand-dollar coupon to go shopping."

"So you and I could have lunch together," Randal said with a smile. "That was pleasant, wasn't it?"

"It was until I found out I'd been lied to. You —"

"I think he means Raye," Jack said. "You talked to her that night at the Brigade. What else did she tell you besides that Tayla may have shot a man?" Jack's eyes were on the verge of fire.

Everyone looked at Randal.

"Not much," he said. "Just that —" He glared at Jack. "Do you turn Roy's temper onto my daughter?"

"Do I what?" Jack sounded like he was about to hit him.

"Stop it," Sara hissed at her brother, then looked at Jack. "He's baiting you. Getting you away from whatever he doesn't want to talk about. He used to do it to your father. It was like taking a leash off a mad dog." She turned back to her brother. "Tell us what you're hiding or I'll let Jack have you."

Randal sighed. "That girl, Raye, saw me with Charlene. I guess she could see that we care for each other, so she told me that Charlene's marriage isn't happy."

"That's wrong!" Kate said.

Randal was unperturbed. "Her lawyer husband was overheard saying that Charlene should be in prison."

Kate and Jack leaned back in their chairs, speechless.

When Sara spoke, she was calm. "Whether that comment about prison is true or not doesn't matter. But that Leland would say it is a lie. Every time there's a problem, he hides Charlene. That's love in its truest form. Now tell us what else this person said."

Randal spoke. "She told me that Tayla talked to somebody who rode a motorcycle. When that girl, Raye, mentioned it, Tayla denied it."

"Why didn't Raye tell *me* this?" Jack asked. "If I have to wear this blasted uniform, it should have a purpose."

"I think she's a bit afraid of you," Randal said.

"Ha!" Kate said. "It's the opposite. I've seen her watching Jack. Anything else she said?"

"Uh . . ." Randal hesitated while they waited. "I showed her a photo of the dead man at the barn and she said he was the one Tayla was talking to. And his motorcycle was small, not like Roy's big Harley."

"Like the one that was used to attack us," Kate said, and Randal nodded.

"That's a lie," Jack said. "The dead guy was muscular, broad shouldered. You described the person on the bike as smaller, thin. Right?"

423

"What a good memory you have," Randal said. "And yes, that's true."

"Is that everything?" Kate asked.

"Every word of it," Randal answered.

"And you didn't think any of this was important to tell us?" Jack said.

"I had other things on my mind."

"Yeah, all about *you*," Sara said, then paused. She looked at her brother with a bonding of understanding. He wanted something and he got it. "She sure told you a lot, didn't she?"

Randal gave a little smile. "Yes, she did. An extraordinary amount, but then people do tend to talk to me."

Ava spoke up loudly. "How old is she? How often do you see her?"

Her jealous outburst was so far from what they were thinking about that they almost laughed.

Sara pushed her empty plate away. "I think we need to do some research."

"Digging holes in root-infested ground like that takes strength," Jack said. "I'd like to know who dug a hole that big. Anybody know where Noah is?"

Kate stood up. "Noah certainly does have the muscle to do that. I know that when Noah works outside, he does it shirtless."

Standing, Jack gave Kate a look of disgust.

424

She smiled.

Only Ava remained sitting. "What about dessert? Pie à la mode?"

Kate looked down at her. "We *Medlars* —" she emphasized the name "— gain weight easily."

"I'm a Medlar too," Ava whispered. "That's my name." She was on the verge of one of her poor-me fits but no one paid any attention to her. They were almost to the exit before Ava ran to join them.

While Jack paid, Sara made a phone call. Since Sara didn't like using the telephone, Kate knew the call must be important.

"There's one person who knows the truth," Sara said then paused. "Dora? This is Sara Medlar. Does Tayla own a big basket? Something she likes to carry around?" Sara waited. "Okay, thanks a lot." She clicked off and looked at Kate. "No. Tayla owns no baskets, inside or out. She never was the rustic type."

Sara looked at Randal and Jack. "That's another lie this Raye told. Let's find out more."

When they were back in the car, Ava said, "We're going to go arrest her? How exciting!" She looked at Kate. "No wonder you want to stay here in the midst of all this sin. It's so different from your peaceful, sin-free

425

life at home with my brothers."

"*You* are the one who is the sinner!" Sara half yelled. "You —"

Loudly, Jack said, "Since Raye likes Randal, he can take her out to dinner. Sweet-talk her. Learn more."

"No!" Ava said. "Just go arrest her right now!"

"She can't be arrested since we have no proof of anything," Randal said.

"People can't be put in jail for lying," Sara said pointedly. "You proved that."

Ava's voice was a whine. "But she's after my husband. That has to be a crime."

"Do I get sent back to prison for that? To 'protect' me from any woman talking to me?" Randal sounded ready to fight.

Kate cut in. "It doesn't matter because he's too old for her."

Randal stiffened. "I beg your pardon. She did come to me first."

Kate said, "Really, Dad? Raye is what? Early thirties?"

Sara said, "Maybe she only likes older men who she believes are sitting on millions in jewels."

Randal groaned. "Not that again! It's some earrings I last saw when I was about ten. They're probably glass."

Sara snorted. "Ha! At six you could tell

426

diamonds from crystals."

Randal smiled. "What a lovely compliment. Thank you."

Ava clamped her arms over her chest. "No dating allowed."

Randal said, "Sister dear, do you know a divorce lawyer?"

Kate looked at Ava. "I think you'd better keep quiet."

Sara turned to Kate. "Tayla will have some info about her employee. We can start from there."

Jack said, "I'll run her through the database. Now that the sheriff is back, I'll have more time to look into things. Maybe now we can find out —" He stopped talking.

Abruptly, the atmosphere in the car changed. As Jack pulled into the drive of Sara's house, everyone was silent.

"What is it?" Ava demanded.

"The unknown DNA," Sara said softly. "To whom does it belong?"

TWENTY-SIX

As soon as they got inside the house, everyone disappeared. Kate thought it was like pepper sprinkled in a cup of water. Stick your finger in and the pepper runs away.

It didn't take insight to see the reason: Kate was left alone with Ava. No one else wanted to deal with her.

Ava was standing in the living room and smiling like the angel she believed herself to be. "I can stay with you. In your little side apartment. We'll be like girlfriends and wear each other's clothes. Yours will be too big for me but you can alter them."

Kate closed her eyes and counted to ten. There was a murder to solve but first she had to deal with Ava. But wasn't that the story of her childhood? Her mother always came first. She opened her eyes. "Let's go to the hotel and get you checked out."

"That's wonderful. Then we'll go shopping for things I need to be able to live in this hot climate. I need cotton tops and sandals. And where do you get your hair cut? Let's make an appointment for me."

Kate started to say something but didn't. She'd spent her entire childhood dealing with her mother's extreme narcissism and somehow, it had seemed normal. But then, her mother was preferable to living with the uncles.

Now, after years away, Kate could see how ridiculous Ava's self-love was.

More importantly, Kate knew there would be no use trying to make her see that she'd been wrong in sending her husband to prison. Wrong in taking a baby that wasn't hers.

Ava was smiling at Kate in a way that said everything was now solved.

What am *I going to do with her?* Kate thought. If Ava stayed in the guesthouse she'd have no qualms about showing up in the house for three meals a day. She'd make all of them miserable. Eventually, Jack would move out and Sara would go back to traveling twelve months a year.

What to do with Ava? Kate thought. Was that the title to a mystery novel? Hey! Maybe Everett would like to write it. Maybe he'd need Ava to live with him while he researched it.

Ava was still smiling in that self-satisfied way. "Let's go," Kate said with a sigh. Maybe she'd stick her mother in a hotel in Boca. Was that far enough away? What about Orlando? Jacksonville? Georgia was a pretty state.

Kate led Ava to her sedan.

"Oh good!" Ava said. "Your car. Not that tiny circus toy of hers. When I live here, I'll have her get rid of it. And that truck! That has to go too. Who has a truck in this day and age? I'll —"

Kate didn't listen as she drove to the four-star hotel where Ava was staying.

Once inside, Kate paid Ava's bill. The amount for room, meals, minibar, the gift shop and laundry was so much that Kate's stomach clenched. In a cowardly move, she added another night to the bill, but she didn't say so. Let Ava stay over one more night. That would give Kate time to coax Jack and Sara and her father into helping her decide what to do with Ava. Would there actually be a divorce? Questions needed to be answered, and Kate did not want to do this alone.

And what about Noah? Kate thought. Maybe he could be persuaded to take Ava back to Chicago. If Kate agreed to pay child support, that is. She couldn't help but smile at that idea. Paying "child support" to someone to take care of an adult woman.

They went up the elevator to the seventh floor. The room was luxurious. It had a kitchenette along one wall, complete with a dishwasher. Kate didn't have to ask to know it was unused. Ava didn't do housework.

Feeling defiant, Kate sat down in a chair and took out her phone. "I'll wait here while you pack."

"But . . ." Ava began, then put on her martyr face. "Right. You're with *them* now. You no longer help your own mother."

In the past, that look and those words would have made Kate do anything to prove she wasn't what Ava was saying she was. But not now.

Jack had texted that he'd been to see Melissa. *Bet she liked that,* Kate thought. He said Melissa had given him all the documentation he asked for. *She'd give him* anything *he asked for.*

Kate chided herself. Her thoughts were as jealous as Ava's.

Jack texted:

Raye's references don't exist. She's not at her apartment or work.

Sara texted,

Can't find her anywhere online. I think her name is fake.

Randal texted,

My darling daughter. How are you holding up? I hope Ava is being kind to you.

Kate frowned at the last one. Her father had given no information about anything. Not where he was or what he was doing. And instead of admitting that he'd dumped Ava onto her, he was sending Kate his love. How could she possibly complain?

She texted back.

Coward! Help me with her.

Randal sent her an emoji of a face laughing to the point of tears.

"At least he's honest," Kate muttered.

"What was that?" Ava asked, sounding very tired from filling a suitcase.

When Kate looked at her she saw that Ava actually was sleepy. She'd always been good at napping. Great emotion wore her out.

Kate stood up. "Why don't you take a nap? I'll . . ." She couldn't think of what she was going to do with a whole ninety minutes of peace.

"You'll leave!" Ava said. "I'll never see you again."

"I won't leave the hotel. I'll just go downstairs, buy a magazine and read it."

Ava looked skeptical but her lids were drooping so she nodded.

A minute later, Kate was outside the door. She leaned against it and closed her eyes. *Peace!* she thought.

When she opened her eyes, Noah was standing there.

"Kate? What are you doing here?"

"I brought my mother . . . I mean Ava here."

"She fell asleep?"

"Like a toddler," Kate said.

Noah reached out and put his arm around her shoulders. "Let's go downstairs and I'll buy you a margarita."

"It's early and I have to drive and . . ." She couldn't think of any more excuses. She'd like nothing better right now than a vat of alcohol. Anything to calm her mind.

They were the only two in the bar and the waiter brought Kate a big, salty margarita.

Noah had a sparkling water. "I have a feeling I may be the one who does the driving." He put down his glass. "I'm sorry I didn't return yesterday, but my new job needed some work done now. I was given some equations to figure out."

"You're the one to do it." Kate downed half of her drink in one gulp and Noah waved at the waiter to bring another one. "What am I going to do with her?" There was no need to explain who she was talking about.

"I'll take her back with me."

"Oh, Noah, would you? That is so good of you. Drop her off, then you can go to Arizona. The brothers know how to handle her. I'll have to send her money." She finished her first drink. "I was thinking of it as 'child support.' " She giggled.

Noah didn't smile. "Tell me about you and Jack. How serious is that?"

Kate sipped her second drink. "Jack is a bit of a free spirit. He seems to have been in love with several women. And lots of sex with lots of women."

"But with you, it's only been me," he said softly. "At least I thought so."

She put her hand over his. "You were always so good to me."

He gave her a hard look. "That's *all* I was to you? Are you forgetting sex in the back seat of cars? In the row boat? When I sneaked through your bedroom window? What about the pregnancy scare?"

With every word, Kate's face grew redder.

434

"I know. It was all lovely."

"Lovely?" he said. "You left me. You found out you had an aunt and you were out of there instantly. I get here and find out you've not even mentioned me to anybody. And there's this guy Jack. Is he a better lover than me?"

"No!" Kate said. "I mean, Jack and I have never had sex."

Noah fell back in the seat. "So that's the key? You want what you haven't had?"

"Please don't do this. I've had enough anguish in the last few days. Father come alive, new mother. Dead people lying about."

For a moment Noah kept his angry look, but then his face softened. "I'm sorry. I should have listened more closely to Aunt Ava while you were here. But I was trying to finish school and get a job away from the uncles and Dad. I did ask Aunt Ava about you often, but she only talked about your aunt. She said Sara liked criminals. I didn't know she meant Jack, didn't know he *lived* with you. I didn't know . . ." Noah calmed himself. "So what's your future with him?"

Kate finished her second drink and her problems seemed far away. "I don't know. We've never spoken about it. About *us*, I mean." She shrugged. "Or maybe we have.

We were going to take a trip to Scotland and Jack said he'd put on a kilt. That seemed like an invitation to romance. A few days ago, he said we should go to Italy and do the 'borrowed and blue.' I'm not sure what he meant by that."

"That's it?" Noah asked. "Kate, trust me, if after years of *living* with a woman and nothing happens, nothing *will* happen. I'm asking you to *marry* me. Move to Arizona with me. Sell houses there. Let's have kids. Your red hair and my blond will make truly beautiful babies."

In her inebriated state, Kate could picture all of it. Noah's reminders of their former sex life made it all come back to her. She'd adored him since she was four years old. She realized that he'd come into her life just as her beloved father was taken away. Just when she needed him.

When she was sixteen, the kisses began. They'd had to keep them secret, of course. The uncles and Ava would have gone into raging fits if they'd known. But maybe the secrecy had added fire to their lives. Besides, Ava made Kate's regular dating life so impossible that Noah had become everything to Kate.

So why did she leave him? Why didn't she give him so much as a thought when she headed for Florida to go to an aunt she'd never met? Did getting away from her mother's depressions and the uncles' oppressive rules overshadow her relationship with Noah? Had Kate craved freedom so much that she'd left behind the good with the bad?

Noah was kissing the back of her hand. She remembered his lips well. "Wasn't it good between us?"

"Yes," Kate said. Her mind wasn't clear enough to think. "We found a dead man today. Mother — I mean Ava — used to stalk him. She said she did it for me but I didn't want balloons *that* much. Even pink and purple ones." She gave a little laugh.

Noah let go of her hand. "I've been told about what the three of you have done while you've lived here. Is it your responsibility to investigate murders?"

"Not really. We just do it. Although, since Jack was deputized it sort of is his responsibility now. And Jack knows everyone. He even went to Melissa and asked her questions. If you knew the things Melissa said about her insatiable lust for Jack, you'd appreciate what he did. But Jack wanted to know so he went."

"Jack," Noah said softly. "King of it all." He lifted his head. "So what did he ask this

Melissa about?"

Kate ran her straw around in her empty glass. "About Raye."

"Raye. Who is he?"

"She. It is a bit of a boy's name, isn't it? She's great at running our office. I hope she isn't a murderer. But then, some murderers are fairly likable people. They —"

Noah groaned. "I'm getting you out of here. You need to sleep this off." He practically picked her up from the chair. When she wobbled, he put his arms around her and they started walking.

"Don't tell Jack about, you know, us. I swear he thinks I'm a virgin. I told him I wasn't, but I didn't tell him about cars and boats and . . ." She waved her hand. "About all that. And don't tell Mother Ava either. Hey! That's what I should call her."

Noah got her into the elevator and as soon as the door closed, he kissed her. It was familiar, but at the same time, it wasn't.

She drunkenly pushed him away. "Jack wouldn't like this. I mean —"

Noah stepped away. "Wouldn't like that you kissed someone else?" He took a deep breath. "It looks like I lost."

Kate was too relaxed to be serious. "But you put up a really good fight." She gave a one-sided grin. "Jack hasn't offered me children. But then his would be dark. His whiskers are as black as midnight, as Aunt Sara would say about one of her romantic heroes. Pure ebony. As dark as —"

"Kate," Noah said, "shut up."

As the elevator door opened, she giggled.

TWENTY-SEVEN

When Kate woke up, she was only mildly surprised to find herself sitting on the ground and leaning against a palm tree. A root was sticking into her leg. Her surprise came when she saw that her wrists were bound together with a plastic snap tie. Her shoes were gone and there was another tie around her ankles. She was immobile.

Déjà vu, she thought. *Been here; done this.* Her mind was still blurry from her two drinks. Actually, it was more befuddled than it should be from just two shots of tequila. Had drugs been added?

She knew she had only to lift her head to see who was behind this, but she had an idea of who it was.

Since Noah had arrived, she'd been lashing herself with guilt. Why did she leave him so abruptly? They'd been lovers. He'd always been kind to her, always caring. It was true that there hadn't been as much between them while they were both at different universities. And after Kate got her job as a Realtor, she hadn't had time for anything except work and dealing with her mother's moods and demands.

But still . . . Why had she been so cold, dismissive even, when she'd driven away? She'd left Noah behind without even a thought of a heartbreaking goodbye.

Now she wondered what she'd seen — or more likely felt — that had warned her. Maybe when she so eagerly ran from her mother and the uncles, she was also escaping from Noah.

As her mind cleared a bit, she realized she was behind the old Medlar house, where Sara and Cal used to meet.

And where her father had dug up a box that contained some earrings he'd stolen. It was also where lots of holes had been dug, including one that contained a dead body.

Kate knew, down to her very soul, that this was all about those blasted jewels. It occurred to her that maybe Noah wasn't angry because she'd left him. He — like everybody else — wanted the sparkles.

She lifted her head. Noah was sitting on the old steps, his long, muscular legs stretched out, a pistol nestled on a thigh.

"Ah. The Golden Girl awakens," he said.

She lifted her shackled hands. "How am I a Golden Girl?" She gave a little smile of friendship, as though nothing was out of order. "I'm sober now, so could you please take these off?"

He held up her phone. "I sent Randal a text. He should be here soon. He'll come running to give anything to his perfect daughter." With a smile, Noah nodded toward her bound wrists. "But I so enjoy seeing you in those."

She could understand Noah wanting great riches but not his animosity toward her. They'd never once had so much as an argument. She was genuinely confused by what he was saying and the way he was looking at her.

"You really don't know, do you?" He stood up, gun in hand, waving it about as though it were nothing.

"I don't think I do. Is this about the proposal? Noah, you're a great guy. When you get to Arizona, you'll find someone and —"

"There is no Arizona!" he shouted, then drew a breath to calm himself. "The uncles contacted the president of the university where I had the job and told lies about me. They won't let me escape. I was brought into that hell group for one reason and I

442

was to do it."

Kate was afraid to hear what he was going to say, but she could see that he was suppressing rage. This was more personal than stolen jewels.

"From the time I was six years old, I heard 'be nice to Kate. Make her love you. That's what you're here for.' Aunt Ava was told to let you go to Florida to Sara to ensure that you become her heiress. The plan was for me to show up after you two had bonded." He snorted. "Aunt Ava said Jack was of no importance."

Kate was trying to comprehend the depth of what he was saying. "I get it. The uncles wanted to make sure that I inherited because they knew that one day it would all implode. Ava isn't my biological mother and my father would eventually be released from prison." Her eyes widened. "It was a scheme twenty-plus years in the planning. That's impressive."

"Clever girl. At least now you are. You weren't then. And nobody was smart enough to see Raye Kirkwood and me."

"Kirkwood?" Kate said. "That's Tayla's last name. And Walter's."

Noah looked at his watch. "Randal had better show up soon. Raye and I need to leave."

After you kill us? she thought, then, *Keep talking. Ask questions. Delay.* "How is Raye related to them?"

"She's the daughter of Walter's second wife. Never heard that he remarried, did you? She was a sweet woman, as unlike his first wife as possible. And Raye was her pretty thirteen-year-old daughter."

"Did Walter . . . ?"

Noah's face turned angry. "No! All of you disparage that man. Raye adored her step-father. She followed him everywhere." He paused. "She *listened* to him."

"Oh," Kate said. "Walter told her about the jewels."

"Exactly! Walter told her what Randal had done, how he'd stolen so much and shared so little." Noah sat back down. "The summer that Walter and Raye came to us in Chicago, they changed my life. I was seventeen and Raye was a glorious twenty-two. You know what my life was like with all the rules and the endless criticism. Raye was sophisticated and . . ." He smiled. "And angry. She was furious at how Walter had been cheated by all of life. She said that if Walter hadn't been betrayed by Tayla and Randal, they'd both be rich now. He'd send her to a top university and she'd end up with a rich husband and a mansion."

444

Kate had opinions about Walter's fantasy but she didn't voice them. Instead, she said, "I can see that. She's been great as an office manager. She can anticipate problems and solve them before they happen."

Noah smiled in a way that could only be described as love. "That's my Raylene. Anyway, Walter and Raye came because he planned to get Aunt Ava to help get the jewels Randal had taken. He just needed to know where they were hidden and he hoped Aunt Ava could find out. I have to give it to her that she tried. She went to Randal in prison and cried poverty. But your father is a clever old fox. He knew that his sister was paying a lot, so he asked Ava who was putting her up to it. Of course she lied and said no one was. It was all maddening. But the good was that Walter ended up staying most of the summer. Raye and I had that time together."

Again, Kate saw the love in his eyes. "Where was I during this?"

"You were fifteen and taking care of Aunt Ava. Her brothers put so much pressure on her that she was one long fit. She didn't let up on you for even minutes."

"I remember that summer." Kate shuddered at the memory. "So the uncles always knew about her so-called depressions? They

445

knew I was taking care of myself?"

"Of course. They encouraged her as it kept you busy. But then, as I said, you were the Golden Girl. You're the heiress to Sara Medlar's fortune, and I had been adopted and groomed to become your husband."

Just like Jack said, Kate thought. "I guess that summer was when you and Raye made plans about the jewels."

"Oh yes. We had days and nights of imagining a different future. One of freedom and wealth." Noah sighed. "Walter's life had been ruined by Randal keeping the lion's share."

"My father says he did share equally. He said he didn't keep anything extra."

Noah's eyes flashed with anger and his hand tightened on the gun. "Do you think I didn't use my brain to check that out? That I'm not capable of rational thinking? Of research?"

Kate whispered, "No, I don't believe that."

"I found out that as soon as the old woman was put into a hospital, the son got an appraisal of everything. It included photos and estimated values. The insurance company paid for much more than what your father said he'd taken. Roy and the sheriff were content with what they were given, but Walter wanted his true cut."

446

Kate wanted to calm Noah's anger. She wanted as much time as she could get. Maybe her father would show up and . . . What? She didn't want to think about that. "Everything that's happened here was planned by you and Raye?" She sounded admiring.

He smiled a bit, seeming to be proud. "There've been some snags but I think it's going to work out. Raye shouldn't have talked to Randal in that beer joint. I told her not to but she's always been impatient. She said that unless she encouraged him, he'd do nothing, that all Randal Medlar cared about was who sent him to prison. I said the cut was enough but . . ." He shrugged.

"The cut? Oh. Right. Was it Raye on the motorcycle and she cut Dad?"

"Yes. She hoped to scare Randal enough that he'd make a move. She wanted to force him to lead us to the jewels."

"What about the man in the barn?"

Noah smiled. "I was the one who hired him. He'd done other jobs of . . . you know. But he said he didn't like being told to kill a woman."

"Charlene?" Kate tried to keep the horror out of her voice.

"Yeah. Randal's great love. We wanted to

447

make him know we meant what we said. Besides, Aunt Ava's hatred of her fueled us."

"The DNA?"

Noah grimaced. "I didn't like that! Raye kissed him just before he left. But it didn't matter. Everything was falling apart because of that guy hired to watch over her."

"Lenny," Kate said. "So who shot him?"

"Me. He was spying and getting in the way. Seeing too much. But he jerked to one side and didn't die."

How inconsiderate of him, Kate thought. "I'm not sure he remembers anything."

"Doesn't matter," Noah said. "Raye will fix it. She went to the hospital to finish him off but she was interrupted. She'll finish him later. When she's in scrubs, she fits right in."

Kate swallowed at the sheer callousness of his words. "You two dug the holes?"

"Yeah. Raye was here when Randal started digging. She's good at hiding. She thought he was going to dig up the jewels, but then *you* showed up and stopped it all."

"What if he had dug them up?"

Noah chuckled. "He would have been found dead. Guess you saved his life. That time."

"And the Bentley man?"

"He was worse than a mosquito. He was

448

always figuring things out. He went to Aunt Ava when she was in jail and tried to blackmail her about those damned balloons! That didn't work. She told him to get lost. That skinny little body of hers is made of steel. It all would have been fine, but he saw Raye and me together and added it all up." Noah shrugged.

"So he had to go."

"Yes, he did."

"So now, your plan is to . . . What?"

"Get the jewels, kill you two, then go back to work. Raye and I will be bereft at your senseless deaths. In a few months, we'll start moving about."

"And enjoying your diamonds."

"Thoroughly."

"No regrets? No remorse?"

"None whatever."

Part of Kate could understand what he was saying. It seemed that he was adopted for the purpose of obtaining money. Not for love. Just money. Kate had been forced on him. No wonder they'd never had a disagreement. She knew the uncles too well. Children who disobeyed were given the belt. An uncle had once threatened Kate after she stood up to him. He was unbuckling his belt when Ava stopped him — with a hard hit with a piece of firewood.

"I'm sorry," Kate said softly, and she meant it. "What was done to you wasn't fair. It wasn't even human. I wish I'd known."

"And what could you have done?"

For a moment their eyes locked and there were memories between them. Sunset trysts. Moonlight. Shared laughter. Joy at occasionally defying an uncle.

"Yeah," Noah whispered. "You should be sorry for all of it." He raised his gun and aimed it at her.

That's when, seemingly out of nowhere, Ava rose up from the foliage, holding the metal handle of a tire jack like a baseball bat.

Kate's eyes must have widened enough that they warned Noah. He whirled around and shot as Ava struck. All Kate saw was a flash of red on Ava and she fell backward. But when Noah turned back to Kate, she saw that his head was bleeding.

"The lazy bitch hit me," he muttered. "She —" His eyes rolled back and he sank to the ground, unconscious.

Kate put her bound hands against the tree trunk and managed to get herself upright. She didn't know how long she had before Noah regained consciousness. She needed to get to the gun.

450

She gave two hops before she fell. She heard a groan from Noah and knew he was waking up. She was trying to get back up when, suddenly, Jack was there and he had his arms around her.

"Mom!" Kate said. "She was shot. She saved me."

Jack buried her face in his shoulder and stroked her hair. "It's okay. Everything is all right. Hear that? It's an ambulance on the way. Your dad and the sheriff are here and they have your boyfriend in cuffs."

"Not my boyfriend," she mumbled. "He was adopted for me. To seduce me. To —"

"Shhh." He was holding her very tightly. "We know. Your dad called the uncles and made some threats. They told him most of it. And besides, the text from you was too sweet. He knew you didn't send it. Did you know your dad set your phone to keep track of you?"

"No. And to think, he had me teach him how to use it." She held out her hands. "Could you . . . ?"

"Sure." He pulled out his pocketknife and cut the plastic, then bent and cut the ties around her ankles.

When Kate started to take a step, she nearly fell. Jack swept her up into his arms. "I'm taking you to the hospital to get you checked out."

When he turned around, she saw her father and Sheriff Flynn standing there. EMTs had Noah strapped down on a gurney. She couldn't see his face — and didn't want to.

"Mother?" Kate asked. "Is she — ?" Her eyes were full of fear.

"She's fine," Randal said. "Barely grazed. She's in the front of the truck, giving the men hell. They're going to let her talk to Noah all the way to the hospital. That's his punishment." He and Daryl chuckled at that.

Sara came around the corner, the last one to arrive.

Kate pushed at Jack to let her down, and aunt and niece hugged hard. And at last, Kate released her fear. No more being brave. The tears came.

"Come on," Sara said, "let's go tell Cotilla how we solved yet another murder."

"One that was caused by the Medlars," Daryl added.

"Let's leave that part out," Sara said.

"Raye?" Kate asked.

"In custody," Jack said. "She was at the airport. So much for fidelity to her lover boy. She was running from him."

"I'll meet you at the office," Daryl said,

and turned away.

Kate was flanked by Jack and Sara, but Randal was standing alone on the crumbling concrete base.

"Come on," Sara said with a sigh.

With a smile that was almost tearful, Randal joined them. They were a family.

Ava loved to tell how she'd hidden herself in the trunk of Noah's car. For once, her paranoia that Kate was going to abandon her had paid off. "Big-time," as she repeatedly told everyone.

For three long weeks, Ava, bandaged and on pain pills, was quietly tolerated by everyone. She told her story of saving Kate over and over — then told it again. The story grew. It blossomed like some all-consuming flower that was about to devour the earth.

Ava moved herself into Kate's little apartment and took the bed, leaving Kate on the lumpy pullout couch. Ava ate all meals with them and went everywhere they did. However, she didn't like anything they did and told them how to change it.

Since Ava had taken a bullet in the shoulder and had saved Kate, no one contradicted her. Even Randal, living in the guesthouse, was polite and quiet around her.

It was the beginning of the fourth week when Kate spoke up. It was during Ava's afternoon nap and they were whispering.

Kate said to Jack, "Let's get married and move to North Dakota."

"Not far enough away," he said without looking up.

"I get on the ship on the sixth of January," Randal said. "I may never return." He looked at his sister.

"I already checked. The ship is full," she said. "No room for me."

For a moment they were silent.

"This has to be fixed," Sara said. "I can't take it anymore."

They all nodded — then turned to look at Kate.

"Me? What am *I* supposed to do?" She looked at her father. "All of this is *your* fault. If you hadn't . . ." She stopped as she didn't have the energy to say everything again.

"She needs a job," Jack said.

The Medlars snorted in derision. Impossible!

"There has to be something she can do," Jack persisted.

"She can talk," Randal said.

"Order people about," Sara said.

"Take all my clothes," Kate said.

455

"She eats as much as Everett," Jack said.

Kate and Sara looked at each other, their eyes lighting up.

"You're a genius," Sara said to Jack.

He looked at Randal, who shrugged. They had no idea what the women were thinking.

It took Kate four long weeks to set things up. Next door to Charlene's little farm was a giant six-bedroom house. Kate talked the owner — who was rarely there — into selling.

It turned out that Lenny had money, and when he was released from the hospital, he moved in. He loved helping Charlene build birdhouses.

Arthur sold his house and contributed to the purchase price. Jack and Gil outfitted the house for his wheelchair in a blazing eight days.

Everett was so thrilled to have so many possible bestselling true crime novels that he ate a dozen doughnuts — with chocolate and cream filling. He took the third bedroom.

Ava claimed the bedroom that looked out over Charlene's house. She wanted to make sure that Randal didn't visit her.

It was Sara who suggested that Dora take the fifth bedroom. She'd still be stuck with cleaning, but she didn't have to run all over town to do it. And she'd have someone to talk to instead of her late husband.

A few days after they all moved in — with Everett and Ava fighting for control, and Lenny winning — the lot of them disappeared for three whole days.

"Where could they have gone?" Kate asked, sounding worried.

"To pester the devil," Jack said. During the remodel, they'd driven him and Gil crazy with their "suggestions."

When the lot of them returned, they were quieter and didn't argue as much. In fact, they seemed to have settled into a semblance of a family. All of them, including Arthur, looked to Lenny as the patriarch, and he quickly settled any disputes. Even Ava behaved around Lenny.

In the Medlar house, one morning Sara wore a look of triumph. She held out a print of a small newspaper article.

It seemed that a lawyer named Melvin Hopkins, who had been falsely imprisoned for seventeen years, had been cleared of all charges. His family said they were eager to see him again. "I've missed my daddy so much," said his adult daughter. She went on to say that she was looking forward to introducing her father to his three grandchildren.

The article said that it wasn't told to the court how the information that cleared Mr. Hopkins was obtained, but the reporter had done some digging. He said no one knew exactly when the information, which was on a USB drive, was stolen from a locked safe, but a receptionist at the big law firm told of an extraordinarily chaotic afternoon. She said that a man in a wheelchair, a thin woman and a man who ate all three bowls of chocolate candies set out for guests caused such confusion and agitation that no one knew what was happening. There was also talk of an elegantly dressed man being seen in one of the offices in the building where Mr. Hopkins used to work, but the man was not identified.

"And there was a man with a scar on his head," someone said. "He was frightening looking. I ran after him but I tripped over the cleaning woman's mop and he got away."

The police were called but someone was quoted as saying, "The police didn't take us seriously. They thought it was all a prank."

It wasn't until weeks later, when new evidence was presented in court, that people began to wonder what really happened on that chaotic afternoon.

Whatever, whoever, the president of the

law firm was taken away in handcuffs, and Mr. Hopkins was going home to his family.

The reporter concluded by saying, "I guess it's true that all's well that ends well."

In January, Sara, Jack and Kate drove Randal to Port Everglades to board the ship for the world cruise. Even Sara was going to miss him.

When Kate got home, she found a package on her pillow. Inside was a diamond and sapphire pin in the shape of a hummingbird. It was one of the jewels that had been stolen before Randal was sent to prison. More importantly, it was one of the jewels that Randal swore he hadn't stolen.

"I'm shocked," Sara said. "My brother is usually so truthful."

The three of them, alone at last and finally together, laughed until they were crying.

ABOUT THE AUTHOR

Jude Deveraux is the author of forty-three *New York Times* bestsellers, including *For All Time, Moonlight in the Morning* and *A Knight in Shining Armor.* She was honored with a Romantic Times Pioneer Award in 2013 for her distinguished career. To date, there are more than sixty million copies of her books in print worldwide.

The employees of Thorndike Press hope you have enjoyed this Large Print book. All our Thorndike, Wheeler, and Kennebec Large Print titles are designed for easy reading, and all our books are made to last. Other Thorndike Press Large Print books are available at your library, through selected bookstores, or directly from us.

For information about titles, please call:
(800) 223-1244

or visit our website at:
gale.com/thorndike

To share your comments, please write:

Publisher
Thorndike Press
10 Water St., Suite 310
Waterville, ME 04901